Silent Game

Alina Ford

Published by Alina Ford, 2024.

SILENT GAME

First edition. November 5, 2024.

ISBN: 979-8227309204

Written by Alina Ford.

Chapter 1: A Chance Encounter

I first laid eyes on Marcus Kane at a bustling coffee shop in downtown Asheville, North Carolina. The air was thick with the scent of freshly ground beans, mingling with the crisp autumn breeze that slipped through the open door. He was seated in a corner, hunched over his laptop, his dark hair tousled and his jawline sharp enough to cut glass. I was there to drown my sorrows in a caramel macchiato after my latest art exhibit had received scathing reviews. Our eyes met, and in that moment, the world around us faded, replaced by a magnetic tension that left my heart racing.

"Do you know what's worse than bad reviews?" I muttered to my friend Sophie, who was engrossed in her own latte. "Having to come to a coffee shop where every sip feels like a reminder of failure." I gestured dramatically at my cup, as if it were the embodiment of my woes. Sophie shot me a look that was equal parts sympathy and amusement, her blue eyes sparkling as she attempted to stifle a grin.

"Maybe the universe is telling you to take a break from art and start a career in interpretive dance," she teased, tilting her head in mock contemplation. "I can already see the headlines: 'Local Artist Turns to Dance—It's a Disaster, but at Least She's Happy!'"

"Ha ha. Very funny," I said, rolling my eyes but unable to suppress a smile. It was true that life had thrown me a curveball recently. My latest collection, a passionate exploration of solitude, had flopped spectacularly. Each canvas, painstakingly crafted, now felt like an embarrassing confession laid bare for the world to judge. I took a deep breath, letting the aroma of coffee momentarily distract me from the gnawing frustration lodged in my chest.

Marcus glanced up from his screen again, his gaze piercing through the noise of the café. There was something intriguing about him, an air of intensity that made it hard to look away. My heart did a little flip, a treacherous traitorous leap. The way his brow furrowed in concentration sent an inexplicable flutter through me, a flicker of curiosity wrapped in hope. What could such a captivating man possibly be doing here, alone in this sanctuary of caffeine?

"Maybe you should go talk to him," Sophie suggested, her voice dropping to a conspiratorial whisper.

"Absolutely not," I shot back, though a part of me stirred at the thought. "I'm not exactly in prime flirting condition right now. My heart is still nursing its wounds."

"Then maybe it's time for a band-aid. Or at least a distraction," she insisted, her playful nudging making me squirm. But before I could muster a retort, she had already stood up, smoothed her shirt, and set off in the direction of Marcus. "You just sit here and look miserable while I break the ice."

"Sophie, wait!" I called, but she was already on her way, determination in her stride. I sank lower in my seat, my cheeks warming as she approached him, my heart pounding in protest at the impending humiliation.

I watched, half fascinated and half mortified, as she gestured animatedly, her hands painting the air with the enthusiasm of a toddler in a candy store. To my surprise, Marcus's lips curled into a faint smile, his posture relaxing as he leaned back, intrigued. Sophie was clearly winning him over, and it felt like I had unwittingly volunteered for a game of awkward charades.

Suddenly, Marcus turned his gaze towards me, his smile broadening as he caught my eye. "Is she always this dramatic?" he asked, the deep timbre of his voice reaching me like a warm breeze.

"Only when she's trying to impress the men," I replied, unable to help myself, my tone a blend of sarcasm and admiration for her audacity.

"Is that so?" His eyebrows raised in playful disbelief. "Then I'd say she's doing a commendable job."

Sophie shot me a triumphant thumbs-up before retreating, clearly satisfied with her successful introduction. My heart fluttered with an odd mix of embarrassment and excitement. I couldn't believe she'd actually managed to drag me into this unforeseen social interaction.

"I'm Marcus," he said, a hint of amusement dancing in his dark eyes.

"Margot," I replied, my voice steadier than I felt. "Your honorary spokesperson, it seems."

His laughter was genuine, rich and infectious. "I'll take that as a compliment. If only my coffee could talk, it would probably have a lot to say about my procrastination levels."

We both chuckled, the moment sparking an unexpected connection. As we exchanged playful banter, I felt the weight of my recent failures begin to lift, replaced by a lightness I hadn't felt in weeks. "So, what are you working on?" I asked, motioning to the screen that glowed in front of him.

"Just some freelance design work. Trying to make the world a bit more aesthetically pleasing, one pixel at a time," he replied, his eyes sparkling with passion.

"I feel you. I just wrapped up a show that went... well, let's just say it wasn't what I'd hoped for." I grimaced, but his interest remained undeterred, a warm light of encouragement in his gaze.

"Art is subjective, after all. What matters is that you created it," he said, leaning closer, as if the noise of the café had faded to an echo. "I'm sure there's a spark in your work that others just haven't seen yet."

His sincerity ignited a flicker of hope within me, a gentle reminder that perhaps this wasn't the end of my artistic journey. I felt a flush creep across my cheeks, an unexpected warmth blooming from our connection.

"So, how about you take a break from drowning your sorrows and join me for a coffee?" he suggested, tilting his head slightly, a spark of mischief glimmering in his eyes. "We can commiserate together over bad reviews and procrastination."

The weight of my doubts and insecurities drifted away like autumn leaves in the wind. "Why not? I could use a partner in crime for this caffeine-fueled pity party," I replied, a smile breaking free from the corners of my lips.

As we settled into easy conversation, the world outside faded away. In that moment, I could almost believe that perhaps, just perhaps, this serendipitous encounter could be the turning point I so desperately needed.

The sound of our laughter mingled with the ambient noise of clinking cups and low conversation, creating a cocoon around our table. I found myself leaning in closer, eager to absorb every word Marcus had to say, as if he were sharing secrets only I was meant to hear. His tales of freelance design projects morphed from amusing anecdotes into impassioned discussions about color theory and the importance of aesthetics in everyday life.

"People think design is just about making things pretty," he said, rolling his eyes, his expressive hands emphasizing his points. "But it's so much more than that. It's about functionality, about making something that speaks to the user, that resonates with them." His enthusiasm was infectious, and I felt myself drawn deeper into the conversation, my earlier melancholy slipping away like autumn leaves caught in a gentle breeze.

"I get that. Art should evoke something, right? Even if it's just confusion," I replied, grinning. "I mean, isn't that what the critics say about my work? I should just change my artist statement to, 'Confusing people since 2020.'"

Marcus laughed, a rich sound that warmed me more than the coffee ever could. "You'd think they'd appreciate a little mystery.

After all, isn't life one big riddle? We're all just trying to figure it out one brush stroke at a time."

Our conversation flowed effortlessly, and before I knew it, we had fallen into a rhythm that felt both exhilarating and terrifying. I could sense the undercurrents between us, that tantalizing spark, yet I was acutely aware of the fragile nature of this moment. What if I said something stupid? What if he realized I was a complete mess of insecurities hiding behind a façade of casual charm?

"So, what's your art about?" he asked, tilting his head slightly, his curiosity evident. "What do you want people to feel when they look at your work?"

The question caught me off guard. It wasn't one I had prepared for. "Honestly? I want them to feel something... anything. I want them to see the solitude I try to capture—the quiet beauty in being alone. But apparently, that's not very marketable." I tried to maintain a light tone, but the truth was that sharing my artistic vision felt like baring my soul.

"Art is a reflection of you, right?" he mused, his gaze unwavering. "You can't control how others interpret it, but you can certainly make it authentic. Your voice matters more than their opinions."

His words resonated, sinking into me like a balm for my bruised ego. I had spent too long worrying about external validation, forgetting the sheer joy of creation. "You sound like you should be on a motivational poster," I teased, nudging him playfully. "You could be the next big thing in inspirational quotes: 'Marcus Kane, the Picasso of Positivity.'"

"Now that's a title I can work with," he grinned, leaning back in his chair with a mock flourish. "Just imagine the merchandise! T-shirts, mugs, probably a line of scented candles. I'd be rolling in it."

We bantered back and forth, the coffee shop fading away into a warm blur of laughter and shared stories. I learned that Marcus had moved to Asheville not long ago, chasing a dream that felt as nebulous as my own. He talked about his love for the vibrant arts community, the breathtaking landscapes that inspired him, and the challenge of starting fresh in a new city.

As the afternoon slipped into evening, the sunlight softened, casting a golden hue over the room. My heart raced, caught up in the moment, but the looming thought of reality nagged at the edges of my mind. I'd walked into this café a defeated artist, yet here I was, laughing with a man who had somehow ignited a flicker of hope within me. But how long could this last?

"I should probably get going," I said reluctantly, glancing at the time. "I have a mountain of rejection letters waiting for me at home, and they're getting anxious."

"Rejection letters? You're not really going to let a few harsh critiques keep you from creating, are you?" he challenged, a spark of defiance in his voice.

"Easier said than done, Marcus," I replied, shaking my head. "It's hard to separate the art from the artist, you know? Every critique feels like a personal attack."

He leaned forward, his expression earnest. "Then don't let them define you. Use that energy, that frustration, and channel it back into your work. Transform it into something beautiful."

His passion ignited something within me, and I couldn't help but smile, a warmth spreading through my chest. "Maybe you're right. Maybe I do need to shake things up. Just like you've shaken up my afternoon."

His eyes sparkled with mischief. "If you're looking for a partner in creative crime, I'm all in. You seem like someone who knows how to turn a good cup of coffee into an adventure."

"Adventure? Is that what we're calling it?" I laughed, my heart racing at the thought of taking such a leap. "What kind of adventure are we talking about? Art heists? Coffee shop recon?"

"Something like that," he said, grinning widely. "Or perhaps we could collaborate on a project—something that merges your artistic vision with my design skills. We could take on the world, one canvas at a time."

The idea was tantalizing, a thrilling proposition that sent my imagination spinning. "Collaborate? Just like that?"

"Why not?" His smile was infectious, and for the first time in a long while, I felt the weight of my doubts lifting. "It could be fun. Plus, I can't think of a better excuse to keep talking to you."

I felt a rush of excitement, my heart leaping into my throat. What had started as an ordinary day had transformed into something extraordinary, something unexpected. "Okay, then. Let's see where this crazy idea leads us," I agreed, my heart racing at the thought of diving into the unknown.

As we exchanged numbers, I felt an electric buzz of anticipation. We both stood, lingering for a moment, caught in the palpable energy of the moment. "So, this is where it begins?" I asked, half-joking, half-holding my breath.

"Definitely," he replied, a confident glint in his eye. "Just think of me as your guide to the wild side of art and design. Adventure awaits, Margot."

With that, we stepped out into the vibrant Asheville streets, where the air felt charged with possibility. The evening sky blushed with the hues of twilight, and I could sense that life, for all its chaos, was about to take a wonderfully unexpected turn.

The excitement of the day carried me forward as Marcus and I stepped out into the crisp Asheville air, the evening sun casting a golden hue over the colorful storefronts lining the street. The town buzzed with life, a blend of laughter, music, and the tantalizing scent of gourmet food wafting from nearby restaurants. My spirits soared, buoyed by the promise of new beginnings and a strange sense of partnership that I never expected to find.

"So, what's our first order of business, oh great guide to the wild side?" I teased, nudging Marcus playfully with my shoulder. He glanced sideways, a grin playing on his lips, and I could see the spark of mischief in his eyes.

"Well, I was thinking we could stop by the art supply store first. You can show me what you're working with. I need to gauge your artistic arsenal before we embark on our epic collaboration," he replied, his tone light yet earnest.

"Art supply store? You think that'll give you a good impression of my skills?" I laughed, unable to suppress the thrill of being so understood. "Be warned, I'm rather fond of impulse buys. Who knows how many tubes of paint I might have hoarded?"

"That's the spirit! The more chaotic, the better!" he said, matching my enthusiasm. "A true artist thrives in chaos."

As we wandered toward the shop, I couldn't help but feel like I was rediscovering a part of myself that had been overshadowed by self-doubt. It was like the very air around us crackled with a shared ambition, a creative energy that promised an adventure far beyond my wildest expectations.

Inside the store, the vibrant colors of paint tubes and sketchbooks surrounded us, the walls lined with canvases and art supplies that beckoned for exploration. I felt my heart quicken as I moved through the aisles, Marcus close beside me, his presence both comforting and exhilarating.

"Show me your favorites," he said, leaning casually against a shelf, his eyes alight with curiosity.

"Okay, but you have to promise not to judge my questionable choices," I said, shooting him a playful glare. I led him to a section filled with bold, unconventional colors. "This—this is my secret weapon. The neon pink? It's not just for highlighters and graffiti. It's for making statements."

"I like it. You're going for 'notice me, world!' I can respect that," he replied, inspecting a bright tube of paint as if it were a rare artifact. "What else you got?"

As I rifled through my stash of beloved supplies, I felt an exhilarating sense of freedom wash over me. Marcus watched, his playful banter encouraging me to embrace my creativity without restraint. "And here we have the classic: ultramarine blue. A staple for any self-respecting artist." I held it up, presenting it like a prized possession.

"That's the color of ocean dreams and late-night art parties, I presume?" he quipped, arching an eyebrow.

"Exactly! A little touch of adventure." I smirked. "It pairs wonderfully with a splash of chaos."

"Then we're off to a good start. Adventure and chaos should be our mantra!" he said, tossing a random assortment of brushes into the cart. "These are essential tools for any artistic escapade."

"Are you sure you want to be my partner in crime? The last time I dragged someone into my art projects, we ended up painting a mural on my living room wall that was equal parts masterpiece and disaster," I warned, biting back laughter as I recalled the hours spent cleaning paint splatters from my hardwood floors.

"That sounds perfect! I'm ready for a good disaster," he replied, his smile widening. "Just think of it as performance art—chaos transformed into creativity."

With a basket brimming with supplies and a promise of collaboration hanging in the air, we left the store, the sun dipping lower in the sky, casting long shadows that danced across the pavement. The vibrant atmosphere of downtown Asheville felt electric, the world outside now pulsing with potential.

"Okay, where to next, adventurous spirit?" I asked, my eyes sparkling with excitement.

"Let's find a spot to brainstorm our artistic endeavor," he suggested, glancing around. "I know a quaint little park nearby that's perfect for sketching out ideas."

"Lead the way, fearless leader," I replied, falling in step beside him.

As we walked, the laughter of children echoed in the distance, mingling with the strumming of a street musician's guitar. I felt an exhilarating sense of freedom wash over me as we entered the park. The trees, dressed in autumn colors, painted the landscape with fiery reds and mellow yellows, creating a picturesque backdrop that inspired a deep sense of tranquility.

Marcus led us to a secluded bench nestled beneath an old oak tree, its branches swaying gently in the breeze. As we sat down, I pulled out my sketchbook and began flipping through the pages, revealing a mix of half-finished pieces and wild doodles. "Here's my brain, unfiltered," I said, gesturing to the colorful chaos.

He leaned closer, studying the sketches with genuine interest. "These are incredible. You have a unique style, Margot. It's whimsical yet thought-provoking," he said, tracing a finger over an abstract piece.

I felt warmth bloom in my chest at his praise, a spark of confidence igniting within me. "Thanks, but they're just ideas. I often get stuck in my head about what they should be."

"Then let's break that barrier. We can create something together that's outside of your usual style. How about we merge your whimsical with my... well, whatever it is I do," he replied, winking playfully.

"Your mysterious charm?" I suggested, laughing.

"Exactly. Let's embrace the unknown!" he declared, his enthusiasm contagious.

Just as we began brainstorming ideas, an unexpected shout caught our attention. A group of teenagers nearby erupted into laughter, a football spiraling through the air, nearly colliding with our peaceful retreat. Marcus instinctively raised an arm to shield us, but it was too late. The ball landed with a thud right in front of us, and the laughter turned into an invitation.

"Hey! Can you toss that back?" one of the boys called, his voice filled with playful challenge.

Marcus looked at me, a gleam of mischief in his eye. "What do you say? Think we can make a solid throw?"

"Only if you promise to catch it," I quipped back, a smile breaking across my face.

Before I could second-guess myself, Marcus leaned forward and effortlessly tossed the ball back. The cheers erupted, and I felt a rush of exhilaration as I joined in their playful banter, laughing alongside him.

Just as we were settling back into our brainstorming, I noticed a figure lingering at the edge of the park, watching us intently. A chill ran down my spine as I squinted to get a better look. The stranger's expression was inscrutable, shrouded in the shadows of twilight.

"Everything alright?" Marcus asked, sensing my unease.

I hesitated, glancing back at the figure, who now seemed to vanish into the trees. "Yeah, I just thought I saw someone watching us. Probably just my imagination," I replied, shaking off the feeling.

"Don't let it ruin our creative flow. We're on the brink of greatness!" Marcus encouraged, but a knot of tension had begun to tighten in my stomach, whispering warnings I couldn't quite ignore.

We resumed our sketches, but my focus wavered, darting back to the place where the stranger had stood. The fleeting sense of being observed lingered, a shadowy presence that clung to the edge of my thoughts. As the air grew colder and darkness wrapped around us, I couldn't shake the feeling that our peaceful escape was about to be interrupted in a way neither of us anticipated.

Suddenly, Marcus's phone buzzed violently on the bench, startling us both. He glanced at the screen, his expression shifting to one of surprise and concern. "I need to take this," he said, standing up.

"Is everything okay?" I asked, anxiety bubbling within me.

"I'm not sure," he replied, glancing back at me, his brow furrowing. "I'll just be a moment."

As he stepped away to answer the call, I couldn't help but feel an unsettling shift in the atmosphere, a sense of foreboding settling over me like a heavy cloak. I stared into the shadows of the park, where the trees loomed like dark sentinels, whispering secrets I was too afraid to decipher.

Then, out of the corner of my eye, I caught a movement. The figure from earlier emerged from the darkness, their face now partially illuminated by the soft glow of a nearby streetlamp. My heart raced as the stranger took a step forward, locking eyes with me, their expression unreadable yet full of intent.

Just as Marcus turned back, his phone still pressed to his ear, I opened my mouth to say something, but the words caught in my throat. The world seemed to hang in the balance, the moment suspended in time, leaving me breathless and uncertain of what was to come next.

Chapter 2: Crossing Wires

Sunlight poured through the café's large windows, casting warm golden patterns on the wooden floor that seemed to dance in rhythm with the soft jazz drifting from the speakers. The rich aroma of freshly brewed coffee mingled with the buttery scent of croissants, creating an atmosphere that was both comforting and electrifying. I stepped inside, my heart racing as I spotted him nestled in a corner, laptop perched precariously on the table like a crown atop a king's head. Marcus was engrossed in his work, fingers flying over the keys with the kind of fervor usually reserved for passionate lovers or determined artists. My pulse quickened, a mix of excitement and apprehension stirring within me.

How could a man be so infuriatingly handsome and yet possess a wit sharp enough to cut through steel? His dark hair fell just above his striking blue eyes, which glinted with mischief as he caught my gaze. That smirk of his was infuriating—a blend of confidence and arrogance that made my stomach churn and my heart flutter all at once. I swiped a breath, steeling myself for our inevitable clash.

As I approached, I half-expected him to look up and acknowledge me with a smile, perhaps even a compliment. Instead, he barely lifted his gaze, his focus firmly on the glowing screen before him. "You know," he began, his voice dripping with condescension, "art is just a way for you creatives to express your inability to engage with reality."

I narrowed my eyes, indignant. "And what makes you the authority on reality, Marcus? Your three months in Paris studying 'the art of the coffee break' doesn't qualify you to critique a world you barely understand."

The words spilled out before I could stop them, but I couldn't help myself. His presence stirred a fire in me, a desire to challenge him, to push back against the walls he'd built around his opinions.

He finally looked up, his eyebrows arching in surprise before settling into that infuriating smirk. "Touché, but I'm not the one who's emotionally attached to a canvas."

"Emotionally attached? Hardly," I shot back, crossing my arms. "It's called passion, and you wouldn't know it if it hit you over the head with a paintbrush."

He leaned back in his chair, amusement dancing in his eyes. "Passion? Is that what you call creating endless variations of the same overused theme? I bet if I looked at your portfolio, it would scream 'I have daddy issues' at every turn."

My cheeks flushed with a mix of embarrassment and fury. He was infuriatingly right, but I refused to let him see the cracks forming in my defenses. "You really should try reading something other than art critiques and your own social media posts. Maybe then you'd grasp that art reflects the artist's soul, not just a regurgitation of traumas."

"Touchy, touchy," he said, a mocking tone slipping into his voice. "But perhaps you're right. A deeper understanding of your angst might be enlightening."

In that moment, it felt like the café had closed in around us, the sounds of laughter and clinking cups fading into the background as our verbal sparring took center stage. Patrons nearby turned to watch the spectacle unfold, their interest piqued by the tension crackling in the air. I could practically feel the heat radiating off my skin, a cocktail of irritation and something else—something more exhilarating.

"You know," I said, leaning closer, "for someone who pretends to be so enlightened, you're remarkably adept at being a complete jerk. What's the deal? Did your last girlfriend break your heart or just your ego?"

He chuckled, and the sound sent an unexpected thrill coursing through me. "Ah, the classic 'let's tear down the walls to build a better connection' maneuver. It's cliché, but I respect the effort."

My jaw dropped in disbelief. "Is that what you think this is? A desperate plea for understanding? Newsflash: I could care less about your opinion."

"Yet here you are, investing time and energy into this conversation. You're welcome," he replied, his tone light, as if we were engaged in some sort of playful game rather than a fierce argument.

The banter spiraled, drawing in snippets of laughter from our audience, and I suddenly felt less like a wounded artist and more like a player in a farcical play. "Fine, you want honesty? I think you're a pretentious blowhard who thinks being a critic is the same as creating. Your opinions mean nothing to me."

"Ah, the classic 'I'm going to insult you to hide my attraction' strategy. It's charming, really," he shot back, a grin spreading across his face.

At that moment, I could either succumb to the intoxicating pull of his charm or maintain my indignation. I opted for the latter, refusing to let my heart race at the idea that beneath the layers of arrogance and wit, there might be a flicker of something real. "Attraction? Hardly. You're about as appealing as a flat tire on a rainy day."

His laughter filled the space, a rich sound that wrapped around me, disarming my defenses, even as I tried to cling to my annoyance. "If only I could bottle this chemistry and sell it. I'd be a millionaire. Or maybe I should just paint your portrait and call it 'The Artist's Frustration.'"

The playful jab ignited an unexpected warmth in my chest, but I shook my head, forcing a frown. "Good luck with that. I have plenty of better options than being your muse."

"Is that so? I'd love to hear about these 'better options.' Perhaps they involve a gallery where no one critiques you, or maybe a secret artist retreat where you can hide from the world?"

His words felt like an invitation, a challenge wrapped in silk. But the thought of engaging with him on any level beyond this witty sparring felt perilously close to the edge of a cliff, and I wasn't sure if I was ready to leap.

The next day, I returned to the café, the familiar blend of coffee and freshly baked pastries enveloping me like a warm hug. I had convinced myself it was fate, an inexplicable force pulling me back into Marcus's orbit. But as I stepped closer to his table, my bravado slipped like the last vestiges of autumn leaves in a brisk wind. There he sat, typing away, exuding an effortless charm that made my heart race and my blood boil all at once.

His handsome features were cast in soft afternoon light, illuminating the sharp angles of his jaw and the hint of a smile that danced on his lips as he composed his latest critique. I cleared my throat, determined to approach him with a cool confidence that had eluded me the day before.

"You know, I was just thinking about how predictable you are," I said, feigning nonchalance as I slid into the chair across from him.

He looked up, surprise flickering in his blue eyes before that signature smirk returned. "And here I thought you were the one who was predictably late. It's a pleasure to see you again, though I'd hoped for more of a grand entrance."

"Grand entrances are overrated," I replied, crossing my arms. "Besides, I figured I'd save the theatrics for my art."

"Ah, art. That nebulous realm where feelings float freely but meaning is as slippery as a fish," he teased, leaning back in his chair, a playful glint lighting up his expression. "Tell me, what masterpiece are you working on now? A portrait of your cat perhaps? Or maybe another depiction of your existential dread?"

"Funny you should mention that," I shot back, my cheeks flushing with irritation. "My cat is actually my most profound muse. Unlike some people, he understands the delicate balance of authenticity and artifice."

"Is that so?" He leaned forward, genuinely intrigued now. "And here I was thinking your art was just an extension of your inner turmoil. I never took you for someone who could find such calm amidst the chaos."

"Calm is a luxury I can't afford," I retorted, feeling the tension thrum between us like a taut string. "And honestly, who wants calm when you can have a rollercoaster of emotions instead? It's far more interesting."

He chuckled, the sound deep and rich, sending a thrill down my spine. "Interesting is a double-edged sword. It cuts both ways, doesn't it? The artist's struggle is only as meaningful as the audience's interpretation."

A flicker of understanding passed between us, momentarily bridging the gap that separated our opposing worlds. I found myself leaning in, drawn to the magnetic force of his wit and intellect. "You keep saying that, but isn't it more about the journey? The art of creating is often messy, unpredictable, and absolutely exhilarating. It's not about how others interpret it but how it resonates with you first."

His gaze narrowed, considering my words. "You're saying the creator is paramount to the experience? That's an interesting stance for an artist. Most would argue the audience holds the true power."

I waved a dismissive hand. "Power, schmawer. If I cared about that, I'd be selling my soul for likes on social media. I create because I need to express what's inside me, not to pander to some fickle audience."

"Brilliant," he said, feigning applause. "Next, you'll tell me you paint for the sheer pleasure of it, ignoring the fact that you're on a hamster wheel of validation."

"Maybe I do paint for pleasure," I countered, feeling a surge of confidence. "What's wrong with that? It's my outlet, my rebellion against the mundane."

"And yet," he replied, his tone shifting, "the very act of rebelling indicates a desire for recognition. You can't escape the paradox of your own creation."

I was tempted to throw my napkin at him, but instead, I took a deep breath and leaned back, allowing a moment of silence to hang between us. The café buzzed around us, the distant sound of laughter and clinking cups blending into a gentle hum, yet it felt like we were suspended in our own world—one fraught with tension and intrigue.

"You have a knack for twisting my words, Marcus," I said finally, unable to suppress a smile. "Maybe that's your true art form. You should add 'verbal gymnast' to your résumé."

He smirked, eyes dancing with amusement. "And you should consider a career in philosophy. You're clearly adept at complicating the simple."

Just then, the barista called out an order, breaking our banter like a glass shattering on the floor. I turned my attention to the counter, and when I glanced back, I caught him studying me with a contemplative expression, as if he were trying to decipher a particularly cryptic puzzle.

"Why do you do it, then?" he asked suddenly, his tone shifting to something more serious. "Why do you create?"

I hesitated, the weight of the question settling over me like a thick fog. "I create because it makes me feel alive," I finally admitted, my voice softer now. "When I paint, the world fades away, and I lose myself in the colors and shapes. It's the only time I truly feel free."

Marcus nodded, his previous bravado momentarily stripped away. "I can respect that. There's something beautiful in the pursuit of freedom through creation."

I blinked, surprised by the sudden shift in his demeanor. "You're not just a critic, are you? You're an artist yourself."

He opened his mouth to respond, but before he could say anything, his phone buzzed insistently on the table. He glanced at it and frowned, a flicker of annoyance crossing his features. "Duty calls," he said reluctantly, running a hand through his hair. "But I'd like to continue this discussion, if you're up for it."

"Continue? You mean you'd actually like to keep talking to me after all that?" I raised an eyebrow, half-serious and half-teasing.

"Believe it or not, you're somewhat entertaining," he admitted, a hint of a smile playing at the corners of his mouth. "I could use a fresh perspective. How about this: let's meet here tomorrow, same time?"

"Tomorrow? And risk the chance of another round of verbal fencing?"

"Exactly," he replied, a mischievous glint in his eyes. "I promise to be just as insufferable."

I couldn't help but laugh, the sound spilling out in a way that felt liberating. "Fine, I'll be here. But be warned, I'm bringing my best arguments."

With that, he stood, gathering his things with an air of confidence that only added to my curiosity. As he walked away, I felt a mix of exhilaration and confusion—a cocktail of emotions that left me questioning everything. There was something about Marcus that ignited a spark within me, an urge to dive deeper into his world, even as I steeled myself against the heat of our exchanges. Little did I know that the next encounter would challenge not just my artistic sensibilities but the very core of my beliefs about connection, art, and the tangled threads of attraction.

The café buzzed with its usual morning energy, the aroma of espresso swirling around me like a warm embrace. I settled into my favorite corner table, my heart fluttering with a mix of anticipation and dread. Today was the day I'd face Marcus again, the man who had unwittingly challenged my entire artistic philosophy and, more alarmingly, stirred something deep within me that felt dangerously close to attraction.

When he walked in, I was struck anew by the way he commanded the room, all sharp angles and easy confidence. His eyes scanned the café, and when they landed on me, that infuriating smirk spread across his face as if he'd found the punchline to a joke only he understood. "Look who's here, the queen of self-righteousness," he teased, sliding into the chair opposite me without waiting for an invitation.

"Funny how you're always the first to throw around insults," I shot back, my voice laced with playful defiance. "I should have brought a crown to match your royal demeanor."

"Ah, but insults are the lifeblood of art, don't you think? I'd expect nothing less from a tortured soul like you," he replied, leaning back with an air of casual superiority.

"Maybe your understanding of art needs to be tortured a bit more," I quipped, feeling the familiar rush of adrenaline that came with our banter. "Art is about more than just throwing shade; it's about connection, expression, and sometimes even catharsis."

"Catharsis?" He raised an eyebrow, clearly amused. "So you admit your work is just an emotional dumping ground? How refreshing."

I narrowed my eyes, resisting the urge to throw my coffee at him. "My work is an exploration, Marcus, not a dumpster fire. It's about peeling back layers, revealing truths—unlike your art critique that feels like a pre-packaged opinion from a shallow pool."

"Touché," he conceded, the glimmer of respect evident in his gaze. "But don't you find it tedious to keep rehashing your 'truths' to an audience that rarely comprehends the depth of your struggles?"

"Better that than to wallow in ignorance, don't you think?" I retorted, my heartbeat quickening. It was exhilarating to spar with him, each word a step on a tightrope stretched between annoyance and intrigue.

"Ah, the eternal struggle of the artist, forever misunderstood," he mused, an almost genuine note breaking through the sarcasm. "But really, what are you trying to say? That people are incapable of grasping your genius?"

"Not genius, just—" I hesitated, suddenly aware of how vulnerable the question made me feel. "Just genuine emotion. My art isn't meant for everyone, and that's okay."

"I suppose that's a healthy way to look at it," he said, his expression shifting as if he were really considering my words. "But what if the audience doesn't show up? What then?"

The question hung between us, heavy and unyielding. I stared at him, searching for the clever retort that usually flowed so easily. "Then I create for myself. Isn't that enough?"

"Perhaps," he replied, his voice dropping an octave. "But you must know the fear that comes with that, the dread of pouring your soul onto a canvas only for it to be met with indifference."

"Of course I know," I whispered, the admission a raw nerve laid bare. "But I can't let that fear paralyze me."

Marcus leaned forward, his intensity palpable. "That's where you and I differ. You create to fight the fear; I critique to keep my distance from it."

A moment passed, the noise of the café fading as we locked eyes. It was a strange intimacy that settled over us, weaving a thread of understanding between our opposing viewpoints. I felt the air crackle with unspoken words, with the kind of tension that could unravel or ignite something deeper.

But before I could respond, his phone buzzed again, breaking the spell. He sighed, irritation flickering across his features as he glanced at the screen. "It's always something," he muttered, shaking his head. "My editor thinks my life revolves around his deadlines."

"Maybe you should get a life outside of your critique columns," I teased, though the thought of him tied to someone else made my stomach twist uncomfortably.

"Maybe," he said, a hint of distraction lingering in his tone. "But here's the thing: my work is my life. It's hard to separate the two."

"Is it? Or is it an excuse?" I pressed, intrigued by the glimmer of vulnerability behind his bravado.

"Maybe we're all just hiding behind our art, afraid to step into the light," he replied, an unexpected sincerity in his voice.

"Maybe," I echoed softly, contemplating the complexity of the man before me. As he rose to leave, I felt a pang of disappointment mixed with something else—a fleeting wish that this moment could stretch into something more.

"I'll see you tomorrow?" he asked, glancing back at me over his shoulder, a flicker of uncertainty crossing his face.

"Count on it," I replied, a smile breaking through the tension. "But prepare yourself. I'm not going to make it easy for you."

With a final nod, he turned to leave, his confident stride cutting through the café's atmosphere like a knife. I watched him go, a rush of conflicting emotions swirling within me. The encounter had deepened my resolve, igniting a spark of curiosity about what lay beneath his layers of sarcasm and critique.

Just as I was about to gather my things, a commotion at the entrance pulled my attention. The door swung open with a force that sent a chill through the warm café air, and a figure stumbled in, disheveled and breathless. My heart raced as I recognized him—a fellow artist, known for his troubled work and reckless behavior.

"Help!" he gasped, eyes wide with fear. "They're after me!"

The café fell silent, patrons glancing around in confusion, their conversations halting as they processed the sudden intrusion. My mind raced, adrenaline flooding my veins as I instinctively rose from my chair. The last remnants of the moment with Marcus slipped away, replaced by an urgent need to understand what was happening.

"Who's after you?" I asked, my voice steady despite the chaos brewing inside me.

"People who think they own me!" he exclaimed, his panic palpable. "I can't go back. Not now!"

Before I could respond, a loud crash erupted outside, the sound of shattering glass sending shards of fear slicing through the air. Instinctively, I turned, dread pooling in my stomach as I caught a glimpse of shadows moving outside the café windows.

"Get down!" I shouted, adrenaline kicking in as I dove toward the back of the café, heart pounding with the uncertainty of what was to come.

And then, as the shadows loomed larger, a voice boomed from outside, clear and chilling. "We know you're in there! Come out now, and no one gets hurt!"

My breath caught in my throat, realization crashing over me like a wave. This was no ordinary confrontation; this was the beginning of something I could never have anticipated—a collision of worlds that threatened to unravel everything I thought I knew about art, fear, and the fragile threads of connection that bound us all together.

Chapter 3: Threads of Conflict

The gallery buzzed like a hive, each whisper and laughter melding into a symphony of nervous anticipation. I stood in the corner, my fingers tracing the rim of my wine glass, its cool surface a balm against the rising tide of anxiety. Paintings danced before my eyes, colors bleeding into one another, each canvas whispering secrets I was too afraid to unravel. The air was thick with the scent of linseed oil and freshly cut flowers, but the atmosphere carried an electric charge—one that hinted at the friction between ambition and artistry.

Marcus was at the center of it all, his presence commanding, draped in a tailored suit that seemed to absorb the light rather than reflect it. He moved through the crowd with an effortless grace, his expression meticulously neutral, a mask that concealed the tempest I had begun to sense roiling beneath. As he stood before the first piece, a chaotic explosion of color and form, I could see the subtle tightening of his jaw, a flicker of something akin to disdain crossing his features. The artist, a nervous newcomer with hopeful eyes, awaited his judgment like a deer in the headlights.

"Daring, I'll give you that," Marcus began, his voice smooth yet laced with a cold edge. "But this is little more than a study in chaos—confusion masquerading as creativity. The lack of focus is disheartening." I flinched at his words, the harshness echoing in my ears like a gunshot, while the artist's face fell, their excitement crumbling into dust at Marcus's feet.

With each critique, I felt my heart thump harder in my chest, a rhythm of protest against the silence that enveloped the room after his comments. It was almost as if I were watching a dissection, the artist's work laid bare for scrutiny. I admired the vulnerability of my peers, who stood there, raw and exposed, their dreams offered up for slaughter, but there was something about Marcus's unyielding scrutiny that left a bitter taste in my mouth.

As the night wore on, I could not shake the feeling that I was watching a tragic play unfold. Beneath the critic's icy exterior, I glimpsed glimmers of vulnerability, small fissures in his armor that revealed a man far more complex than the harsh words he wielded. In a brief moment between critiques, I caught him staring at a piece that was almost painfully beautiful—a soft portrayal of two figures entwined in a midnight embrace, painted with the brushstrokes of longing and regret. The lines of his face softened, and for a heartbeat, the mask slipped.

Later, as the gallery began to empty and the echoes of laughter faded, I found myself approaching him, the weight of unspoken words heavy on my tongue. "You don't know what it's like to create," I accused, the challenge ringing in the air between us. The intensity of the moment held my breath captive, as if the world had narrowed to just the two of us, circling each other like wary animals.

He looked at me then, his gaze searching, the flicker of regret I had seen earlier returning to his eyes. "And how would you know what I know?" His voice was low, measured, a contrast to the storm I felt raging inside. "Creating is not just about splattering paint on a canvas; it's about the willingness to expose your soul. It requires a level of honesty that most artists are not prepared to face."

I crossed my arms, a gesture of defiance. "Maybe you're just afraid to face it yourself," I shot back, my voice sharper than I intended. "You critique from a distance, hiding behind your words as if they're a shield."

He laughed, but it was a bitter sound. "And what would you have me do? Shower them with praise that isn't deserved? I'm doing them a favor, preparing them for a world that is often crueler than my reviews."

"And yet here you are, alone in your critique. You hide behind your words, Marcus, but they're a veil you wrap around yourself to keep the world at bay." I could feel the pulse of the gallery's afterglow around us, but within that charged atmosphere, there was an unsettling tension—a recognition of our shared solitude, perhaps.

A moment passed where I felt as if we were two ships passing in the night, our paths momentarily intertwined. But just as quickly, he shifted, the walls he had built around himself rising again. "Perhaps you should take your own advice," he said coolly, the warmth from before extinguished. "It's easy to throw stones when you're standing on solid ground."

I couldn't help but recoil at the truth in his words, the sting of recognition slicing through me. I was standing on a precipice, balancing my own insecurities against my dreams, and yet here was this man, so determined to wield his words like weapons, afraid to let anyone see the cracks in his own armor.

I turned away, the laughter and chatter of the remaining patrons suddenly feeling like a world away. The connection we had sparked moments before faded into the cold night air, leaving me feeling unmoored. Outside, the city pulsed with life, the distant sounds of music and laughter promising a world filled with possibility, yet I felt anchored in place, caught between the vibrant chaos of creativity and the numbing chill of critique.

As I stepped out into the night, I couldn't shake the feeling that our paths would continue to cross, that the threads of our conflicts were only just beginning to unravel. The lingering taste of wine and disappointment lingered on my tongue, and I wondered if I was brave enough to forge ahead, to challenge not just him, but the very nature of my own artistic journey.

As I walked away from the gallery, the cool night air wrapped around me like a disheveled shawl, tugging me toward the subway station a few blocks away. The streets were alive with the hum of late-night diners and the occasional burst of laughter from clusters of friends spilling out of bars. My mind, however, was a whirlpool of thoughts, each one pulling me deeper into the conflicting currents of my encounter with Marcus. His words replayed in my mind like an old record, skipping at the most painful parts. It struck me that our confrontation had peeled back a layer I hadn't anticipated—one that revealed the frailty behind his polished facade.

I stepped onto the subway, the lights flickering overhead, casting fleeting shadows that seemed to dance with my thoughts. The car jolted forward, and I held onto the metal pole, trying to anchor myself amidst the sea of humanity. Strangers swayed together, an unspoken bond formed by the rhythm of the train. Each face reflected a unique story, yet mine felt like a cacophony of emotions, struggling to find coherence.

My phone buzzed in my pocket, pulling me from my reverie. I pulled it out and saw a message from Claire, my best friend and fellow artist, who had witnessed my interaction with Marcus. What did you say to him? You looked like you were ready to duel!

I chuckled softly, imagining Claire's wide-eyed expression as she watched us. It was more of a verbal sparring match, I typed back, but I think I might have scored a few points.

Her reply was almost immediate: Only a few? You've got to knock him out next time. He needs it!

As the train rattled on, I couldn't help but wonder about Marcus. Who was he beneath the snark and sharp critiques? There was a fine line between honesty and cruelty, and I suspected he often strayed into the latter territory. Maybe I was the one who had to break through that ice, the one who could reveal the humanity he tried so hard to conceal.

The next day, I found myself in my tiny studio apartment, surrounded by canvases in various states of completion. Each one felt like a reflection of my mood—vibrant with promise or muddied with uncertainty. I set to work, splashing color across the canvas, trying to channel the tumultuous emotions swirling within me. I needed to express my frustration and confusion, to let the paint dance freely without the constraints of critique.

As I layered the paint, the sunlight streamed through my window, illuminating the dust particles that floated lazily in the air. My brush moved with a frenetic energy, the strokes becoming more animated as I lost myself in the rhythm of creation. My mind drifted to Marcus and the sting of his words. It was tempting to see him as a villain in my artistic story, but I knew there had to be more to him.

Suddenly, the doorbell rang, breaking my concentration. I wiped my hands on my apron and made my way to the door, half-expecting it to be the landlord with another complaint about the noise. Instead, I found Claire standing there, her dark curls bouncing as she waved frantically. "I come bearing caffeine and gossip!" she announced, shoving a steaming cup of coffee into my hands.

"Perfect timing," I grinned, taking a sip. The rich flavor slid down my throat, grounding me in the moment. "What's the gossip?"

She plopped down on my couch, her enthusiasm infectious. "I heard through the grapevine that Marcus is holding a workshop next week. The nerve! Can you believe it? After that massacre he called a critique?"

My heart quickened. A workshop? The thought was both exciting and terrifying. "Is it open to everyone?"

"Apparently! He wants to get more people involved in the art scene—his words, not mine. But can you imagine being in a room with him? It would be like walking into a lion's den wearing a steak dress." Claire leaned forward, her eyes sparkling with mischief.

"Sounds like a challenge I might need to accept," I replied, my pulse racing at the idea. "What if I go and confront him again? Show him that artists are more than just the sum of his critiques?"

"Or you could just throw paint at him," Claire suggested, her voice laced with laughter. "You know, a good old-fashioned artistic protest!"

"Tempting," I admitted, a smile creeping onto my face. "But I think I'll save the paint for the canvas. I want to get a glimpse behind that tough exterior."

The rest of the afternoon flew by in a flurry of laughter and planning. Claire and I concocted a strategy for the workshop, envisioning how I would approach Marcus without letting my nerves overshadow my intent. With her support, the idea of facing him transformed from daunting to exhilarating.

As the week crawled toward the workshop, my anticipation grew. I prepared a piece to showcase, a canvas embodying my journey as an artist—a mix of vibrant colors and chaotic brushstrokes that reflected the tumult of emotions within me. I wanted Marcus to see the heart behind my work, the vulnerability that seemed so foreign to him.

When the day finally arrived, I arrived early, the gallery space filled with a quiet hum of expectation. I could see Marcus setting up at the front, his posture rigid, fingers tapping away at his notes, seemingly oblivious to the energy swirling around him. I felt the knot in my stomach tighten as I took a deep breath, steeling myself for what was to come.

The workshop began, and as he spoke, I could feel the tension coiling within me. His voice was confident, authoritative, a stark contrast to the vulnerable artist I knew lay beneath. He dissected the elements of art, offering his critiques with a mix of insight and cutting commentary. I struggled to focus, my mind swirling with the unresolved conflict between us.

And then, when the moment was right, I raised my hand, the heat of my gaze locked onto his. "Marcus," I began, the room quieting as all eyes turned toward me. "Can you explain how you reconcile the passion of creation with the harshness of your critiques?"

A flicker of surprise crossed his face, the carefully crafted mask slipping just for an instant. "It's not about passion; it's about the work," he replied, his voice steady, though the slight tremor revealed the depth of his conviction.

"Isn't the work only half the story? Art comes from a place of vulnerability. It's an extension of ourselves. You have to admit there's more to it than just what's on the surface." My words hung in the air, charged with the electricity of our unspoken tension.

He paused, the silence stretching between us, a delicate thread threatening to snap. In that moment, I sensed a shift, a crack in his carefully constructed armor, as though my words had reached him in ways I hadn't expected. The workshop wasn't just about critique; it was about connection—something I hoped we could build together, even amidst the layers of conflict that still lingered between us.

The sun hung low in the sky, casting a golden hue across the gallery as I paced the polished wooden floor, wrestling with my thoughts. The announcement of the competition had sent shockwaves through the art community, and my stomach twisted with anxiety. I could almost hear the whispers behind my back, the well-meaning friends who would inevitably say, "Oh, it's just a competition; it's not worth losing your head over!" As if they understood the weight of every brushstroke, every late night spent pouring my soul onto canvas. But the truth was far more insidious. This competition had the potential to derail my career entirely.

Chapter 4: How It Began

I needed an edge, something to ensure that my work not only stood out but also made a resounding statement. The irony of seeking help from Marcus wasn't lost on me. He had been my staunchest opponent, a man who could turn the simplest critique into a dagger, his words laced with the sort of disdain that could make even the most confident artist falter. But deep down, beneath that polished exterior and sharp tongue, I sensed a flicker of something—perhaps respect, or maybe it was the thrill of competition that had him on edge.

After a moment's hesitation, I dialed his number, the screen lighting up with his name. My heart raced as I listened to the ringing. Would he even pick up? I braced myself for his inevitable snark, the kind that could peel paint off walls.

"Hello, if this is about a personal loan, I'm afraid I'm not interested," he drawled, his voice as smooth and sarcastic as a fine whiskey.

"Very funny, Marcus. I need your help," I replied, forcing the words past the knot in my throat.

There was a pause, thick with disbelief. "Help? From me? This is either a prank or a sign of the apocalypse."

"Can you be serious for one second?" I shot back, fighting the urge to roll my eyes. "I'm facing a threat to my career here. That gallery is trying to outshine everyone, and I can't afford to be left in the dust."

"Is that so?" He chuckled, an amused note creeping into his voice. "And why would I, your most illustrious rival, choose to help you?"

"Because I know you're capable of appreciating real talent," I shot back, perhaps a little too confidently. "And I'd be willing to bet you don't want to see me crash and burn. At least, not yet."

There was a silence on the line, and I imagined him leaning back in his chair, contemplating my audacity. "Alright, I'll consider it. But know this: my intention is to make you fail spectacularly. Nothing personal; it's just how I operate."

"Perfect," I said, an unexpected grin tugging at my lips. "I'll take that as a yes."

Our first meeting was set for the following afternoon, and I arrived at his gallery, which loomed like a fortress with its imposing glass facade. Inside, the walls were lined with his art—each piece a vivid testament to his skill, yet they were infused with an air of arrogance that I had grown accustomed to. I braced myself as I stepped through the threshold, the scent of fresh paint mingling with something sharper, something distinctly Marcus.

"Welcome to my lair," he said, leaning against a wall, arms crossed. "Do try to resist the urge to admire my brilliance while we work."

"Very generous of you," I replied dryly, surveying the space. "Shall we get to it?"

He motioned for me to follow him into a bright studio filled with canvases in various stages of completion. "First, I want to see what you're working on," he said, gesturing dismissively. "Then I'll tell you exactly what's wrong with it."

The familiarity of our banter was both comforting and infuriating. I set up my easel and unveiled my latest piece—a swirling explosion of color that represented the chaos of my emotions. "It's a work in progress," I said, attempting to mask my vulnerability with bravado.

He studied it for a moment, his brow furrowing. "You're trying too hard," he finally stated, a hint of genuine critique in his tone. "The chaos feels forced. It lacks authenticity."

"Thanks, I'll just whip up a masterpiece while you're busy analyzing it," I shot back, crossing my arms defensively.

"Oh, I didn't say I was done. You need to find the balance between chaos and clarity. Right now, it's all noise and no melody," he countered, a glint of something more—perhaps camaraderie?—in his eyes.

His critique, while laced with sarcasm, struck a chord. For the first time, I felt the walls between us begin to crack. I picked up my brush and began to paint, the colors flowing more freely as he offered suggestions, each one a sharp jab that pushed me to dig deeper.

Hours melted away as we argued over strokes and shades, the atmosphere electric with the tension of our rivalry turned collaboration. "You might actually be worth the effort," he quipped as I stepped back to assess my progress.

"Don't flatter yourself," I shot back, my heart racing. "This is just a temporary alliance. Once I win, it's back to hating you."

"Looking forward to it," he said, a smirk playing on his lips.

But beneath the banter, I felt a growing connection, something that caught me off guard. We were not enemies but two sides of the same coin, both striving for excellence in a world that thrived on competition.

As the sun dipped below the horizon, casting shadows across the room, a sense of camaraderie hung in the air. Just as I was beginning to enjoy this unorthodox partnership, Marcus's phone buzzed, shattering the moment. He glanced at the screen, his expression hardening as he read a message.

"What's wrong?" I asked, curiosity getting the better of me.

"Nothing you need to worry about," he replied curtly, the tension shifting like a storm cloud.

But I could sense the change in his demeanor. His walls were back up, and I couldn't help but wonder what secrets lay hidden behind those carefully constructed defenses. As he turned away, his silhouette framed against the dim light, I felt an unexpected pang of concern.

"Hey," I said, my voice softer than before. "You know you can talk to me, right?"

He glanced back, a flash of vulnerability flickering in his eyes before it vanished, replaced by that familiar arrogance. "You don't want to know what's in my head. Trust me."

But I could see it in the way he clenched his jaw, the way his fingers tightened around his phone. Something loomed just beneath the surface, a tension that had nothing to do with our artistic rivalry. As the shadows deepened, I knew I had stumbled onto a deeper mystery—one that could change everything.

"Then enlighten me," I said, stepping closer, but he shook his head, the moment slipping away like sand through fingers.

Before I could press further, the sound of shattering glass echoed through the gallery, a sudden and terrifying crash that echoed like thunder. My heart raced as we both turned toward the source, dread settling in the pit of my stomach.

"Stay here," he ordered, moving toward the sound with an intensity that made my skin prickle.

"Like hell," I shot back, trailing behind him. Whatever was happening felt bigger than either of us. The tension between us shifted again, now charged with urgency and fear.

As we reached the edge of the gallery, I froze, my breath hitching in my throat. What lay before us was a scene of chaos that had nothing to do with our earlier argument. Something was shrouded in darkness, lurking just beyond the reach of the flickering lights, a shadowy figure slipping through the cracks of our reality.

In that moment, our rivalry faded away, overshadowed by the gravity of the unknown. We were no longer competitors; we were allies bound by something far greater. The air thickened with suspense, each heartbeat drumming in my ears as I stepped closer to the precipice of what lay ahead.

"What the hell is that?" I whispered, dread pooling in my stomach.

Marcus glanced back at me, his expression a mix of determination and apprehension. "I don't know," he said, his voice low, "but we're about to find out."

With that, we plunged into the dark, our unexpected alliance sealing our fates as we stepped into the unknown.

Chapter 5: Shadows from the Past

The dim glow of the studio's fairy lights cast a warm, inviting hue across the canvas, the scattered paintbrushes, and the half-empty coffee cups that served as silent witnesses to our late-night discussions. Marcus stood at the easel, his silhouette framed against the vibrant chaos of color. The tension in his jaw told me he was battling something far deeper than the splashes of paint he effortlessly swirled on the canvas. It was as if every stroke unleashed a torrent of emotions that he had bottled up, each swirl a hidden fragment of his past.

"Do you think if I mix this shade of cerulean with just a hint of violet, it will convey the depth of sorrow I feel about my lack of talent?" He tossed the brush onto the palette with exaggerated flair, a crooked smile forming on his lips. The sarcasm was a shield, one I had come to recognize. Beneath the bravado, I sensed the shadows looming just out of reach.

"Only if you want to scare off all your potential admirers," I shot back, rolling my eyes with a dramatic flourish. My heart fluttered at the sight of him, the way his dark hair fell across his forehead and the way his eyes sparkled even under the weight of unspoken words. "But seriously, have you ever considered that art might be more about the emotion behind it than the technique?"

"Emotion?" He scoffed, though his eyes betrayed a flicker of intrigue. "What do you know about emotion, Miss I-paint-with-a-broad-brush-and-hope-for-the-best?"

"More than you think," I replied, feigning indifference as I picked up a brush and dipped it into the vibrant magenta. "But if you're afraid of showing your true colors, just stick to the sarcasm. It suits you."

With a dramatic flourish, I swiped the brush across my canvas, splattering magenta against the cooler tones Marcus had chosen.

A messy blend of hues danced in a beautiful chaos, mirroring the growing tension between us. It was in those moments, amid our playful banter, that I realized how much I had come to care for him. I admired the way he navigated the darkness of his past, even if it meant retreating behind layers of humor. But I wanted more from him—needed more.

As our conversations deepened over the weeks, I discovered fragments of Marcus's past—fleeting glimpses of a time when laughter didn't feel so far away. He spoke of his sister in hushed tones, as if saying her name too loudly would summon her ghost back into the room. I learned about the reckless nights spent waiting for her to come home, the heartache of watching someone you love slip through your fingers like sand. It felt like a privilege to hear these stories, an invitation into his world that he rarely offered to anyone.

One evening, the air was thick with the scent of paint and a hint of jasmine from the window left ajar. The warm breeze carried the faint sound of laughter from the street below, a stark contrast to the somber mood that had settled between us. I had just finished my latest creation—a blend of colors that mirrored the chaos of my heart—and turned to Marcus, ready to break the silence that loomed like a storm cloud.

"Tell me about your sister," I urged gently, meeting his gaze. "You don't have to, but... I want to know."

He hesitated, the flicker of vulnerability passing over his features like a shadow. "She was... everything. The kind of person who could light up a room with just a smile. But life... it has a way of extinguishing even the brightest flames." His voice was low, heavy with the weight of memories.

"I'm sorry," I whispered, feeling the ache of his loss wrap around my heart like a vise. "You don't have to carry that burden alone, you know."

"Easy for you to say," he shot back, but there was no venom in his tone, just a weariness that settled in his eyes. "You don't know what it's like to lose someone and have the world keep spinning as if nothing happened. To feel like you're stuck in a time capsule, and everyone else gets to move on."

"Maybe not," I admitted, my voice softening. "But I know what it's like to feel alone in a crowded room, to pretend everything is fine when it's not. We're all haunted by something, Marcus."

In that moment, we were both vulnerable, exposed. The laughter of the street faded into the background, and the only sound was the soft brush of bristles against canvas. My heart raced as I took a step closer, feeling the heat radiate between us, an invisible tether drawing us together.

Just then, the door swung open with a dramatic creak, and our world was shattered. A figure loomed in the doorway, silhouetted against the light. I squinted, trying to make out the features, my heart racing with a mixture of dread and recognition.

"Marcus," the voice was cold, dripping with malice. "Looks like you haven't changed much."

My stomach twisted as I recognized the intruder—someone I had only heard whispers of, a name that hung like a dark cloud over Marcus's past. A knot of tension tightened in my chest, the atmosphere crackling with uncertainty. The warm glow of our shared moment evaporated, replaced by an icy dread that seeped into every corner of the studio.

"What do you want?" Marcus's voice was steady, but I could see the flicker of fear in his eyes.

"Just wanted to see how my favorite artist is doing," the figure sneered, stepping into the room with an air of entitlement. My heart sank, knowing that whatever bond Marcus and I had forged in our late-night discussions was now under threat.

The air grew thick with tension as the figure in the doorway stepped forward, the harsh light casting long shadows that danced across the studio floor. My pulse quickened, and instinctively, I shifted closer to Marcus, though I could feel the strain radiating from him like heat waves on a summer day. The intruder smirked, his presence an unwelcome specter, instantly reminding me of the complexities we had begun to untangle together.

"Just wanted to check in on you, Marcus," he said, his voice smooth yet laced with an unsettling undertone. "Missed our little chats." He leaned casually against the door frame, arms crossed, as if he owned the very air we breathed.

Marcus straightened, a defensive posture I'd never seen before, the casual bravado slipping away to reveal a raw, almost palpable vulnerability. "I'm not interested in your games anymore, Aaron," he replied, his tone clipped, each word heavy with unspoken history. The warmth of our earlier conversation felt like a distant memory, washed away by the cold tide of confrontation.

"Oh, come on," Aaron drawled, his eyes glinting with mischief. "You think you can just cut me out like I'm some old sketch you don't need anymore? We've got unfinished business, don't we?" He pushed off the door frame and took a step inside, the tension in the room tightening around us like a noose.

"Unfinished business?" I interjected, my voice steadier than I felt. "What does that mean? Who even are you?" I shot Marcus a quick glance, hoping for some indication that he had a plan, but his face was a mask of conflicted emotions.

"I'm just a friend helping Marcus remember what he left behind," Aaron replied, flashing a disarming smile that sent chills down my spine. "Isn't that right, Marcus? Or have you decided to forget the past completely?"

"Enough," Marcus growled, stepping forward. "You need to leave. I'm done with you and whatever hold you think you have over me." His voice wavered, but the fire in his eyes ignited a spark of courage I hadn't expected.

"Such defiance," Aaron chuckled, the sound oozing with condescension. "It's amusing, really. But you know, ghosts have a way of coming back to haunt you, no matter how hard you try to forget." He glanced at me, a predator assessing his prey. "And it looks like you've got a new little distraction now. A pretty one, too."

My heart raced, anger bubbling beneath my skin. "I'm not a distraction, and neither is Marcus," I shot back, crossing my arms defiantly. "You don't know anything about us."

"Ah, feisty. I like that," he replied, raising an eyebrow in mock admiration. "But really, you should be careful. Some pasts are better left buried." With that, he turned on his heel and strolled toward the exit, pausing only to look back at Marcus, a cruel smirk playing on his lips. "You know where to find me, brother. I'll be waiting."

As the door swung shut behind him, the studio felt emptier, the warmth evaporating like steam from a freshly brewed cup of coffee. I looked at Marcus, who stood frozen, the color drained from his face. "What just happened?" I asked softly, my heart aching for the storm brewing within him.

"I—I thought I had put all that behind me," he stammered, running a hand through his hair in frustration. "But I guess you can't just erase memories like paint on a canvas."

"What did he mean by 'unfinished business'?" I pressed gently, hoping to peel back the layers of his guarded exterior.

He sighed, a deep, weary sound that echoed through the silence. "Aaron and I were close once, back when my sister was alive. He was part of that world—the dark one that consumed her. I thought I was leaving all of it behind when I distanced myself from him, but clearly, he doesn't share the same sentiment."

"Is he dangerous?" I asked, my voice barely above a whisper, the air thick with apprehension.

"He has a way of twisting things. He knows how to play on fears, how to dig up scars." Marcus's gaze was distant, lost in the memories that threatened to resurface. "He'll say anything to regain control, to remind me of what I tried to escape."

"Marcus," I began, searching for the right words, "you don't have to face this alone. We can figure it out together."

He turned to me, a mixture of gratitude and fear reflected in his eyes. "I didn't want to drag you into this mess. You deserve better than my baggage."

I stepped closer, emboldened by my own feelings. "And you deserve someone who won't run when things get tough. You're not just a collection of your past mistakes."

He studied me, his expression shifting from uncertainty to something softer, something that made my heart leap. "You make it sound so easy. But the past is... complicated."

"It always is," I replied, my voice steady. "But facing it is the first step. You've already made progress by opening up to me."

His lips curled into a small, grateful smile that warmed the edges of the tension. "You're remarkable, you know that?"

"Remarkable? I just throw paint around and pretend I know what I'm doing." I chuckled, the mood shifting slightly as we danced around the heavy weight of our emotions. "But I'll gladly accept the compliment if it helps keep your spirits up."

The faintest flicker of lightness returned to his eyes, but I could still feel the undercurrent of fear swirling beneath the surface. "You have no idea how hard it is to break free from the chains of the past," he murmured, almost to himself.

"And you have no idea how much I'm willing to help you break those chains," I countered, my voice unwavering.

As he leaned against the easel, his shoulders slumped, the weight of his struggles more pronounced. "If I let you in, you might regret it. I don't want to be the reason you get hurt."

"I'd rather face the storm with you than hide in a corner," I insisted, stepping into the space between us, closing the distance. "Let me be part of your story, the good and the bad."

He took a deep breath, and for a moment, it felt like the world outside had faded away, leaving just the two of us suspended in this fragile moment of understanding. "You really want to do this?" he asked, a mixture of hope and fear in his voice.

"More than anything," I replied, feeling the weight of my own resolve. "But only if you promise to meet me halfway."

With that unspoken agreement, the walls between us began to shift, the past still looming, but now with the faintest glimmer of hope threading through the darkness.

The stillness that followed Aaron's departure was deafening, wrapping around us like a thick fog. The echoes of his taunts lingered in the air, a chilling reminder of the shadows that had reentered Marcus's life. I stood there, the space between us charged with unspoken fears and the weight of a new reality. My heart raced, caught between the urgency to comfort him and the dread of what lay ahead.

"I can't believe he showed up like that," Marcus muttered, running his fingers over the canvas, now splattered with remnants of our earlier creativity. "I thought I had cut ties, but I guess he's not so easily forgotten."

"Some people cling to the past like a lifeboat," I said softly, moving to stand beside him. "But you're not drowning anymore. You've fought your way back."

His eyes flickered to mine, uncertainty mingling with gratitude. "I just don't want to drag you into this mess. You deserve—"

"—someone without baggage?" I finished for him, shaking my head. "Sorry, but I'm not that person. We all carry something, Marcus. I'd rather face the storm with you than run away."

He smiled, but it didn't quite reach his eyes. "It's just that this isn't the fairytale you're used to. You have no idea what I've done, what I've seen."

"Neither do you," I replied, my voice firm. "You have no idea what's waiting for you on the other side of this fear. Let's turn this mess into something beautiful, together."

Marcus turned toward me, his expression shifting. "Together? That sounds nice, but... what if I mess it up?"

"Then we'll mess it up together," I said, the warmth of connection sparking between us again. "Trust me, I'm pretty good at finding the silver lining in chaos."

Before he could respond, a loud knock echoed through the studio, the sound sharp and demanding, slicing through the fragile atmosphere we'd built. I glanced at the door, heart racing. "Who could that be at this hour?"

Marcus stiffened, his gaze darting to the entrance as though he could sense a storm brewing outside. "I don't know, but I'm not in the mood for surprise visitors."

"Neither am I," I muttered, moving cautiously toward the door, my instincts on high alert. "Stay behind me."

I pulled open the door, half-expecting to find a harmless neighbor or a delivery person, but instead, I was greeted by a familiar face that sent a chill racing down my spine. It was Jenna, Marcus's childhood friend, the one person I had heard Marcus mention only in fleeting memories, always cloaked in shadows and secrecy.

"Jenna," Marcus breathed, stepping forward, disbelief etched across his features. "What are you doing here?"

"I had to find you." Her voice was urgent, almost frantic, eyes darting around as if she expected someone to leap from the shadows. "You need to listen to me. It's important."

I felt the tension crackle like static in the air, each heartbeat resonating with the weight of her words. "What's going on?" I asked, shifting my position to protect Marcus, though my own heart raced with confusion and concern.

"Not here," she insisted, glancing over her shoulder, her voice barely above a whisper. "We need to talk somewhere private."

Marcus exchanged a look with me, uncertainty etched across his brow. "This isn't the best time, Jenna. Things are... complicated."

"Complicated doesn't begin to cover it," she shot back, her frustration boiling over. "I know about Aaron. I know what he's capable of, and you need to be careful."

"What do you mean?" I asked, stepping closer, desperation creeping into my voice. "What does he want?"

Jenna shook her head, her eyes wide and frantic. "He's not just playing games. He has something on you, Marcus. Something he's willing to use against you. You need to trust me."

The air turned electric with fear and uncertainty, the atmosphere heavy with unspoken truths. "You know about my past?" Marcus asked, his voice tight.

"Enough to know that you can't let him get into your head," Jenna replied, stepping fully into the room. "I've seen what he does to people, Marcus. He'll use everything against you—your fears, your guilt."

I could see the conflict swirling within Marcus, the raw vulnerability exposed once more. "I thought I was done with him. That I had moved on."

Jenna placed a hand on his arm, grounding him, her expression softening. "I know. But he won't let you go that easily. You have to be ready for anything."

"What do you want from me?" he asked, frustration spilling over into his voice. "I can't keep living in fear of what he might do. I thought I was strong enough to face him."

"You are strong," Jenna assured him, but her voice wavered slightly. "But strength isn't just about facing the storm; it's knowing when to take shelter. And right now, you need to listen."

I glanced between them, sensing the gravity of their shared history, the bond that had been forged in both light and darkness. "What do we need to do?" I pressed, my determination hardening.

"There's more at stake than just your past," Jenna said, her voice steadying. "Aaron has been making threats, and he's gotten to people close to you. We need to figure out his next move before it's too late."

The implications of her words hung in the air like an ominous storm cloud, dark and heavy. My heart raced, a mixture of fear and resolve building within me. "What do you mean 'people close to you'?"

"That's just it. He's already reached out to others, trying to draw you back into that world," Jenna said, her gaze locking onto Marcus. "You need to prepare for a fight."

Marcus's expression hardened, the facade of bravado returning as he squared his shoulders. "I won't go back to that life. I refuse."

"Then let's make a plan," I chimed in, determination coursing through me. "We can outsmart him. Use his own tactics against him."

A flicker of hope danced in Marcus's eyes, but it was quickly overshadowed by the weight of the situation. "And what if that's not enough?" he asked, the vulnerability creeping back into his voice.

Jenna's gaze grew serious, the shadows deepening in her eyes. "Then we'll have to face him head-on, together."

A sudden noise echoed from outside—a distant shout, followed by the unmistakable sound of glass shattering. My heart dropped, instinct urging me to look out the window. A small group of people were gathered in the street, their faces contorted in panic, the chaos unfolding beyond our safe haven.

"Marcus, we need to go. Now," I urged, my voice laced with urgency.

As we turned to leave, a dark figure emerged from the shadows at the edge of the street, a sinister grin spreading across his face. I froze, recognition crashing over me like a tidal wave, the nightmare of Marcus's past converging with our present.

"Aaron," Marcus breathed, a mix of disbelief and dread flooding his expression.

And just like that, the world around us spiraled into chaos, the past and present colliding in a way that threatened to unravel everything we had fought to build.

Chapter 6: The Unraveling

The night wrapped itself around us like a thick fog, muffling the city's usual cacophony and drawing the edges of our world into shadow. I sat across from Marcus in the dimly lit corner of my living room, the glow of a single lamp illuminating the furrow of his brow as he reviewed the latest information we'd gathered. The remnants of takeout lay abandoned on the coffee table, their cardboard boxes growing cold, but we hadn't noticed. We were too engrossed in our growing entanglement with danger, our breaths heavy with tension and the unspoken words that lingered just out of reach.

"I still think we should go to the police," I said, my voice barely a whisper, as if saying it too loudly would somehow draw the threat closer. Marcus looked up, his eyes catching the light, revealing a storm swirling in their depths. "You know they can't help us," he replied, his tone edged with a weariness that felt too familiar. "This isn't just some petty crime we're dealing with. They won't understand."

His words hung in the air, weighted with the gravity of his experiences, and I couldn't shake the image of him—always slightly on edge, like a coiled spring ready to snap. Marcus had once been an ally, a man who seemed to glide through life with effortless charm, but now he wore his secrets like armor, every guarded glance revealing just how much he had yet to share. The thought sent a shiver down my spine, not just from fear but from an undeniable attraction that crackled between us, a tension so palpable it made the hair on my arms stand on end.

I leaned forward, elbows resting on my knees, an attempt to bridge the distance that felt like a chasm growing wider by the day. "Then what's the plan?" I asked, determination replacing the trepidation that had gripped me moments before. "We can't just sit here and wait for something to happen."

He ran a hand through his tousled hair, a gesture that was both exasperating and oddly endearing. "We need to draw them out. If they think we're scared, they'll keep coming. But if we show them we're not afraid..." His voice trailed off, a wicked glint sparking in his eyes. "We can take the fight to them."

A mix of exhilaration and dread rushed through me. I knew the risks; I'd seen enough movies to recognize the thrill of the chase—the allure of danger mingled with the excitement of outsmarting an adversary. But this wasn't a film; it was our lives, and every decision felt like a dance on the edge of a precipice.

"What do you have in mind?" I asked, intrigued despite the rational part of me screaming for caution. Marcus leaned back, a slow smile spreading across his face, the kind that made my heart race. "A little misdirection. We'll set up a fake meeting, bait them into revealing themselves. It'll be risky, but I think we can manage it."

I couldn't help but laugh at the absurdity of it all. "You make it sound so easy. 'We'll just lure them in, throw caution to the wind, and hope for the best.'" My sarcasm hung heavy in the air, but Marcus didn't flinch.

"Trust me," he said, his gaze steady and intense. "I've dealt with worse. This is just another puzzle to solve." The way he looked at me, with that fierce determination in his eyes, made my stomach twist in a way that felt almost pleasurable. It was both frightening and intoxicating, the thrill of being swept up in his world.

As we plotted late into the night, the boundaries between us began to blur. I caught glimpses of the man behind the secrets—his laugh, a quicksilver thing that cut through the tension, revealing a sense of humor as sharp as a well-honed blade. Each word exchanged sparked something in me, igniting a flame that was impossible to ignore.

But there was also an undeniable weight pressing down on us. We both knew that this plan was precarious at best, and the stakes were rising. As dawn approached, casting pale light through the curtains, I caught Marcus's eye, and for a fleeting moment, the world outside faded away. "What if this goes wrong?" I asked softly, my heart racing at the thought.

He leaned closer, his voice barely above a whisper, "Then we adapt. Together."

In that moment, something shifted in the air between us. I felt the magnetic pull drawing us closer, like the inevitability of night following day. Yet the reality of our situation loomed larger than any fleeting connection, a constant reminder of the danger we faced.

As we prepared to enact our plan, the streets of the city felt different, a palpable tension crackling in the air. The hum of the world outside was replaced by the sound of my heartbeat, loud and insistent. I couldn't shake the feeling that we were walking a tightrope, and any misstep could send us tumbling into the unknown.

Each day passed in a blur of frantic planning, stolen glances, and hushed conversations. The chemistry between us intensified, blooming amidst the chaos, yet the threat always lingered, like a shadow that refused to fade. We were teetering on the edge of something monumental, and I wondered if we were strong enough to weather the storm brewing on the horizon.

With each passing hour, the uncertainty grew. The line between ally and adversary began to blur, the tension around us thickening as we drew closer to the date of our confrontation. I didn't just feel a sense of dread; I felt an exhilarating rush, the thrill of the unknown driving me forward. In the quiet moments between strategy sessions, I caught myself lost in thoughts of Marcus—his laughter, the way his smile lit up his face, and the darkness that lurked just beneath the surface.

Whatever secrets he carried, I was determined to uncover them, not just for my safety but for the connection that was undeniably forming between us. The stakes were rising, and as the sun dipped below the horizon, I braced myself for the unraveling that lay ahead.

The day arrived with a shroud of gray clouds, a stark contrast to the vibrant colors of the autumn leaves outside. The air was thick with the scent of impending rain, mingling with the musk of damp earth and the faint sweetness of decaying foliage. I stood by the window, watching droplets gather on the glass, the rhythmic tapping echoing the frantic drumming of my heart. Today was the day we would confront whatever lay hidden in the shadows, and I could feel the weight of our plan pressing against my chest like a vise.

Marcus was pacing in the small living room, his movements restless, each step echoing the tension simmering between us. "Are you sure about this?" he asked, stopping to look at me, his dark eyes searching for any hint of doubt. I knew what he was really asking. It wasn't just about the plan; it was about us, our precarious connection woven through layers of danger and unspoken longing.

"Of course," I replied, adopting a tone of bravado I didn't entirely feel. "What's the worst that could happen? We'll either win or... we'll win," I added, attempting to inject some humor into the moment. Marcus raised an eyebrow, a hint of a smile playing at the corners of his mouth, and for a brief second, the weight of the world fell away.

"Right, that's a comforting thought," he replied, crossing his arms and leaning against the wall, his posture casual but his expression anything but. "But seriously, we need to be ready for anything. These people aren't playing games."

The memory of the threats that had started as whispers now echoed in my mind—muffled voices in dark alleyways, shadowy figures lurking just out of sight. I nodded, steeling myself against the rising tide of anxiety. "I know. But we're prepared. We've got a plan, and I trust you." My words hung in the air, heavy with the promise of vulnerability.

He stepped closer, the space between us crackling with unarticulated emotions. "Trust is a dangerous thing," he murmured, his voice low and thick, as if it were a fragile thing that could shatter at any moment. I swallowed hard, feeling the heat of his gaze like a tangible force. "I'd rather be cautious than naïve."

As the clock ticked closer to our meeting time, we moved through our final preparations, each action infused with an urgency that heightened my senses. I couldn't shake the feeling that we were stepping into a well-laid trap, one designed to ensnare us both. The thought made my stomach churn, yet a part of me reveled in the thrill of danger, the way it ignited something deep within me.

When we finally stepped outside, the world felt different, imbued with a kind of electric anticipation. The sky was a slate gray, heavy with clouds, as we made our way down the rain-slicked streets. My heart raced with each step, the city humming around us, a living organism pulsating with secrets. Every passerby could have been an ally or an enemy, and I felt the sharp edge of paranoia slice through me.

We arrived at the designated spot, a quiet café tucked away in a side street, where the smell of brewing coffee mingled with the faint notes of baked goods. It should have felt cozy, but the air was thick with tension. I took a deep breath, trying to steady my nerves as we entered. The soft murmur of conversations blended into an ambient noise, a stark contrast to the chaos swirling in my mind.

Marcus led the way to a table in the back, his presence both reassuring and intimidating. I couldn't help but admire the way he moved through the world, an effortless confidence that drew attention without him even trying. As we settled into our seats, I caught a glimpse of myself in the reflection of the café window. I looked composed, yet inside, I was a whirlpool of emotions—anticipation, fear, and an undeniable thrill that curled in my stomach like a cat ready to pounce.

Just as I opened my mouth to voice a thought, the door swung open, and in strode a figure cloaked in darkness, a tall man with a presence that commanded attention. My heart raced as he approached our table, the weight of his gaze pinning me in place. "Marcus," he said, his voice smooth and unsettling. "I see you're still playing with fire."

"Elias," Marcus replied, his voice steely. The familiarity in their exchange sent a shiver down my spine, an unspoken history crackling in the air between them. I sat up straighter, acutely aware of the tension that had shifted palpably in the room.

"Do you have what I asked for?" Elias leaned forward, his eyes glinting with something dangerous. I exchanged a quick glance with Marcus, whose jaw clenched at the obvious insinuation. "Let's just say I'm here for business, not to reminisce," Marcus retorted, his voice calm but firm.

The game had begun. My pulse quickened as I watched the two men engage in a silent standoff, words barely exchanged, yet their body language spoke volumes. I was merely a pawn in this dangerous chess match, caught between their unresolved pasts and the threat that loomed just beyond our understanding.

Elias smirked, his expression condescending. "You're in over your head, Marcus. You know that, right? This isn't just about you anymore."

I felt Marcus tense beside me, the energy in the air shifting like a storm about to break. "I can handle myself," he snapped, his voice low and dangerous, and I felt a surge of admiration for his defiance. But beneath it all was a flicker of fear that worried me.

"Let's cut to the chase," Elias said, his demeanor shifting to one of calculated menace. "You're looking for answers, but I have to warn you, some secrets are best left buried." The implication hung in the air, a sharp blade poised to strike.

"Are you threatening us?" I interjected, my voice steady despite the tremor of uncertainty that clutched at my heart. Both men turned to me, surprise flickering across their faces. Marcus's gaze held mine, a mixture of pride and concern reflected in his dark eyes.

"Not a threat, just a warning," Elias replied smoothly, though I could see the irritation beneath his façade. "People have lost everything digging too deep."

"Then I guess I'll have to make sure we don't lose," I shot back, surprising even myself with the strength of my voice. I was tired of being sidelined, tired of letting fear dictate my actions. Marcus shot me a glance, a flicker of admiration sparking in his eyes, and I felt emboldened by it.

"Bold move," Elias sneered, but there was an undertone of respect in his tone, as if he hadn't expected me to stand my ground. "You're playing a dangerous game, little girl."

I met his gaze unflinchingly, refusing to back down. "It's a game we intend to win."

In that charged moment, I sensed a shift in the air. The stakes had been raised, and our little plan had spiraled into a showdown far beyond what we had anticipated. With a final flicker of intrigue, Elias turned to Marcus, the tension palpable, the threat unmistakable. "You may have chosen your path, but be careful what you wish for."

As he walked away, the air felt charged, a sudden rush of adrenaline flooding my veins. I turned to Marcus, breathless. "What just happened?"

He leaned back, his expression a mix of frustration and admiration. "We just put a target on our backs, and I hope you're ready for the storm that's coming."

The air was thick with anticipation, every heartbeat echoing the unspoken truth: we were in deep, and there was no turning back.

The café buzzed with the hum of conversations and the clinking of cups, but all I could hear was the pounding of my heart, matching the relentless drumming of the rain outside. Marcus's gaze lingered on the door long after Elias had disappeared into the misty streets, a mix of irritation and concern etched into his features. I couldn't shake the feeling that we had crossed some invisible line, stepping into a game with stakes higher than either of us had anticipated.

"Are you okay?" I asked, though I knew the answer. His shoulders were tense, the muscles rigid under the fabric of his shirt, a telltale sign of the storm brewing within him. He turned to me, a flicker of vulnerability surfacing in his otherwise stoic demeanor.

"I'm just... processing." His words hung heavy, laden with unspoken fears. "Elias isn't just a name; he's a shadow from my past, a reminder of everything I've tried to leave behind."

I leaned in, drawn closer by an invisible thread of empathy. "What did he mean by secrets?"

Marcus rubbed the back of his neck, a gesture I'd come to recognize as a signal of discomfort. "There are things I never wanted you to know, things I thought I could protect you from. But now..." His voice trailed off, leaving a cavern of uncertainty between us.

"Now what?" I pressed, my heart racing as curiosity mingled with concern. "You can't just drop a bomb like that and expect me to let it slide."

He hesitated, his expression a tapestry of regret and longing. "I didn't want to involve you in this. I thought I could handle it on my own."

"But here we are," I interjected, a playful defiance dancing on my lips. "In this delightful mess together. You've let me in, so let's deal with it together."

Marcus's lips twitched, caught between a smile and a grimace. "You're stubborn."

"I prefer determined," I shot back, feeling a spark of warmth amidst the tension.

He chuckled softly, the sound easing some of the heaviness that had settled between us. "Alright, determined it is. But you need to understand, this isn't just about us. This goes deeper."

A flash of uncertainty flickered in his eyes, and I felt the weight of his words settle around us. The café around us continued its dance, oblivious to the tempest brewing in our corner. "So, what's the plan now?" I asked, steering us back to the task at hand.

"We wait," he replied, his voice low, the seriousness returning. "Elias may think he has the upper hand, but he's just as curious about us as we are about him. We need to play it cool."

"Playing it cool is not exactly my forte," I admitted, my mind racing with possibilities. "What if he's already one step ahead?"

Marcus met my gaze, a spark of challenge igniting in his eyes. "Then we need to be smarter. Outthink him at every turn."

With that, we moved into a strategic rhythm, our conversation a blend of ideas and theories, plans and contingencies. We plotted our next steps, our laughter occasionally punctuating the tension as we sketched out scenarios on the backs of napkins. For a fleeting moment, the world outside faded into a dull roar, leaving just the two of us navigating this uncharted territory.

As the hours slipped away, the rain intensified, a steady drum against the windows, creating a barrier between our little haven and the chaos beyond. But just as I began to feel a sense of control, the café door swung open again, a rush of cold air preceding a figure cloaked in darkness. My stomach dropped as I recognized the sharp angles of the man striding toward us.

Elias.

"Did you really think I'd let you go so easily?" he purred, his voice smooth but laced with a menace that sent chills racing down my spine. Marcus instinctively shifted, placing himself between me and the approaching threat.

"Back off, Elias," Marcus warned, his tone low and edged. "This isn't your territory."

Elias smirked, a self-satisfied glint in his eye. "Territory? Oh, I believe we're well past that. This is a game, my friend, and I have no intention of losing."

"Then why don't you play fair?" I shot back, my courage ignited by the adrenaline coursing through me. "If this is a game, why are you trying to intimidate us?"

He turned his gaze to me, the flicker of surprise quickly replaced by intrigue. "Feisty, aren't you? I'll admit, it's refreshing."

"Don't flatter yourself," I snapped, my heart pounding, willing myself to maintain composure. "What do you want?"

Elias stepped closer, the air thickening with tension, his presence both compelling and threatening. "You have something I want, and I'm willing to make a deal."

Marcus's posture stiffened, protective instincts kicking in. "We're not interested in your games, Elias."

"Oh, but you should be," Elias replied, a glimmer of something predatory in his eyes. "I know where to find the answers you're seeking, Marcus. All you have to do is cooperate."

"What answers?" I demanded, stepping around Marcus, unwilling to hide behind him any longer. The thrill of defiance coursed through me. "You're just trying to manipulate us."

He raised an eyebrow, the corners of his mouth curling into a smile that sent shivers down my spine. "You're smarter than I thought. But manipulation is part of the game, my dear. Besides, there's much more at stake than you realize."

Marcus's hand found mine beneath the table, a silent gesture of reassurance. I squeezed back, bolstered by his presence, even as dread coiled in my stomach. "What do you know?" I pressed, unwilling to back down.

"Everything," Elias said, his tone dripping with a confidence that felt almost predatory. "And nothing at all. I know Marcus has secrets, but I also know there are things that should stay buried. But if you're willing to play, I can help you find what you're looking for."

"And what's the price?" Marcus asked, his voice low and tense, the warning clear in his tone.

Elias leaned in closer, the scent of danger swirling between us. "Oh, I think the price will be quite personal. You'll have to decide how much you're willing to sacrifice to uncover the truth."

My heart raced as a wave of unease washed over me. I glanced at Marcus, searching for answers in his eyes. The atmosphere crackled with unresolved tension, every heartbeat amplifying the danger lurking beneath the surface.

"I'll never trust you," I stated firmly, trying to reclaim some sense of control, my voice steady despite the whirlwind of thoughts racing through my mind.

"Trust is overrated," Elias replied, leaning back with an air of satisfaction. "But remember this: in this game, knowledge is power, and power can change everything."

As he turned to leave, the tension in the café seemed to shift, an unseen weight pressing down on us. I could feel the storm brewing not just outside but within our own hearts, a tempest of uncertainty and unresolved emotions.

"What do we do now?" I asked, my voice barely above a whisper, the gravity of the situation settling heavily between us.

Marcus squeezed my hand again, determination radiating from him like heat. "We prepare for the worst. Whatever Elias is playing at, we need to be ready."

As we stood up to leave, I caught a glimpse of a figure lurking just outside the café window, a shadow blending into the rain-soaked street. My pulse quickened, dread pooling in my stomach. "Marcus," I breathed, my voice trembling.

But before I could say another word, a blaring siren sliced through the air, the sound sharp and discordant, followed by the rush of police cars barreling down the street. My heart sank as I turned to Marcus, the realization dawning like a cold wave crashing over me.

"We've been found," he said, his voice steady but laced with urgency.

Just as the door swung open again, and a figure clad in black stormed inside, I felt the world shift around us, spinning toward an inevitable confrontation that neither of us could escape. The storm was here, and we were right in the eye of it.

Chapter 7: Confrontation

A chill settled over the room, wrapping around us like an unwelcome blanket. I could hear my heartbeat thundering in my ears as I paced back and forth, my fingers running anxiously through my hair. Outside, the world was drenched in twilight, shadows stretching and merging as the sun succumbed to the horizon. I had always loved this time of day—the way the sky painted itself in hues of lavender and gold, promising the intimacy of evening. But tonight, the beauty felt like a cruel joke, taunting me with its serenity while turmoil brewed within my heart.

Marcus stood by the window, his broad shoulders silhouetted against the last rays of sunlight. He looked so imposing, so infuriatingly calm, as if the storm brewing inside me was nothing but a passing drizzle to him. I could feel anger bubbling just beneath my skin, the kind that ignited flames rather than mere irritation. "You can't keep running from your past, Marcus!" I snapped, the words escaping my lips like firecrackers.

He turned to me, his eyes narrowed, a flicker of something fierce dancing across his features. "And you can't keep pretending to be someone you're not. This isn't a fairy tale, Emily." His voice was low, gravelly, and it sent a shiver down my spine. I could feel the weight of his accusation settling over me like a lead blanket.

"I'm not pretending!" I shouted, frustration pouring out with each syllable. "I'm just trying to understand why you keep pushing me away! Do you really think I can't handle it?" The words hung in the air between us, heavy and charged.

A silence enveloped the room, thick and suffocating, as we stared at each other. I wanted to claw at the tension that sparked in the air, to rip apart the unspoken barriers he had constructed between us. I took a step closer, my heart racing, adrenaline coursing through my veins. "You let me in just enough to feel connected, but then you shove me out like I'm some kind of disease!"

He inhaled sharply, his jaw tightening. "You think it's easy for me? You think I want to feel like this?" He gestured around, as if indicating the invisible strings tying us together and pulling us apart. "You're not the only one who's scared, Emily."

The admission hit me like a rogue wave, knocking the breath from my lungs. I'd seen the pain in his eyes, the shadows that loomed behind his bravado, but hearing him say it felt like uncovering a raw nerve. "Then why don't you let me help you? Why don't you let me in?" I pleaded, my voice softening. I was desperate to peel back the layers of his guarded heart, to uncover the man beneath the armor.

He stepped toward me, closing the distance until there was barely a breath between us. The scent of sandalwood and something distinctly him enveloped me, intoxicating and maddening all at once. "Because it's easier to push you away than to let you see the real me," he confessed, the vulnerability in his voice disarming. "You deserve better than this."

"Better than you?" I scoffed, surprised by the sting of his words. "You think I want some perfect prince? I want you—flaws and all. But you have to meet me halfway."

His brow furrowed, and for a heartbeat, I thought he might actually relent. But the flicker of hope in my chest dimmed when he crossed his arms, shutting me out once more. "You don't know what you're asking for," he warned, his voice low and strained.

I stood there, frustration boiling over, the urge to shake him until he understood clashing with the overwhelming desire to reach out and touch him. "Try me," I said, my challenge hanging in the air like an invitation to battle.

He smirked, a flicker of amusement dancing in his eyes that only served to ignite my anger further. "You're brave, I'll give you that. But bravery doesn't make you invincible."

"Maybe not. But it makes me willing to fight for something worth having," I shot back, my resolve hardening.

With every word, the air thickened between us, crackling with tension. I could almost feel the electric charge hovering, waiting for the right moment to ignite. And then, as if pulled by some invisible force, we leaned into each other, breathless and wide-eyed. My heart hammered against my ribcage, and for a fleeting moment, the world around us dissolved.

Our lips brushed, a whisper of contact that sent shockwaves through my body. It was unexpected and electrifying, awakening something deep within me that I hadn't realized was dormant. But just as quickly, Marcus recoiled, as if the simple touch had burned him.

"What the hell was that?" he breathed, shock flickering across his face.

"I... I don't know," I stammered, my cheeks heating, embarrassment rushing in to take the place of courage. "But it felt real, didn't it?"

He ran a hand through his hair, frustration etched into his features. "Real or not, this isn't the time. You need to understand—my past is dangerous. I don't want you to get hurt."

"Then let me choose that risk!" I exclaimed, my voice rising. "You can't decide for me, Marcus! Let me be part of your life—however messy it is. I won't shy away from your truth. I refuse to!"

His expression softened for a moment, the hard lines of his jaw easing as if he were considering my words. But the clouds of uncertainty still loomed, and I could see the conflict battling behind his eyes.

"Maybe I'm not ready to share that truth," he finally admitted, his voice barely above a whisper, but the weight of his confession settled over me like a leaden weight.

"Then let me help you find that readiness," I said softly, reaching for his hand. The warmth of his skin against mine sent a thrill coursing through me, a flicker of hope igniting in the darkness. "I'm not going anywhere. You can push me away, but I'll keep coming back. Just know that."

A heavy silence enveloped us once more, but this time it felt different—like a fragile truce hanging delicately between us, waiting for one of us to shatter the tension and claim what lay unspoken in the space between our hearts.

The air felt heavy with unspoken words, thick as the storm clouds gathering outside. Each raindrop tapped against the window like a persistent reminder of the chaos that enveloped us—both inside and out. I could still feel the warmth of his hand lingering on mine, as if it held the power to soothe the tumult that raged within me. The clash of our emotions hung in the atmosphere like an impending thunderstorm, charged and electric, waiting for the right moment to unleash its fury.

"Emily," he said, his voice a low rumble, breaking the silence that had settled in the aftermath of our almost-kiss. "You think you can just waltz into my life and everything will be sunshine and rainbows? It doesn't work that way."

"Waltzing, huh? You must think I'm a ballerina," I shot back, my voice dripping with sarcasm. "If I were, I'd have pirouetted out of here the moment you started playing your emotional charades." I took a deep breath, trying to rein in my temper. "Look, I'm not here for the fantasy. I'm here for the mess. And I know your mess is deeper than you let on."

His brow furrowed as he crossed his arms, the tension in his body radiating like heat from a flame. "You think you know me? You don't know what I've been through. You don't know the kind of people I've had to deal with, the kind of choices I've made." His voice trembled with a mix of anger and something softer, almost vulnerable.

I leaned forward, driven by a mixture of defiance and compassion. "Then tell me. Let me in. Stop acting like you're some tortured hero and let me see the real you." The challenge hung between us, daring him to take a leap of faith.

"I can't." The quiet despair in his voice struck a chord deep within me. It was like the crack in a dam, a glimpse of the flood of emotions held at bay. "You wouldn't understand."

"Try me," I insisted, refusing to back down. "I may not have lived your life, but I'm not blind to the struggles around me. I see you. And I see how hard you're fighting against whatever is dragging you down."

His defenses faltered for a heartbeat, and in that moment, the world around us felt still. I could almost hear the thrum of his heartbeat echoing in my ears, a silent rhythm that pulled at the edges of my resolve. "It's not just my past," he admitted, his gaze dropping to the floor. "It's my present, too. There are things in my life that you couldn't even begin to understand."

"What's in your present, then? Tell me about it." My voice softened, the heat of our earlier argument cooling to a simmer. "I want to know."

He shook his head, the weight of his secrets pressing down on him. "You really don't want to get involved with my world. It's dangerous, and I don't want you to get hurt."

"Is this one of those classic 'I'm protecting you' lines? Because I've had enough of that." I placed my hands on my hips, leveling a look that would make a lesser man back down. "If you think I'm going to tiptoe around you while you hide in the shadows, you've got another thing coming. I deserve better than that."

Marcus's expression shifted, a mix of admiration and frustration dancing in his eyes. "You're infuriatingly stubborn, you know that?"

"Stubbornness is a virtue in my book. It means I'm not afraid to fight for what I want." I took a step closer, closing the distance again, desperate to connect. "And what I want is you, Marcus—every messy, complicated piece of you."

He looked torn, his jaw tightening as if he were battling an internal war. "And if I fall apart? If I drag you down with me?" The question hung heavily in the air, an unspoken fear cloaked in bravado.

"Then we'll figure it out together. I'm not going anywhere." I stepped even closer, my heart racing as the space between us shrank. "We can be messy together. Isn't that what real relationships are about?"

He hesitated, his vulnerability cracking through the hardened exterior. "You're not afraid of the mess? Most people run from it."

"Most people don't know what they're missing," I countered, a playful smile breaking through the tension. "Besides, I've seen enough chaos in my life to know it doesn't always mean disaster. Sometimes it leads to something beautiful."

Just then, the heavens opened outside, rain pouring down in torrents, a wild symphony of nature mirroring the storm brewing in our hearts. I could see the raindrops racing each other down the glass, like the urgency of our unspoken feelings. "See that?" I pointed toward the window, the downpour providing a surreal backdrop to our heated exchange. "That rain is perfect chaos. But it makes the world cleaner, brighter. And sometimes," I said, leaning in closer, "the best things come from the mess."

His eyes sparkled with a hint of mischief, and for a moment, the storm inside him seemed to calm. "You're quite the optimist, aren't you?"

"Only when the situation calls for it," I quipped, unable to resist the banter that felt so natural between us. "But I'd say the current situation calls for a little optimism mixed with some stubbornness."

He chuckled, a rich, warm sound that made my heart leap. "You're unbelievable."

"And you're unbelievable for not seeing how incredible you are," I replied, my tone softening again. "You have so much potential, Marcus. Stop hiding from it."

With a deep breath, he ran a hand over his face, the lines of tension beginning to ease ever so slightly. "You really mean that?" His voice was softer now, more vulnerable, and it sent a wave of warmth through me.

"Absolutely," I said, my sincerity pouring through every word. "You've already shown me more than you realize. Let's take that next step together."

He met my gaze, the flicker of hope igniting in his eyes almost palpable. But just as the moment felt poised to shift, his expression hardened once more. "I can't be the reason you get hurt, Emily. I refuse to put you in danger because of my past."

"Then let me help you break free from it," I urged, willing him to see the truth in my words. "If you're so determined to protect me, maybe you should let me help you carry that burden instead. We could face it together."

As the rain drummed steadily against the window, I realized we stood on the precipice of something monumental. My heart raced, each beat echoing with the possibility of connection. The vulnerability hung in the air between us, shimmering like the droplets on the glass, both delicate and daring, filled with the promise of a storm that could wash away our fears.

The silence that followed felt like a taut string ready to snap. I could sense the charge in the air, thick and electric, as Marcus's gaze bore into mine, each breath between us weighted with unspoken thoughts. My heart raced as I searched his eyes for clarity, for a glimpse of the man who lurked beneath the armor of defiance. "Are you going to push me away again?" I asked, my voice barely above a whisper, fear creeping into my words.

His expression shifted, revealing the war waging inside him. "You don't get to dictate my choices, Emily. If you want to stay, you need to know what you're getting into."

"Then tell me!" I pleaded, desperation clawing at my throat. "I can't help if you keep me in the dark. I won't be your secret."

A flicker of pain crossed his features, and I hated that I was the cause. "You really want to know what I deal with? Fine," he snapped, the walls he'd built starting to tremble. "I've got people in my past who don't take kindly to someone poking around. And you," he took a step closer, "you're in the crosshairs now."

I felt the gravity of his words hit me like a wave, pulling me deeper into his reality. "You mean, they'd come after me?" I inhaled sharply, a surge of adrenaline coursing through my veins. "What, so I should just walk away?"

"Exactly!" His frustration flared, and I could see the glimmer of fear hiding beneath the anger. "This isn't a game, Emily. You think love conquers all? This is real life. There are consequences."

I crossed my arms, unwilling to back down. "So you want me to live in fear because of your past? That's not love; that's control. You can't keep me at arm's length because you're scared of what might happen."

He ran a hand through his hair, his frustration evident as he paced back and forth, the tension coiling tighter around us. "You don't understand what I've done, who I've been," he muttered, almost to himself. "I can't let you get caught in the crossfire of my mess."

"Then let's clean up the mess together," I insisted, stepping closer until I could feel the warmth radiating from him. "I'm not afraid of the chaos. I'm not afraid of you. I care about you, and that means facing the danger, not running from it."

He paused, his eyes searching mine, as if weighing the truth of my words against the doubts gnawing at him. "You're serious, aren't you? You'd really stand by me?"

"Absolutely," I replied, my voice steady. "I'm not some damsel waiting to be rescued. I'm more like the sidekick who'll kick your butt if you try to do this alone." A smirk tugged at my lips, hoping to ease the tension, to remind him that even in darkness, there was still light to be found.

His expression softened for just a moment before the storm returned. "You have no idea what you're inviting into your life. People can be ruthless when it comes to protecting their own."

"Then let's protect each other," I countered, my heart pounding against my chest. "I'm tired of living in a world of shadows. It's exhausting."

The rain hammered against the window, a relentless rhythm that echoed my pulse. I took a deep breath, determination flooding through me. "Let me help you find a way out of the shadows, Marcus. We can be stronger together."

For the first time, I saw a flicker of hope dance in his eyes, and it sent a shiver of anticipation down my spine. "You really mean it? You're not just saying this because of the adrenaline rush?"

"No, I'm saying it because I believe in you," I replied, my voice firm. "I don't need the fairytale version of you. I need the real one. All the parts, even the messy ones."

He looked at me, uncertainty warring with something deeper, something that felt like yearning. "What if I'm not worth the risk?"

I stepped even closer, our breaths mingling, the world around us fading into a blur. "You are," I whispered, and in that instant, I could feel the connection deepening between us, like threads of a tapestry weaving together.

But before he could respond, the shrill ring of his phone sliced through the moment, shattering the fragile cocoon we had created.

He pulled away, his face hardening as he glanced at the screen. "It's them," he said, his voice dropping to a whisper, the joy in his eyes extinguished like a candle snuffed out in a gust of wind.

"Who?" I asked, dread pooling in my stomach. "Marcus, don't answer it if—"

"I have to." His voice was taut, determination edging out fear. "I can't ignore this."

He answered, his voice steady yet strained as he spoke. "What do you want?"

I couldn't hear the response, but I could see the change in his posture, the way his muscles tensed and his jaw clenched. It was like watching a soldier brace for impact, and my heart raced as unease settled in. "I told you to leave me alone," he said, his voice rising slightly, laced with anger.

"Marcus?" I urged, reaching for him. "What's going on?"

His eyes darted to mine, panic mingling with resolve. "They know about you. They want to meet."

"Meet? Why?" I could barely breathe, the implications crashing over me like a tidal wave. "What do they want with me?"

He cut off the call, his gaze darkening. "I don't know, but we can't let them. Not like this."

"Then we need to go to the police or—"

"No." He interrupted, shaking his head fiercely. "I can't put you in that kind of danger. You need to leave—now."

"Leave?" My heart dropped at the suggestion. "I'm not running away, Marcus. Not when we're so close to finding a way through this."

"Trust me, Emily. This is bigger than you think."

As the rain lashed against the window, I felt the weight of the storm closing in around us. I couldn't tell if it was the world outside or the tumult brewing inside me. "What are you planning?" I asked, desperation lacing my words.

"Something reckless." His voice dropped to a whisper, the seriousness in his tone sending chills down my spine. "And you're going to hate me for it."

Before I could respond, there was a sharp knock at the door, slicing through the tension. My heart raced, adrenaline coursing through my veins as fear took hold. I glanced at Marcus, who was already tensed and ready, a warrior poised for battle.

"Who is it?" I called, my voice barely more than a whisper.

"Open up, Marcus. We know you're in there." The voice from the other side was deep and gravelly, a sinister undertone that sent a chill racing through me.

My stomach dropped as Marcus and I exchanged a glance filled with horror and urgency. He moved closer to me, determination etched on his face. "Whatever happens, don't open that door."

The knock came again, louder this time, demanding. "We need to talk, and it's better if you let us in."

Panic surged as I took a step back, the reality of our situation crashing down like a freight train. This was no longer just an emotional confrontation; this was the beginning of something much darker.

"Marcus, what do we do?" I breathed, the weight of uncertainty heavy on my shoulders.

His eyes bore into mine, fierce and protective, yet shadowed with fear. "We fight."

Just as the door began to rattle on its hinges, the world around us teetered on the brink of chaos. My heart raced, the air thick with impending danger, and I realized with a sinking feeling that nothing would ever be the same again.

Chapter 8: Revelations

The city was a labyrinth of shadows and shimmering lights, each street whispering secrets as the night enveloped it. I stood on my balcony, a glass of merlot in hand, gazing at the kaleidoscope of colors painting the skyline. The rhythmic pulse of the city below matched the thumping of my heart, which was still reeling from the recent tempest in my life. It wasn't just the art I poured my soul into that felt raw and unrefined; it was everything—the confusion, the doubts, and most importantly, Marcus.

He had always been a tempest of emotion, a chaotic whirlwind that swept through my life when I least expected it. The late-night phone call had been an impulsive choice, borne from a blend of frustration and longing. As I dialed his number, the weight of my insecurities felt almost tangible, like a shroud I couldn't quite shake off. I hadn't expected him to pick up, but when his voice crackled through the receiver, it was as if a dam had burst.

"Are you still there?" he asked, his voice a rich baritone that somehow soothed the jagged edges of my anxiety.

"I'm here," I replied, my heart racing. "Can we talk?"

Silence stretched between us like a taut string ready to snap. "About what?" he finally asked, a hint of weariness in his tone. I could picture him, probably pacing in his dimly lit apartment, fingers raking through his hair, just as he always did when he was agitated.

"Everything," I said, the word escaping me like a breath I didn't know I was holding. "About us, about where we stand. I feel like we're two ships passing in the night."

He sighed deeply, the sound echoing with unspoken fears and frustrations. "I know. I feel it too. There's so much happening, and I—" His voice faltered, and I could hear the struggle in his silence. "I don't know how to make sense of it all."

The vulnerability in his words broke something open within me. "I'm scared, Marcus. Scared that I'm not good enough, that my art will never resonate with anyone." I swallowed hard, feeling the sting of unshed tears. "And I'm scared that I'm losing you in the process."

"Losing me?" His voice was suddenly sharper, igniting a spark of tension between us. "I don't want to be lost, but you can't keep pushing me away. I want to be there for you."

His earnestness wrapped around my heart like a warm blanket, but I could also feel the simmering heat of our unspoken desires rising between us. The uncharted territory of our relationship had been fraught with misunderstandings and unfulfilled expectations. But in that moment, as I shared my fears, a shift began to happen, softening the edges of our discord.

"Can we just... let go?" I suggested, the words tumbling out of me like paint splattering onto a blank canvas. "Let's be honest about what we want."

"Okay," he murmured, a palpable tension thrumming through the line. "Then let's be honest."

In a flurry of confessions, I poured out my soul, recounting the relentless self-doubt that plagued my artistic endeavors. The fear of vulnerability in my work echoed the vulnerability I felt in our relationship, each confession unraveling the tightly wound thread of my composure. With every word I spoke, I could feel the layers of protection I had carefully constructed around my heart begin to dissolve.

"I've always seen you as a force of nature," he said softly. "Your art is powerful. You just need to believe in it—and in us."

There was a lingering silence, charged with unspoken emotions. It was as if the world around us faded, leaving only the two of us suspended in a moment where time no longer held sway. I leaned against the balcony railing, letting the night air wash over me, cleansing the doubt and fear that had settled like dust in my heart.

"Maybe I just need to let go of my fear of failing," I whispered, each word heavier than the last.

"Then do it," Marcus urged, his voice fierce and compelling. "Let go of the fear. We can face it together."

A spark ignited within me, and I could feel the warmth radiating from our shared vulnerabilities. I wanted to leap across the void between us, to bridge the distance that had been growing with every unspoken fear and every unacknowledged longing.

"Let's meet," I suggested, the words rushing out of me with a sudden clarity. "Let's stop dancing around this."

"Tonight?" he asked, his voice suddenly sharp with anticipation.

"Tonight," I confirmed, my heart racing at the thought of seeing him, of feeling his presence wrap around me like a safety net.

The moments that followed felt suspended in time, each heartbeat echoing with the weight of our decisions. I dressed with trembling hands, the soft fabric of my blouse brushing against my skin like a promise of something beautiful yet uncertain. The vibrant hues of my favorite skirt swayed gently as I moved, embodying the swirl of emotions coursing through me.

When I finally stepped into the evening air, the world around me seemed to vibrate with possibilities. The night had a taste, a delicious hint of intrigue that left me breathless. As I made my way to our usual meeting place, the café tucked away in a quiet corner of the city, anticipation thrummed through me, mingling with the lingering fear of what was to come.

The café was alive with soft music and the comforting aroma of freshly brewed coffee, but all I could focus on was Marcus, standing by the entrance, his silhouette framed by the warm glow of the lights inside. Our eyes met, and in that instant, the distance that had felt insurmountable seemed to vanish, leaving only the electricity crackling between us.

"Hey," I greeted, my voice barely a whisper against the backdrop of clinking cups and muted conversations.

"Hey," he replied, a small, tentative smile breaking across his face. It was a smile that held promises, secrets, and the hint of a journey we were about to embark on together.

The moment stretched out as we moved closer, my heart racing with each step. As we embraced, a wave of warmth enveloped me, and for the first time in what felt like ages, I felt a sense of belonging wash over me, anchoring me in a reality where fears could be faced together, where love didn't have to be a tumultuous sea of chaos, but a steady tide that pulled us in the right direction.

"Let's talk," I murmured into his shoulder, my voice muffled by the fabric of his coat. It was time to explore the depths of our connection, to peel back the layers and reveal the truths that lay hidden beneath the surface.

The café buzzed with the energy of life, the hum of conversation mingling with the clinking of mugs and the hiss of the espresso machine. It was a sanctuary of warmth, and I felt myself soaking it all in as I and Marcus settled into our corner booth. The dim light painted soft shadows across his features, accentuating the familiar furrow of his brow that often signaled deep contemplation. Yet, beneath that façade, I could see the flicker of anticipation glimmering in his eyes—a shared excitement that was both thrilling and terrifying.

"What's on your mind?" he asked, his voice low and inviting. The question was simple, but it felt monumental, like an invitation to peel back layers that had long concealed our true selves. I toyed with the rim of my cup, feeling the steam warm my fingertips, grounding me in the moment.

"I'm just... wondering how we got here," I said, looking up to meet his gaze. "Two people who once barely knew each other, now sharing confessions like they're secrets in a diary." The words felt vulnerable as they hung between us, but honesty was the new currency in our relationship.

Marcus chuckled softly, the sound rich and comforting. "Maybe it's the chaos of life that draws us together. We've both been through the wringer lately." He leaned forward, resting his elbows on the table, his eyes searching mine. "But maybe we're not just drawn together by chaos; maybe we're creating something beautiful from it."

I nodded, the weight of his insight settling in my chest. "It feels like we've both been standing on the edge of a precipice, unsure whether to leap or step back." The vulnerability in my voice was unmistakable, and I could sense Marcus responding to it, the air between us thick with unspoken words.

"Then let's leap," he said, his expression shifting to one of determination. "No more holding back. We can navigate this chaos together."

His conviction ignited something within me, and I felt a swell of courage rising. "Okay. But I need to know what we're diving into. What do you want, Marcus?"

"I want you," he said, his voice steady. "But I also want us to figure out what that means. We're both artists, both trying to make sense of our worlds. And I'm not afraid of the mess that comes with it."

As the words spilled from him, I could feel the atmosphere crackle with the promise of honesty. It was intoxicating, the way he laid bare his heart, revealing the raw edges of his soul. "I've always been a bit of a control freak with my art. Every brushstroke needs to be perfect, every line defined. But life... life isn't like that, is it? It's messy and unpredictable, and I think maybe that's where the real beauty lies."

The way he spoke, so passionately, reminded me of why I had fallen for him in the first place. "It's about the imperfections," I mused, taking a sip of my coffee. "The layers that come together to create something uniquely ours."

"Yes!" His enthusiasm was palpable, and I couldn't help but smile at his fervor. "Exactly! And maybe, just maybe, we can help each other find those layers."

His words lingered in the air, an unspoken promise that our journey together was only beginning. "So, where do we start?" I asked, my heart racing as I leaned in closer, eager to delve into the depths of what we could build together.

He hesitated for a moment, a flicker of uncertainty crossing his face. "How about we create something together? A project, an art piece, whatever you want to call it. We can brainstorm ideas, blend our styles... the chaos of our emotions could lead to something incredible."

I couldn't help but laugh at the audacity of his suggestion. "You want to throw me into a creative collaboration right after we've bared our souls?"

"Why not?" He grinned, a devilish spark lighting his eyes. "You're the one who suggested leaping, remember? Besides, if we can confront our fears, why not face our creative instincts head-on?"

As I pondered his suggestion, a wave of exhilaration washed over me. The idea of merging our talents was both daunting and thrilling. "All right, but if this goes south, I'm blaming you."

"Deal," he said, extending his hand across the table, a playful glint in his eyes.

With a soft laugh, I accepted his hand, the warmth of his skin sending an electric jolt through me. We sat in that café, surrounded by the hum of life, but it felt as if we were cocooned in our own little universe, an enclave where vulnerability and creativity intertwined.

Our conversation flowed like a river, carving out paths of inspiration as we shared ideas, laughed, and occasionally stumbled over words. Each suggestion sparked a new wave of creativity, and

I could feel the tension of uncertainty begin to dissolve. In that moment, it was just us, two artists braving the unknown, ready to blend our colors into something vibrant.

But then, just as the atmosphere grew warm and cozy, a shadow of doubt crept in. What if the project didn't resonate? What if my insecurities held me back from fully engaging in our creative endeavor?

"Marcus," I said, my voice taking on a serious tone. "I need to be upfront about something. What if this project reveals more about our differences than our similarities?"

He leaned back, contemplative, the light shifting as he processed my words. "Then we embrace it. It's not about creating a perfect piece; it's about exploring the journey. What if our differences are what make the collaboration exciting? We could end up with something no one expected."

The wisdom in his words washed over me like a soothing balm. Maybe he was right. Perhaps the beauty of art lay in its unpredictability, in the unexpected twists that could lead to new paths of expression.

The café began to fill with the evening crowd, and with every passing moment, the world outside seemed to blur into insignificance. But in that moment, the focus was solely on us, on our creativity and the raw emotions swirling around the table.

"Okay, let's do it," I declared, feeling emboldened. "Let's create something that's a true reflection of us."

As the words escaped my lips, I could sense the shift, the thrill of a new adventure igniting within me. Marcus smiled broadly, a mix of relief and excitement dancing across his features. "You won't regret it."

"Just remember," I added with a playful smirk, "if we end up on some avant-garde list of 'what not to do in art,' you're the one who suggested it."

"Trust me, I'll take full responsibility," he shot back, laughter lacing his voice.

And with that, the tension in the air transformed into a vibrant tapestry of possibilities. We left the café hand in hand, stepping into the evening's embrace, ready to create our own masterpiece—a collaboration woven with threads of laughter, vulnerability, and the kind of chaos that only life could conjure.

The evening air was thick with anticipation as Marcus and I walked side by side, our fingers intertwined like brushstrokes on a canvas, each movement electric with possibility. The city around us pulsed with life, streetlights flickering like stars fallen to Earth, illuminating our path. We were no longer two solitary artists battling our fears; we were partners in a vibrant dance, ready to create something that reflected our shared struggles and triumphs.

"Where to first?" I asked, tilting my head up to catch a glimpse of his expression, which was a mixture of mischief and focus, like he was plotting some grand scheme.

"How about we head to that old warehouse on 14th?" he suggested, a glint of excitement in his eyes. "I've heard it's filled with all sorts of forgotten treasures. We could find inspiration hiding in the dust."

"An abandoned warehouse? I'm sensing a horror movie subplot here," I replied with a smirk, my pulse quickening at the thought. "What if we find something so creepy that it turns us into a new kind of artist—one who paints portraits of phantoms?"

He laughed, the sound rich and infectious. "Or maybe we'll discover a hidden masterpiece waiting for us. Think of it as a scavenger hunt, but with more cobwebs and fewer prizes."

"Or fewer cobwebs and more prizes. Let's aim for the latter." My heart raced with the prospect of adventure, and I felt the familiar rush of creativity surge through me. With each step toward the warehouse, the uncertainties that had clouded my mind began to lift, replaced by the thrill of exploration.

The warehouse loomed ahead, a relic of the past standing defiantly against the backdrop of the modern skyline. It was a sprawling structure, its brick façade weathered and adorned with graffiti—an artwork of its own that told stories of rebellion and creativity. As we approached, I couldn't help but feel a shiver of excitement mixed with a tinge of trepidation.

"I hope we don't get arrested for trespassing," I said, glancing sideways at Marcus.

He waved a hand dismissively. "We're not breaking and entering; we're merely appreciating forgotten art. Besides, we have each other's charming company to keep us out of trouble."

With a push, the door creaked open, revealing a vast expanse filled with shadows and shafts of moonlight filtering through broken windows. The air was thick with dust, and the smell of aged wood and metal mingled with a sense of nostalgia. It felt like stepping into a time capsule, where echoes of the past were waiting to be rediscovered.

As we ventured further inside, I couldn't help but admire the haphazard arrangement of forgotten objects. Old canvases leaned against the walls, their surfaces faded but still holding traces of vibrant colors. A collection of rusty tools lay scattered on a weathered table, each one a potential muse, whispering tales of craftsmanship and creativity.

"Look at this!" Marcus exclaimed, crouching beside a battered trunk half-buried beneath a pile of old newspapers. With a dramatic flair, he flung it open, and we both gasped at the contents. Inside were a series of forgotten sketches, each one depicting scenes of life long past—a street market bustling with activity, a couple dancing under a streetlamp, children playing in the rain.

"Someone poured their heart into these," I said softly, running my fingers over the fragile paper. "It's beautiful."

"It is," he agreed, his eyes shining with inspiration. "We should take some of these and make them the basis for our project. Let's channel the emotion captured in these sketches."

A surge of creativity flooded through me, fueled by the connection we were building in this intimate space filled with history. "Yes! We can recreate the scenes but through our lenses. Bring them to life with our colors, our interpretations."

As we delved deeper into the warehouse, we uncovered more treasures—a cracked mirror reflecting our excited expressions, an ancient piano that seemed to hum with untold melodies, and even a set of worn-out chairs that had borne witness to countless conversations. With each discovery, the excitement swelled between us, intertwining like the brushstrokes we dreamed of creating.

Yet, amidst our exploration, a peculiar sensation began to creep in—a sense of being watched. I shook it off, attributing it to the eerie ambiance of the warehouse and the flickering shadows dancing in the corners. Marcus seemed oblivious, caught up in his excitement as he pulled me toward a section of the room draped in darkness.

"Come look at this!" he called, his voice echoing with enthusiasm. I followed him, curiosity piqued, but as we turned a corner, we stumbled upon a door slightly ajar, an ominous gap leading into an even darker room.

"What do you think is in there?" I whispered, hesitation creeping into my tone.

"Only one way to find out," he replied, his adventurous spirit evident. "But let's be careful. We're here to create, not to become part of a horror story."

With a shared look that mingled excitement and apprehension, we stepped toward the door. As we pushed it open, a chill swept through the air, sending a shiver down my spine. The room beyond was bathed in shadows, the only light filtering through a cracked window high above.

"Maybe this was a bad idea," I murmured, the sense of being watched intensifying.

"Hey, we're fine," Marcus assured me, though his voice was tinged with uncertainty. "Let's just take a peek. If it's too creepy, we'll hightail it out of here faster than you can say 'ghost.'"

I nodded, though unease curled in my stomach. As we crossed the threshold, a sudden noise echoed through the room, a soft scuffle that made my heart leap into my throat. I froze, and Marcus turned to me, eyes wide.

"Did you hear that?" he whispered, tension creeping into his voice.

Before I could respond, the door behind us slammed shut with a resounding bang, the sound reverberating like a thunderclap in the stillness. My breath hitched, and I glanced at Marcus, who looked equally startled.

"What the—" I began, but my words were cut short as the shadows in the room seemed to thicken, coiling around us like smoke.

"Let's get out of here," Marcus said, taking a step back toward the door, but it wouldn't budge. Panic bubbled within me as I tugged on the handle, but it remained stubbornly shut.

"Try again!" I urged, feeling the walls close in around us.

He slammed his shoulder against the door, but it held firm, an immovable barrier between us and the outside world. My heart raced, an uneasy rhythm echoing in my ears as I turned back to face the room, the dark corners now feeling more like lurking entities than mere shadows.

"Is this really happening?" I asked, half-laughing to mask the fear threading through my voice. "Did we just accidentally stumble into a horror movie? Because if so, I want my money back."

Marcus chuckled nervously, but I could see the anxiety etched across his face. "We just need to stay calm. There's got to be another way out."

But as we scanned the room, the sensation of being watched grew stronger, a prickling awareness that sent chills racing down my spine. I could feel something—someone—lurking just beyond the edges of our perception.

Then, from the depths of the shadows, a soft whisper floated through the air, the words indistinguishable but hauntingly familiar. My heart sank as the temperature in the room dropped, and I clutched Marcus's arm, a bolt of fear shooting through me.

"Do you feel that?" I whispered, my voice barely a tremor.

"Yeah," he replied, his eyes darting toward the darkened corners. "We need to get out—now."

As we turned back to the door, desperation surged within me. "What if it's locked from the outside?"

Marcus's expression hardened with resolve. "Then we find another way. There has to be a window or something."

But just as we turned to scour the shadows, a figure emerged from the darkness, stepping into the sliver of light that spilled from the cracked window. My breath caught in my throat as I realized this was not the art we had sought—it was something far more sinister, an unexpected twist in our chaotic journey that sent a shockwave of fear coursing through me.

The figure loomed, cloaked in shadow, and for a moment, the world around us faded, leaving only the chilling realization that we had entered a realm we were never meant to explore.

Chapter 9: A Dangerous Game

The air crackled with the electric tension of uncharted emotions, each stolen glance between Marcus and me a brush with danger. Our late-night brainstorming sessions had turned into something far more intimate, the edges of our relationship blurring into a vivid tapestry woven with urgency and desire. Sitting across from him in the dim light of my kitchen, the aroma of freshly brewed coffee mingled with the scent of autumn leaves drifting through the open window. The soft rustle of the trees outside mirrored the fluttering in my stomach, a mix of exhilaration and apprehension.

"Do you ever think about how we got here?" Marcus asked, his voice low, a husky undertone that sent shivers down my spine. He leaned forward, a lock of hair falling across his forehead, the soft light catching the sharp angles of his jaw. There was a softness in his gaze that made my heart race, but lurking behind it was a shadow, an unspoken fear that danced just out of reach.

"Here? In this chaotic mess?" I replied, attempting to inject humor into the heavy atmosphere. I wanted to believe we were merely two people caught in a web of unexpected circumstances, but as the thoughts of those messages crept back into my mind, I struggled to maintain the lightness.

"Not just the mess. I mean... us." He gestured between us, as if our very presence was something tangible, a thread connecting two souls in a world that threatened to unravel. My heart swelled at the admission, even as the reminder of danger clawed at the edges of my bliss.

"Yeah, well, it's a beautiful disaster," I quipped, but my smile faltered. It was a fragile veil, hiding the creeping dread that had taken root since the messages had begun. Each ping of my phone felt like a gunshot, loud and jarring, each word from the sender echoing in my mind, mixing with the sweetness of our moments together.

The first message had been a simple threat: Stay away from him. This isn't a game. The words had slithered under my skin, igniting a primal instinct to protect what I had come to treasure. Marcus had brushed it off, his bravado shining through like a shield, but I knew better. I could see the way his hands clenched around his coffee mug, the subtle tension in his shoulders that spoke volumes of the weight he carried.

"Beautiful disasters can have disastrous consequences," he murmured, breaking my reverie. His eyes bore into mine, a silent plea for honesty. The air between us thickened, charged with unspoken truths and the remnants of shared laughter. I could feel the vulnerability radiating from him, and it struck a chord within me.

"Are we playing a game?" I asked, my tone teasing, but my heart thudded with uncertainty. The words hung between us like a pendulum, swinging toward truth or consequence.

"Only if the stakes are high," he replied, his gaze unwavering. "And believe me, they are."

The acknowledgment sent a chill racing down my spine. It was more than the threats; it was the realization that our intimacy had thrust us into a perilous dance with the unknown. As much as I craved to be closer to him, the danger felt like a black cloud looming overhead, threatening to burst at any moment.

"I can't keep pretending everything's fine," I confessed, my voice a whisper. The weight of my words pressed down on us, forcing a silence that hummed with unspoken fears. "Those messages... they're getting worse."

He sighed, running a hand through his hair, a gesture that spoke of frustration and helplessness. "I know, but I won't let it tear us apart. I refuse to let the past dictate our future."

The intensity of his resolve sparked a fire within me, igniting a sense of shared purpose. We were two souls fighting against the current, clinging to what we had built amidst the chaos. "So, what's the plan, then?"

His lips curved into a determined smile, the corners crinkling in that way I had come to adore. "We get proactive. We figure out who's behind this and confront them before they can make a move."

A shiver of fear danced through me, but alongside it, a surge of excitement. The thrill of the unknown beckoned, the promise of unraveling a mystery that could alter the course of our lives. "Sounds like we're in for a wild ride," I said, attempting to mask my anxiety with a playful tone.

"Wild is just the beginning," he chuckled, but the laugh was tinged with a seriousness that belied the levity of his words.

We dove into planning, our discussions morphing into strategies, each idea building upon the last like a fortress of resilience. The ticking clock in the background served as a constant reminder of our dwindling time, yet each moment spent together intensified our connection. We shared secrets and hopes, dreams entwined with fears, forging a bond that felt as unbreakable as the walls we were erecting against the outside world.

Yet, as we navigated through the labyrinth of our fears and ambitions, the shadows of our past loomed larger, the specter of danger clawing at the edges of our fragile sanctuary. I could feel it in the air, a creeping sensation that something was watching us, waiting for the right moment to strike.

That night, as I lay in bed, the weight of our plans settled heavily on my chest, mixing with the thrill of anticipation. The line between our desire and the looming threat blurred, creating a tension that was intoxicating and terrifying all at once. I closed my eyes, summoning the warmth of Marcus's laughter, the spark of his determination, hoping against hope that we could navigate this dangerous game together.

In the quiet sanctuary of my apartment, where shadows flickered like whispers of our past, I poured over the notes Marcus and I had compiled. The kitchen table, once cluttered with coffee mugs and casual conversation, now bore the weight of our plans. Diagrams sprawled across the surface like a map of a battlefield, each line drawn with the intent to outsmart the unseen enemy that had invaded our lives.

"Okay, so let's break it down," Marcus said, leaning over the table, his brow furrowed in concentration. The early morning light filtered through the window, casting a golden glow on his tousled hair, making him appear almost ethereal, as if he were a hero from a novel rather than a man entangled in a dangerous game. "We know the threats are personal, aimed at us, but what's their end game?"

"Good question," I replied, tapping my pen against my chin. "Are they trying to scare us into submission or do they have something more sinister in mind? I mean, if they're this bold, they must feel untouchable."

"Or they're desperate," he countered, the tension in his voice revealing just how deeply this affected him. "We can use that. If we can figure out who's behind it, we can turn the tables."

I admired his resolve, but a thread of fear wove through my thoughts. "And if we can't? What if we're in over our heads?" The weight of my question hung in the air, thickening it with uncertainty. I wanted to believe we could outsmart whoever was lurking in the shadows, but the prospect of failure gnawed at my insides.

He met my gaze, the fierce intensity in his eyes igniting a flicker of hope. "Then we fight. We don't let them dictate our lives."

His conviction wrapped around me like a warm blanket on a winter's day. I took a deep breath, inhaling the rich aroma of coffee mingled with the faint scent of cinnamon from the candles I'd burned the night before. "Right. So, what's our first move? We could try to trace the messages, see if they lead us anywhere."

"That's a start, but I think we need to dig deeper. Someone has to know something." He leaned back, rubbing his temples as if already contemplating the weight of the task ahead. "We need to gather intel. What about your contacts?"

A mischievous grin crept onto my face. "I do have a few friends in high places. They might be able to help us track down the origin of those messages."

"See? That's the spirit!" Marcus exclaimed, his enthusiasm infectious. "Just make sure to choose wisely; we don't want to tip our hand too soon."

We spent the next hour brainstorming, our ideas bouncing off one another with an energy that felt almost electric. The danger outside faded, replaced by a camaraderie that both excited and terrified me. It was as if we were dancing on the edge of a precipice, the thrill of the unknown pulling us closer together.

When the sun began to dip below the horizon, casting a soft glow through the kitchen window, I felt the weariness settle into my bones. The weight of our plans, combined with the dread of what lay ahead, had me leaning heavily against the table. "Maybe we should take a break," I suggested, fatigue creeping into my voice. "You know, regroup and recharge. We can't tackle the world on empty."

"Fair point." He stood, stretching his arms overhead, the muscles in his back flexing with the movement. "But how about we take that break over dinner? I could use a distraction, and I make a mean pasta."

I chuckled, the image of Marcus in a kitchen, wielding a spatula like a sword, brought a sense of levity to the moment. "Pasta? Are you sure you're not setting us up for a culinary disaster?"

"Culinary disaster? Please. I've seen you eat my cooking before, and you didn't die." He raised an eyebrow, the playful banter lighting up his expression. "Unless you were faking your enthusiasm, which I'm beginning to suspect."

"Okay, guilty as charged," I laughed, waving my hands in mock surrender. "But seriously, I'm in. Just don't burn the place down."

As he moved to the kitchen, a flurry of movement and energy, I marveled at how quickly my life had transformed from mundane to thrilling, intertwined with danger and desire. I grabbed my phone, scrolling through my contacts, contemplating whom I could trust. My friends in the business had always been reliable, but now I needed them to be more than just friends; I needed them to be allies in this unpredictable battle.

Marcus's laughter drifted from the kitchen, an infectious sound that wrapped around me, infusing the space with warmth. He was humming a tune, a mix of charm and lightheartedness, and I found myself smiling, the tension in my shoulders easing just a bit.

"I know you're not the world's greatest chef," I called out, leaning against the kitchen doorway, "but let's at least try not to turn this into a horror movie scenario, alright?"

"Fear not! I've got this under control," he declared, feigning confidence as he rummaged through cabinets. A pan clattered loudly, echoing through the small apartment. "Besides, I'll have you know I once saved a dinner party from complete disaster with my spaghetti."

"Right. You mean the time you managed to serve everyone undercooked noodles and called it 'al dente'?" I shot back, crossing my arms with a smirk.

"Hey, that was a culinary choice," he replied, sticking his tongue out in playful defiance. "I'd like to think I've improved since then."

As I watched him move about the kitchen, I felt a swell of warmth bloom in my chest. There was something profoundly comforting about this moment—two people, caught in a whirlwind of chaos, finding solace in the simplicity of sharing a meal. It was a reminder that even amidst the shadows threatening to close in on us, there were still glimmers of light, laughter, and the possibility of something beautiful.

"Okay, Chef Marcus," I called, feigning seriousness. "Just remember, if you burn the garlic bread, I'm out of here."

"Noted. But you'll miss my charming company too much," he shot back, his grin wide and infectious.

"Touché," I laughed, feeling a rush of affection for this man who had unexpectedly become my partner in this dangerous game.

As the scent of simmering sauce filled the air, I felt a renewed sense of determination wash over me. Together, we would face whatever lay ahead, armed not only with our plans but with the bond we were forging in the midst of chaos.

The aroma of garlic and herbs wafted through the air, mingling with the sharp tang of simmering tomatoes, creating an intoxicating backdrop for our culinary adventure. I leaned against the counter, sipping a glass of wine, my eyes following Marcus as he expertly tossed the pasta in a bubbling pot. His movements were fluid, almost graceful, betraying a confidence that made my heart flutter.

"I have to admit, this might be your best dish yet," I teased, swirling the wine in my glass, the deep red liquid catching the light. "What's your secret? Did you channel your inner Italian chef?"

"Ah, you see, it's all in the technique," he said, his voice dripping with mock seriousness as he expertly drained the pasta, the steam curling up around him like a halo. "Also, I have a hidden stash of marinara sauce that I've been hoarding like a dragon with its gold."

I laughed, shaking my head at his antics. The banter flowed easily between us, a delightful distraction from the gnawing tension of the outside world. Yet, the thrill of our connection intertwined with the undercurrent of danger, and I couldn't shake the feeling that our moment of tranquility was fleeting.

"Just make sure your 'hidden stash' doesn't come with a side of crazy exes or dark secrets," I quipped, raising an eyebrow as I set my glass down, letting the humor mask the unease that lurked at the back of my mind.

"Too late for that," he said, turning to face me, his expression suddenly serious. "I think we're already knee-deep in it."

"Right." I took a breath, pulling myself from the lightheartedness. "So, what's the plan after dinner? We have to keep that momentum going."

"We regroup and reach out to your contacts. I'll handle the tech side, see if I can track down any IP addresses linked to those messages. Meanwhile, I can't help but think there's a person behind this, someone who knows both of us," he replied, his eyes narrowing as he pondered the implications.

The thought sent a shiver down my spine. "You think they might be someone we know? That's... unsettling."

"It is, but it's a possibility we can't ignore. People can be unpredictable when they feel threatened." He placed the pasta into bowls, the steam curling invitingly into the air. "Eat first. We'll figure it out after."

The dinner was surprisingly delightful, each bite accompanied by lively conversation that painted a picture of normalcy against the backdrop of chaos. As we laughed and shared stories, I found comfort in the rhythm of our exchanges. He regaled me with tales of his culinary mishaps—like the time he mistook salt for sugar and served a dessert that made everyone question his sanity. I matched him with my own disasters, highlighting how I once tried to impress a date with a complicated soufflé that ended up resembling an eggy pancake.

"Honestly, if the world were ending, I'd rather eat your culinary disasters than face the thought of life without pasta," I joked, savoring the comfort of our shared laughter.

"Flattery will get you everywhere, you know." He leaned in closer, the warmth radiating off him like a gentle wave, momentarily dispelling the chill of our circumstances.

But as the evening wore on, the laughter faded, replaced by the heavy silence of looming uncertainty. We had a plan, but doubt lingered like a stubborn shadow. I couldn't shake the nagging sensation that we were racing against an unseen clock, each second echoing the urgency of our situation.

"Let's clean up and get to work," I suggested, forcing myself to break the silence. "I'll make those calls."

"Good idea. The sooner we start, the sooner we can put this to rest," he agreed, his expression turning resolute.

As we cleared the table, I felt the familiar buzz of my phone vibrating against the countertop. My heart raced, a mix of anticipation and dread flooding my veins. I grabbed it, my stomach twisting as I saw an unknown number flashing on the screen. It could be a lead, or it could be more trouble.

"Who is it?" Marcus asked, glancing over my shoulder.

"I don't know. Might be a wrong number," I said, attempting to sound casual, though my voice betrayed me. I could feel the weight of his gaze, urging me to answer.

With a deep breath, I pressed accept. "Hello?"

The silence on the other end was deafening, stretching into an uncomfortable pause that seemed to echo my rising anxiety. Just as I was about to hang up, a gravelly voice pierced through the stillness. "You should have stayed away from him."

The blood drained from my face, my pulse quickening as the words sank in. "Who is this?" I demanded, my voice shaking slightly.

"Someone who knows your little secret. Someone who can make all your troubles disappear... or escalate them." The voice dripped with malice, each word laced with an undertone of danger that made my skin crawl.

"Stop playing games," I shot back, my mind racing. "What do you want?"

"Want? Oh, sweet girl, it's not about what I want. It's about what you can lose. Keep poking around, and you'll find out just how dangerous it is to get too close." The line went dead, leaving a hollow silence that wrapped around me like a shroud.

I dropped my phone, the sound of it hitting the counter punctuating the tension in the air. "Marcus," I whispered, my voice trembling.

He rushed over, eyes wide with concern. "What happened? Who was it?"

"A threat. They know..." My voice faltered, fear coiling tightly in my chest. "They know about us, about you."

The realization settled over us like a thick fog, heavy and suffocating. The game had changed, and now the stakes were higher than I had ever imagined. "We have to act now. We can't let them dictate our lives," Marcus said, his expression hardening with resolve.

I nodded, but the fear gnawed at me. The danger felt real, palpable, and with it came the undeniable truth that our precarious dance with fate had taken a darker turn. We were no longer just trying to uncover the mystery; we were now players on a board where every move could cost us everything.

Just as we began to strategize, a loud crash echoed from the hallway, followed by the unmistakable sound of footsteps pounding against the floor. My heart raced as adrenaline surged through my veins. Someone was coming, and the realization hit me like a freight train: the game had escalated, and we were about to find out just how dangerous it could be.

Chapter 10: The Deep End

The studio was alive with the chaotic symphony of color. Sunlight streamed through the tall windows, casting a warm glow that danced over the myriad of brushes and canvases strewn about like the aftermath of a wild storm. The air smelled of turpentine and linseed oil, mingling with the faint sweetness of the fresh lilies I had arranged in an old glass vase—each petal a reminder that beauty often bloomed in the most unexpected places.

Marcus stood beside me, his brow furrowed in concentration as he mixed hues of cobalt blue and emerald green. I had invited him in an attempt to create a sanctuary of sorts, a place where we could explore the turbulent emotions we had barely begun to articulate. As I dabbed my brush into a puddle of crimson, I glanced over to find him absorbed in his work, a solitary figure caught in the whirlwind of our shared silence. I often wondered what thoughts churned behind those deep-set eyes, so intense and yet so inviting.

"Do you ever feel like the colors you choose reveal more than just a mood?" I asked, breaking the spell of quiet that had wrapped around us like a comforting shawl. "Like they're whispering secrets about who you really are?"

He paused, the brush hovering over his palette. "Maybe it's not the colors that do the revealing, but the act of painting itself. It's raw, unfiltered—like unwrapping a gift that you're not quite sure you're ready to see." His lips curled into a faint smile, the kind that made my heart flutter as if it were straining against its cage.

Before I could respond, the sharp trill of his phone sliced through the air. My breath caught in my throat as he fished it out of his pocket, the sound reverberating in the quiet studio, turning it into a stage for an unwelcome intrusion. The caller ID flashed an unknown number, and I felt an involuntary shiver race down my spine. There was something unsettling about it—like a whisper of danger threading its way into our fragile moment.

"Sorry," he said, an apologetic frown etching across his face as he stepped away, his voice low and serious. "I need to take this."

I nodded, forcing myself to focus on the canvas. Each stroke felt heavier now, burdened by an inexplicable weight. I could hear his muffled voice, the tension rising like a slow tide as he paced back and forth. My heart thudded against my ribcage, each beat echoing the unease that began to fill the room. The vibrant colors on my canvas started to blur together, bleeding into one another, mirroring the chaos that threatened to spill over in our world.

As he continued his conversation, I caught snippets of his words, punctuated by an urgency that prickled the back of my neck. "I told you I was done with that," he said, the firmness in his tone contrasting sharply with the underlying tremor of fear. "I won't let it drag me back in."

The door to the studio creaked slightly, and I turned my head, catching a glimpse of Marcus's silhouette against the backdrop of sunlight. His body language shifted, tension coiling like a spring, and I felt an instinctual urge to reach out, to ground him. Whatever lay on the other end of that call was more than just a disturbance; it was a specter, an echo of a past that clung to him like a shadow, refusing to be exorcised.

When he finally hung up, I didn't need to ask. The pallor on his face spoke volumes. "Who was that?" I asked, trying to keep my voice steady, though the tremor of worry seeped through.

"An old acquaintance," he replied, his voice low and measured. "Someone I thought I'd left behind."

The words hung in the air, heavy and suffocating. I could see the internal struggle in his eyes, a battle fought in the silence between us, but I didn't push. Instead, I returned to my painting, the vivid hues becoming my sanctuary, a barrier against the encroaching darkness.

I felt a sense of urgency building within me, compelling me to dive deeper into my own emotions, to escape the grip of reality and slip into the solace of art.

Just as I felt the tension begin to lift, Marcus stepped closer, his expression unreadable. "What do you see when you look at your painting?" he asked, his voice barely above a whisper.

"An escape," I admitted, my brush hovering above the canvas. "A world where everything is vibrant and alive, untouched by the murkiness that life sometimes throws at us."

He nodded, a small flicker of understanding passing between us. "What if I told you that sometimes the murkiness is where we find our true selves? Where the real art lies?"

I paused, my heart racing as I processed his words. "But what if the murkiness pulls you under, Marcus? What if it's a darkness you can't swim away from?"

A beat of silence enveloped us, the unspoken fears pooling like paint on a palette, waiting to be mixed into something new. The sunlight streaming through the windows began to dim, shadows stretching and yawning as the day edged toward twilight. In that moment, I realized we stood at a precipice—a choice between diving into the depths of our pasts or stepping back into the light, together.

The atmosphere was charged with a tension that felt palpable, as if the very walls of the studio bore witness to our reckoning. I could feel the pull of the colors around us, each one beckoning with the promise of healing or the threat of despair. The world outside faded, leaving only the two of us, suspended in this fragile moment, where decisions lay heavy in the air like the scent of wet paint.

And then, just as I thought we might find a way through the chaos, the phone rang again, and my heart sank. It was a reminder that the shadows didn't just linger outside; they were right here with us, waiting for their chance to disrupt our fragile balance.

The phone's jarring ring cut through the vibrant chaos of our sanctuary, pulling me back into a reality I wasn't ready to face. Marcus's expression shifted, the playful warmth of the moment evaporating like morning mist under a relentless sun. He glanced at the screen, a furrow forming on his brow, and my heart sank. Whatever awaited him on the other end of that call felt like an unwelcome gust of wind, threatening to extinguish the flicker of connection we had just begun to explore.

"Just a moment," he murmured, stepping away with an urgency that suggested a storm was brewing just outside our carefully painted world. As I watched him, I felt a mix of concern and annoyance. I wanted to dive into the depths of what we were creating together, yet it seemed the universe had other plans, teasing us with fleeting moments of intimacy before yanking them away.

I turned back to my canvas, the vibrant strokes of blue and green suddenly feeling like a lie. My brush hovered over the paint, trembling slightly as I wrestled with the emotions swirling within me. Would we ever get to the place where we could truly be ourselves, where the walls of our pasts wouldn't loom like specters?

Marcus's voice floated back to me, low and tense. "No, I don't want any part of it. I told you, I'm done." His tone held a mixture of anger and regret that sent a shiver through me. I wanted to burst through that veil of uncertainty, to reach out and draw him back into our bubble, but instead, I remained rooted in place, a statue in my own studio.

After what felt like an eternity, he returned, his demeanor shifted, tinged with an urgency that hadn't been there moments before. "That was... not great," he said, running a hand through his tousled hair. "An old colleague from my past is trying to drag me back into something I thought I'd left behind."

"What kind of something?" I asked, my curiosity piqued despite the heaviness in the air.

He hesitated, glancing at the paint-splattered floor as if it might offer him some comfort. "Just... some old business dealings. You know how it is—when you think you're out, they pull you back in."

I felt the sharpness of his words, a reflection of the struggle within him. "Marcus, if it's something that threatens your peace, you don't have to engage. You've made it this far without it, haven't you?"

He looked at me, and for a moment, I saw a flicker of the man beneath the layers of caution and past burdens. "You make it sound so simple," he replied, a sardonic smile playing on his lips. "Just say 'no' and walk away. If only life were that easy."

"Maybe it could be," I challenged lightly, my own smile creeping up in response. "You're the one holding the paintbrush here. You get to decide what the picture looks like."

He raised an eyebrow, the tension slowly easing as he returned to my side, his presence grounding me. "That's an interesting analogy. So, what if my canvas is already smeared with shades of regret and old mistakes?"

"Then you paint over it," I said, gesturing dramatically, my voice playful. "Add layers! Make it abstract! Who's to say what's beautiful or worth keeping?"

He chuckled, a sound that warmed the chilly air around us. "Abstract, huh? So you're saying my past can be a modern masterpiece?"

"Exactly! Who doesn't love a bit of chaos in their art?" I grinned, gesturing to my own chaotic creation, a swirl of colors that resembled a tempest more than a landscape.

With a newfound spark, he picked up his brush again, mixing his palette with vigor. "Alright then, let's see what this masterpiece looks like."

The tension began to dissipate as we lost ourselves in our shared creativity, the studio transforming back into our sanctuary, the outside world fading into a distant murmur. With each stroke, I felt the air grow thicker with unspoken words, the electric charge of possibility wrapping around us like a warm blanket.

"Maybe we should collaborate on a piece," I suggested, the idea bubbling to the surface. "A joint masterpiece that reflects this moment, all the complexities and chaos included."

"Are you sure?" he asked, skepticism lacing his voice. "What if I ruin it?"

I shrugged, feigning nonchalance. "What if we ruin it together? Better to make a mess with someone else than to do it alone, right?"

He laughed, the sound light and genuine. "I like that idea. Let's make the most beautiful disaster anyone's ever seen."

As we worked side by side, the brushstrokes intertwined like the threads of our lives, building layers upon layers, revealing glimpses of something extraordinary beneath the chaos. The colors became a dialogue of their own—vivid oranges clashing against cool blues, soft greens blending into fierce reds. The intensity of our unspoken connection seemed to pulse through the canvas, charging every stroke with an urgency that matched the uncharted territory of our feelings.

Then, just as I felt we were weaving our way into something profound, Marcus's phone buzzed again. The sound reverberated in the space, jolting me from my artistic trance. His expression faltered, the warmth retreating into the familiar shadows of concern.

"Not again," he muttered, glancing at the screen. "I swear, if it's the same number..."

"Maybe it's your long-lost art critic?" I teased, attempting to lighten the moment, though my heart raced with anxiety.

He rolled his eyes but didn't answer. The air between us thickened once more, the playful banter stalling as he took a deep breath and swiped to answer.

"Hello?" he said, his voice taut.

I could hear the low murmur on the other end, but the words were muffled, slipping through my awareness like water through cupped hands. My mind raced with possibilities—who could be calling, and why now, when we were on the verge of breaking through something beautiful?

"Look, I'm not interested," Marcus said, his voice firm yet strained. "You need to stop calling."

He hung up abruptly, turning back to me, the tension evident on his face. "That was—" he began, but the words fell away, his frustration palpable.

"What did they want?" I pressed, my curiosity piqued again, though a nagging fear stirred deep inside.

"More of the same. They think they can sweet-talk me into returning. It's infuriating." His voice trembled slightly, a crack in the façade that revealed the weight he carried.

"Then don't let them. You're not that person anymore," I said, my heart racing with the truth of my words.

"Easier said than done." He crossed his arms, a familiar gesture of self-protection.

"Then paint it!" I urged, grabbing my brush and gesturing dramatically. "Let it out. Let the colors bleed your frustrations onto the canvas, and maybe we can create something new from it. Something they can't touch."

He met my gaze, the fire igniting in his eyes again, and in that moment, I realized we weren't just painting a picture; we were painting our own realities, crafting a space where the past couldn't dictate our futures. With every stroke, we were building our own sanctuary—a defiance against the shadows that threatened to invade our light.

As he picked up his brush again, the air crackled with a newfound intensity, a promise of what lay ahead—a partnership born from chaos, vulnerability, and the audacity to create something beautiful amid uncertainty.

The tension in the studio hung thick as Marcus turned away from me, his expression a tumult of emotions. The brush in my hand felt heavier than usual, weighed down not just by paint but by the gravity of the moment. I could hear him on the phone, words clipped and harsh, but it was the tightness of his jaw and the way his fingers clenched the edge of the table that truly told the story. The intimate atmosphere we had crafted together now felt precarious, like the frail surface of a canvas at risk of being ripped apart by an unseen hand.

"I've told you, I want nothing to do with that anymore," he said, his voice rising slightly. The room felt smaller with every syllable, every utterance vibrating against the walls that had witnessed our flirtation with intimacy only moments before. My heart raced as I painted, the brush strokes becoming erratic under the pressure of uncertainty.

As he hung up, I caught a glimpse of the fear in his eyes, a flicker that sent a chill spiraling down my spine. "Are you okay?" I ventured, the words tumbling out before I could filter them through the veil of my own rising anxiety.

"No. Not really," he admitted, and for a moment, the vulnerability in his voice drew me closer. "It's about the business dealings I mentioned. Someone wants me back in the fold, and I'm not sure how to shake them off."

"What kind of business?" I asked, crossing my arms instinctively, as if shielding myself from the invisible storm brewing in the air.

"Let's just say it's complicated," he replied, his voice barely a whisper. "Not the kind of thing you just walk away from without repercussions."

"Repercussions?" My mind raced, visions of late-night meetings and whispered conversations flickering through my thoughts.

"Marcus, you don't have to go back. You've created a life for yourself here. You're safe."

His gaze was intense, piercing through the chaos like a beam of light through a dense fog. "Safe? Do you really think that? Safety is an illusion. It only takes one call to pull the rug out from under you."

There was a pause, the air thickening with unspoken fears, and I reached out, placing a hand on his arm. "Then let's do this together. Whatever it is. We can paint through it, talk it through it."

The warmth of my touch seemed to ignite a spark in him. He glanced down, his breath catching for a moment, as if he were weighing the gravity of my offer against the fears that loomed large. "You don't know what you're getting into," he warned, but there was a softness in his tone, a hint of longing that spoke louder than the fear.

"Try me," I challenged, a small smile creeping onto my face. "I've dealt with my own shadows. Besides, the idea of us becoming a masterpiece—a beautiful, chaotic mess—sounds far more appealing than being swept up in some corporate drama."

A laugh escaped his lips, and it was as if the tension surrounding us loosened just a little, allowing a fresh breath of air to circulate. "Okay, Picasso," he said, his tone teasing as he began to mix colors again. "Let's see if we can't paint our way out of this mess."

We resumed our work, the rhythm of our brushstrokes creating a symphony of color and emotion, a dance between chaos and order. With every stroke, the heaviness lifted slightly, our laughter weaving a thread of connection that seemed to bind us closer together, even as the shadows outside crept ever closer. The canvas became our escape—a riot of colors mirroring the turmoil within, yet also the hope that flickered like a candle in the dark.

Just as I thought we'd found our rhythm, the phone rang again, its shrill tone slicing through the fragile atmosphere we had built. Marcus froze mid-stroke, his expression shifting from joy to dread in the blink of an eye. "Not again," he muttered, irritation flaring in his eyes.

I felt a rush of protectiveness as he hesitated, uncertainty painting his features. "Don't answer it," I urged, my voice firm, but he shook his head, a decision already forming behind those intense eyes.

"I have to," he said, steeling himself as he grabbed the phone. The moment felt suspended, the world narrowing down to just the two of us and the ringing device, each sound reverberating like a heartbeat echoing in a cavern.

"Hello?" His voice was steady, but I could see the way his fingers trembled slightly, a betraying quiver that whispered of the storm brewing beneath the surface. I held my breath, the weight of anticipation hanging heavy in the air.

"Marcus, it's me," came a voice from the other end, smooth and eerily calm. I didn't recognize it, but the way he stiffened told me everything I needed to know. "We need to talk."

The words slithered through the phone like poison, tainting our moment with a chilling clarity. I felt a surge of protective instinct, ready to dive into the fray, to shield him from whatever ghosts haunted this conversation. But Marcus's expression twisted into a mix of fury and fear, his knuckles whitening around the phone as he turned away, his back to me.

"You have no idea what you're asking," he replied, his voice low but laced with tension. "I'm done with this. You can't just call me out of the blue and expect me to jump back into your game."

"Is that what you think?" The voice was smooth, almost mocking, and my heart raced as I felt the atmosphere thicken with a sense of impending doom. "You're not done, Marcus. You can't escape what's already set in motion. You're in deeper than you think."

"Don't threaten me," he shot back, anger flaring in his voice like a fire igniting in a dry forest. The moment seemed to stretch, a taut line ready to snap. My instincts screamed that this conversation was more than a mere nuisance; it was a warning, a shadow coiling around us as the night began to descend.

But before I could process the implication, the door to the studio creaked open, the sound echoing with an unsettling familiarity. I turned just in time to see a figure slip inside, silhouetted against the dying light. My breath caught, and I felt a wave of icy fear wash over me as I recognized the face staring back at us—a face from Marcus's past, one I had only seen in fleeting photographs and half-whispered conversations.

"Looks like we all have some catching up to do," the newcomer said, a smirk playing at the corners of their mouth.

In that instant, the air crackled with tension, the fragile sanctuary of our studio transforming into a battlefield of uncertainty, where shadows from the past collided with the precarious hope of the present. My heart raced as the stakes rose impossibly high, and I knew without a doubt that we were teetering on the edge of something far greater than ourselves, a confrontation that could unravel everything we had begun to build.

Chapter 11: The Hunter

The streets of Asheville twisted and turned like the trails of my thoughts, each shadowed corner echoing my growing unease. I stood in the dim light of my studio, the scent of linseed oil mingling with the pungent aroma of wet earth seeping in through the cracked window. Outside, the night had draped itself over the town, a heavy blanket that swallowed the flickering street lamps, leaving only vague outlines of the world I once found so charming. But now, charm felt like a distant memory, overshadowed by the weight of uncertainty pressing down on my chest.

Marcus had left with purpose, his silhouette slicing through the darkness, a warrior chasing whispers in a world that thrived on secrets. I could still hear the sound of his voice, a deep rumble that vibrated through me, full of resolve and perhaps a hint of desperation. "I'll find out who's behind this," he had said, his eyes fierce, almost glowing with an intensity that made me want to reach out and tether him to me, to keep him safe. But I knew better than to hold him back. He was driven, a force of nature, and in my heart, I understood the path he had chosen was as much for my sake as it was for his own need for justice.

With a trembling hand, I dipped my brush into a deep indigo, the color swallowing the last remnants of daylight. As the bristles met the canvas, I poured out my anxiety, the fluid motions of my arm guiding the brush like an extension of my very soul. The strokes transformed into a tumultuous sea, each wave a reflection of my turmoil, while whispers of light danced above the chaos—hopes and dreams fighting against the impending storm. But beneath the surface, I sensed the lurking shadows, a tension that tightened my throat.

I let the brush linger, allowing the hues to mingle and clash, creating an emotional tempest that echoed the disarray in my mind.

Marcus's face emerged, chiseled and determined, an anchor in my swirling thoughts. The soft curve of his lips, usually relaxed in laughter, was now a thin line, drawn tight with the weight of what lay ahead. I could almost feel the warmth of his skin beneath my fingers, the reassuring presence that seemed to melt away the world's worries. Yet here I was, wielding paint and canvas, trying to capture his essence while wrestling with the gnawing anxiety that bit at my resolve.

The air around me crackled, charged with the unspoken fears that hung in the corners of the room like specters. I was half-tempted to throw the brush aside and pace the studio, but instead, I continued to paint, as if the canvas might absorb my turmoil and transform it into something beautiful. I painted the stormy sea, the rolling waves swelling and crashing, then transformed them into a dance of light that hinted at hope and rebirth. In the chaos, I found a flicker of solace, but it was fleeting.

Hours passed, and with each flick of the brush, time slipped away, morphing into a nebulous concept I could no longer grasp. The clock ticked away in the corner, each chime a reminder of Marcus's absence, of the darkness he had ventured into. I stepped back from the canvas, my heart racing as I surveyed my work. It was as if I had spilled my soul onto the surface, a vivid tapestry of my fears and desires, and yet it felt incomplete. I needed him here, needed the grounding presence that filled the empty spaces within me.

Just as I turned to collect my thoughts, the sound of footsteps echoed from the street below. My heart leapt, the hope igniting within me like a match struck against the dark. Was it Marcus returning? The urge to run to the window tugged at me, a desire to see him, to know he was safe. But curiosity held me rooted in place, my pulse racing with anticipation. The footsteps paused, and for a moment, I could only hear the distant murmur of the night, punctuated by the faint rustling of leaves in the chilly breeze.

Suddenly, a sharp knock reverberated through the stillness, slicing through the tension that had enveloped me. I jumped, paint splattering against the wall as my heart raced. Approaching the door, my mind whirled with possibilities—had Marcus come back, or was it someone else entirely? I opened the door just a crack, peering into the dimly lit corridor beyond.

"Who's there?" I called, my voice stronger than I felt, a feeble attempt to mask the tremor in my hands.

"Ellie," a voice called back, rough yet familiar. It was one of Marcus's friends from the local pub, Kyle, whose presence had always felt like a warm embrace amidst the cool Asheville air. "You need to let me in. It's important."

The urgency in his voice twisted my stomach in knots, a sense of foreboding washing over me. I swung the door open, revealing him standing there, eyes wide and scanning the darkened hallway as if it were filled with lurking shadows. "What's wrong?" I asked, bracing myself against the frame.

"Marcus... he's—" he hesitated, the weight of his words hanging in the air like a thundercloud. "He's in trouble. We need to find him."

Every heartbeat thudded in my ears as dread settled like a stone in my gut. The hunter had become the hunted, and I was about to dive headfirst into a world I had tried to keep at bay.

The door swung open wider, and Kyle stepped inside, his demeanor a mix of urgency and reluctance. I noticed how he kept glancing over his shoulder, as if expecting something—or someone—to follow him. "Ellie," he began, his voice low and steady, "Marcus is caught up in something we didn't see coming. It's serious."

A chill snaked down my spine, tightening my throat. "What do you mean 'caught up'?" I forced myself to remain calm, though my heart raced like a runaway train. The walls of my cozy studio felt like they were closing in, the vibrant colors of my paintings fading in the harsh light of reality. "He was just looking into the threats, Kyle. How bad could it be?"

Kyle rubbed the back of his neck, a nervous gesture that made my stomach twist. "I don't know the details, but there's a group—more like a syndicate—that's been sniffing around. I overheard some guys at the pub talking about it. They mentioned Marcus's name."

Every word felt like a weight pressing down on me. "And you thought telling me now was a good idea?" My voice came out sharper than I intended, a mix of frustration and fear. "What am I supposed to do with that?"

"Panic isn't an option," he said, his tone calming, though the worry etched on his face suggested otherwise. "We need to find him before it gets worse. He's stubborn, and he's not going to stop until he gets to the bottom of this. You know him."

"I do," I replied, my voice softening. "But he can't keep doing this alone." A wave of guilt washed over me. Had I encouraged his reckless pursuit for answers?

"Exactly. And that's why I'm here," Kyle said, stepping further into the room, the door creaking slightly as it settled behind him. "I was hoping you could help us track him down. He mentioned he'd check in with some contacts in the area, but I don't know who he was meeting."

"Do you think he's in danger?" The thought tightened my chest like a vise.

Kyle met my gaze, the seriousness of the moment stark between us. "If he's tangled up with those guys, then yes. But I don't want to scare you more than you already are. We need to think clearly."

I nodded, trying to draw a breath deeper than my rising panic would allow. "Let's find him," I said, my voice firmer now, steeling myself against the tide of worry that threatened to pull me under. "Do you have any idea where he might be?"

"There's a warehouse on the outskirts of town where some of them hang out," Kyle suggested. "It's not exactly a welcome mat kind of place, but it might be where we need to go."

The thought of Marcus in a potentially hostile environment sent a rush of adrenaline coursing through me. "Then what are we waiting for?" I shot back, my determination surging. "Let's go."

As we hurried through the narrow streets, the crisp night air bit at my skin, an unwelcoming reminder of the darkening world we were stepping into. The moon hung low, casting an eerie glow on the cobblestones, and shadows danced as we navigated the dimly lit alleys. The quaint charm of Asheville felt like a cruel mask over a reality filled with danger, and I couldn't shake the feeling that we were being watched.

"Why are you looking at me like that?" Kyle asked, breaking the heavy silence that had settled between us.

"Like what?" I replied, feigning innocence.

"Like you're planning to save the world with a paintbrush and a can of spray paint," he teased, though I could see the concern etched on his brow. "We're not in one of your art pieces, Ellie. This isn't a metaphorical fight."

"It could be," I said, unable to resist a smirk. "Just think—me, the fearless artist, wielding a palette knife against the forces of evil."

"Please don't let your imagination run wild right now. Focus." He shook his head, half-smiling despite the tension.

I appreciated his attempt to lighten the mood, but the gravity of the situation loomed larger with every step. Soon, we approached the warehouse—a hulking structure cloaked in shadows, its windows dark and uninviting. The air felt electric, thick with the scent of danger that set my nerves on edge.

"Stay close," Kyle instructed, his voice barely above a whisper.

"Isn't that my line?" I retorted, trying to match his intensity with a hint of bravado, but I felt the weight of the unknown pressing heavily on my shoulders.

We crept around the side of the building, the gravel crunching beneath our feet as we surveyed the perimeter. A flicker of light broke through a gap in the boards, illuminating a cluster of figures silhouetted against the glow. My heart raced as I strained to catch snippets of their conversation, the urgency in their voices echoing the fears that had taken root in my mind.

"...he said he wouldn't talk..."

"...it's too risky now..."

"Find him before he brings more heat..."

Each phrase dripped with threat, and a shiver crawled down my spine. "They're talking about Marcus," I whispered, the realization tightening my grip on the wall.

"Let's get a closer look," Kyle said, edging forward cautiously.

I followed him, adrenaline fueling my movements as we crept closer, my heart pounding in time with the pulse of the night. We settled into a shadowed alcove, hearts racing as we strained to listen.

"Yeah, he thought he could play hero," one of the figures sneered, a malevolent edge to his voice. "We need to teach him a lesson he won't forget."

A wave of nausea washed over me. "We have to get him out of there," I said, my voice a raw whisper.

"Agreed," Kyle murmured, determination etched into every feature. "But we can't charge in there blindly. We need a plan."

A plan. It felt absurd to even contemplate as I peered into the maw of uncertainty looming before us. Yet, even as fear clawed at my insides, a flicker of resolve ignited. If Marcus was in danger, then there was no way I was backing down. "Let's figure out how to get inside without turning ourselves into targets," I said, swallowing hard against the lump in my throat.

Kyle nodded, eyes narrowing as he scanned the area, a flicker of mischief sparking in his gaze. "I might have an idea. We can create a diversion—something loud and distracting."

"Fireworks?" I suggested, half-joking, though I found myself entertained by the idea.

"Not quite. How about we give them a little show of our own?" His grin was both mischievous and reassuring, lighting up the shadows that surrounded us.

I felt the weight of fear shifting, turning into a palpable sense of purpose. We might not be able to face this threat head-on, but we could certainly use our wits to level the playing field. As the night thickened around us, the stakes rose higher, but I knew one thing for certain: I wouldn't let Marcus face this alone.

The dim light of the warehouse flickered as Kyle and I huddled together, our breaths mingling in the chilly air like a wisp of smoke—delicate yet laden with purpose. I could feel the pulse of the night thrumming around us, an electric current of danger that both thrilled and terrified me. We were about to engage in a game of shadows, and I was determined to tip the odds in our favor.

"Here's the plan," Kyle whispered, his eyes gleaming with the reckless spark of an adventurer. "I'll create a distraction over by that stack of crates." He pointed to a pile of weathered wood, their edges worn and splintered. "While they're busy figuring out what that noise is, you slip inside through the side door. You'll have the element of surprise."

"Perfect," I replied, though a wave of doubt washed over me. "What kind of distraction are we talking about here? Because if you're suggesting a dance party, I don't think that's going to impress the thugs inside."

"Leave the theatrics to me," he grinned, and the confidence in his voice was a comfort amidst the uncertainty.

"Right, let's get this show on the road before I lose my nerve," I said, trying to inject a bravado I didn't quite feel. With a final nod to each other, Kyle darted off toward the crates, his movements fluid and determined.

I waited, my heart pounding like a drum, feeling the weight of the moment press down on me. The anticipation was almost unbearable, a tight coil of fear and excitement that left me breathless. As Kyle reached the crates, he kicked one, sending it crashing to the ground with a thunderous bang. The sound echoed like a cannon shot, slicing through the stillness of the night.

"Hey! What the hell?" a voice barked from inside the warehouse, sharp and demanding.

That was my cue. I slipped away from the shadows and darted toward the side door, my heart racing as I pushed it open, wincing at the creak of the hinges. It led into a narrow corridor, its walls damp and grimy, the scent of mildew thick in the air. I could hear raised voices, confusion spilling into the air like water rushing through a broken dam.

"Get over there and check it out!" another voice commanded. "We can't have anyone snooping around."

Panic bubbled in my chest, but I forced myself to move forward. The corridor twisted and turned, leading me deeper into the heart of the beast. I pressed myself against the wall, listening intently as footsteps thundered past, oblivious to my presence. Every instinct screamed at me to turn back, but I pushed through the fear, driven by the thought of Marcus and the danger he might be facing.

The corridor opened up into a large room filled with crates and shadows, a makeshift staging area for whatever operations these men were running. The flickering light from overhead illuminated the outlines of several figures, their movements tense and charged. I crouched behind a stack of boxes, peering out to catch a glimpse of the chaos Kyle had unleashed.

"Go check the perimeter! Now!" A man, his voice gruff and commanding, pointed toward the exit. The others scrambled to obey, tension thick in the air like the smell of gunpowder after a shot is fired.

My breath caught in my throat as I spotted Marcus, bound to a chair in the corner, his usually bright eyes clouded with confusion and anger. My heart sank at the sight, and I felt an overwhelming urge to run to him, to tear away the ropes that held him captive. But I knew better; charging in would only put us both in danger.

Instead, I crouched lower, scanning the room for anything I could use to my advantage. There had to be something—anything—that could help me distract them long enough to reach Marcus. My gaze landed on a metal rod lying on the ground, discarded and forgotten. A spark of inspiration ignited within me. If I could create another distraction, maybe I could draw their attention away just long enough.

I glanced around, ensuring no one was watching before inching toward the rod. The shadows enveloped me, a cloak of safety that urged me forward. As I reached for it, my fingers curled around the cold metal, and I felt a rush of adrenaline course through my veins.

I took a deep breath, steeling my resolve. I had to act quickly. Just then, I heard the sound of footsteps approaching again. I ducked back behind the boxes, clutching the rod tightly, my heart thudding wildly in my chest.

"Did you check the back door?" the gruff voice demanded, echoing from somewhere nearby. "I swear if it's another false alarm, I'm going to—"

"Forget the door! We've got bigger problems," another man interrupted, urgency sharpening his tone. "We need to deal with Marcus before he gets anyone else involved."

That did it. The mere mention of Marcus sent a surge of protective instinct racing through me. I stepped back, taking a deep breath to steady myself, then threw the rod with all my strength. It clattered against a pile of crates at the far end of the room, the sound reverberating like a cannon shot.

"Did you hear that?" One of the men shouted, eyes widening as they turned toward the noise. "Go check it out!"

I seized the opportunity, dashing across the room, every instinct screaming for me to move faster. I reached Marcus, and my heart dropped at the sight of him, his face bruised but fierce. "Ellie?" he breathed, a mix of surprise and worry flaring in his eyes. "What are you doing here?"

"No time for questions!" I whispered urgently, fingers working to untie the ropes that bound him. "We have to get out of here!"

"Did Kyle—"

"He's distracting them!" I hissed, my focus zeroing in on the knots, frustration mounting as they refused to yield. "Hold still!"

"Ellie, you shouldn't have come—"

"Can you please stop lecturing me and just trust me?" I snapped, my patience wearing thin. The last knot finally gave way, and I felt a rush of triumph. "There! Now, let's go!"

Just as Marcus stood, a shadow moved at the edge of my vision. I turned, heart plummeting as I saw the figure approaching—a man with a hardened face, his expression a mask of anger and disdain.

"Where do you think you're going?" he growled, eyes narrowing as he took a step forward. The air crackled with tension, a predator scenting its prey.

In that split second, I knew we were trapped. No way out, no backup. I felt the walls closing in, panic clawing at my throat. I shot a glance back at Marcus, his expression shifting from confusion to fierce determination, and my heart pounded with the weight of the moment.

"Run!" I screamed, but the words barely escaped my lips before chaos erupted.

Chapter 12: An Invitation

The soft glow of chandeliers bathed the gallery in golden light, casting flickering shadows that danced along the walls, where art hung in decadent displays. I had never seen anything quite like it. Each piece seemed to whisper secrets of far-off places and long-lost histories, the stories woven into the very fibers of their canvases. But tonight, it was the people that held my attention. They glided through the space, draped in silks and satins, their laughter ringing out like a symphony composed of privilege and pretense. I stood on the threshold, feeling like an intruder in a realm where elegance reigned, and I, with my worn clutch and secondhand dress, was just an unwelcome guest.

Marcus was a whirlwind beside me, his charisma drawing people in like moths to a flame. With each smile he shared, he opened doors—figuratively and literally—as he led me deeper into this shimmering world. His tailored suit hugged him just right, the deep navy accentuating the sharp angles of his jaw and the warmth in his hazel eyes. I had always admired how he could navigate any situation, his voice smooth like aged whiskey, calming yet captivating. I tried to mimic his ease, though I felt more like a clumsy swan than a poised swan gliding through the evening.

The sound of clinking glasses resonated around us, laughter bubbling over in sharp bursts as the elite shared jokes I could barely comprehend. I wrapped my fingers around a delicate flute of champagne, the effervescence tickling my nose as I took a cautious sip, its crispness momentarily distracting me from the tension coiling in my stomach. My heart raced, caught in a tango of exhilaration and apprehension. We were here for answers, yet it felt as if we had stepped into a masquerade where the masks were smiles and the truth lurked just beyond the surface.

"Do you see that man over there?" Marcus leaned closer, his breath warm against my ear, the scent of his cologne—a rich blend of sandalwood and something crisp—sending an unexpected shiver down my spine. He gestured subtly toward a figure draped in an expensive-looking linen suit, his hair slicked back with a sheen that suggested both vanity and control. "That's Sebastian Lark. Rumor has it he's not just a collector; he's involved in some pretty dubious deals."

My gaze shifted to Lark, and I found myself captivated by the way he surveyed the room, a predator among prey. There was a cool confidence in his stance, a self-assuredness that sent a shiver of foreboding through me. "Are we sure this is the right place to be? It feels...dangerous," I murmured, unable to shake the feeling that eyes were tracking our every move, sharp and calculating.

Marcus chuckled, a low sound that vibrated against my arm, his proximity wrapping around me like a protective cocoon. "Dangerous is my middle name, or at least it should be. We're just here to gather intel, nothing more. Besides," he added, tilting his head toward me with a mischievous glint in his eyes, "what's life without a little risk?"

I rolled my eyes, though a smile tugged at my lips. "Easy for you to say. You thrive in chaos. I'm still figuring out if I can handle a full glass of champagne without spilling it all over myself."

He laughed outright, the sound infectious, drawing a few curious glances from nearby guests. "If you spill it, I'll drink it. Consider it a bonding exercise." The way he looked at me, all sincerity and warmth, sent a rush of warmth flooding my cheeks. There was an undeniable chemistry that crackled between us, a blend of tension and unspoken desires. But amidst the thrill, I couldn't shake the gnawing feeling that we were out of our depth, far from the safety of our familiar lives.

As we mingled among the crowd, I felt a ripple of anxiety settle in my chest. The atmosphere felt thick with secrets, as if the air itself was a conspirator in this clandestine affair. Whispers fluttered like moths around the gallery, delicate and fleeting, barely audible yet laden with weight. I caught snippets of conversation—talk of acquisitions and investments, rumors of art thefts that hinted at a darker world behind the velvet ropes. The laughter that echoed around us felt forced, like a carefully curated façade meant to obscure the truth lurking beneath.

Just then, a woman approached us, her presence magnetic. She wore a crimson dress that clung to her curves like a lover's embrace, the fabric shimmering with every step she took. Her dark hair cascaded in loose waves, framing a face that was both striking and intimidating. "Ah, Marcus! So good to see you." Her voice was smooth, a silken thread weaving through the air, and she extended her hand toward him, her nails painted a fierce shade of red that matched her dress.

"Lila, you look as stunning as ever," Marcus replied, his tone warm yet guarded. I felt a pang of jealousy, an unwelcome sensation that twisted in my stomach as I observed their interaction. It was a brief exchange, yet the undercurrents crackled between them, filled with history and unspoken tension.

"Who's your lovely companion?" Lila's gaze slid to me, sharp and assessing, as if she were a hawk sizing up its prey. I offered a smile, trying to appear confident, even as I felt small beneath her scrutiny.

"This is—" Marcus began, but I cut him off before he could finish.

"Just a curious observer," I interjected, forcing my tone to remain light and airy. "I'm trying to soak in all this extravagance. It's quite a spectacle." I gestured broadly, my eyes flitting over the opulent surroundings, desperate to divert attention from the simmering tension.

"Curious, indeed," Lila replied, her eyes narrowing slightly. "You should be careful. Curiosity has a way of leading one into dark places."

Her warning hung in the air like a thundercloud, heavy and foreboding. The words, laced with unspoken implications, sent a chill creeping up my spine. I exchanged a glance with Marcus, whose expression was unreadable, a mask carefully constructed to conceal his thoughts. The evening, once filled with promise and intrigue, now felt as though it were teetering on the edge of a precipice. The vibrant world around us, with its laughter and light, seemed increasingly surreal, as if we were participants in a grand play where the final act was yet to unfold.

The air crackled with energy as Lila's words hung between us, thick with tension. I could feel the weight of her gaze pressing against my skin, a challenge wrapped in silk and charm. There was something about her, a magnetic allure that had a way of drawing people in while simultaneously pushing them away. As Marcus continued to engage her, I felt like a small fish in a vast ocean, floundering beneath the waves of their familiarity.

"Careful is my middle name, Lila," Marcus replied, his voice laced with a playful tone that belied the seriousness of her warning. "But I appreciate your concern." He flashed a charming smile, one that could light up even the darkest corners of this opulent gallery. I wondered if he was aware of the way it transformed him from a mere participant in this gathering to the center of attention, as if the very air bent around him in reverence.

Lila's eyes sparkled with intrigue, yet I sensed an underlying calculation in her smile. "Ah, but curiosity has a way of leading even the sharpest minds astray. Just remember, Marcus, not every piece of art tells the same story." With that cryptic remark, she stepped back, her crimson dress trailing behind her like a comet's tail. She disappeared into the crowd, leaving a trail of whispers in her wake.

"Why do I feel like she just served me a riddle wrapped in a warning?" I turned to Marcus, trying to shake off the unsettling feeling that Lila had dropped a clue I was too dense to decipher. "Is she always that cryptic, or is it just me?"

Marcus laughed, a warm and rich sound that eased my tension slightly. "Oh, she's always like that. Lila thrives on intrigue, the art of the tease. Don't let her words unsettle you. She's just keeping her options open, a player in her own game."

"Great, just what I need. Another player." I took a fortifying sip of champagne, the bubbles sparkling like stars against the backdrop of my escalating anxiety. "What exactly are we doing here again? Gathering intel, you said? What does that mean in a place filled with high-society backstabbers?"

"Consider it an expedition into the unknown," Marcus replied, his eyes glinting with mischief. "And you're the adventurous spirit I've always admired."

"Adventurous? Is that what we're calling it? More like stepping into a lion's den with a steak wrapped around my neck." I sighed, glancing around at the opulence surrounding us. The grand space pulsated with a vibrant energy that felt both thrilling and ominous.

"Embrace the adventure," he said, his voice smooth as silk. "Besides, we're not here to be eaten. We're here to find out what Lark is hiding."

The mention of Sebastian Lark sent another shiver down my spine. The man was an enigma wrapped in a designer suit, with rumors swirling around him like autumn leaves caught in a storm. My instinct told me he was trouble, the kind that came wrapped in a pretty package.

As we moved further into the throng, Marcus nudged me toward a small cluster of people gathered around a piece of art that commanded attention. The canvas was a chaotic explosion of colors, a cacophony of brush strokes that screamed for recognition. It was stunning and disturbing all at once, like a beautiful lie. "What do you think?" Marcus asked, tilting his head as if he were studying my reaction rather than the art itself.

"Honestly? It looks like someone took their emotions and splattered them across the canvas without a second thought," I said, crossing my arms. "It's raw, but I can't say I love it."

"Art is subjective, darling. It's about what it evokes," he replied, his voice teasing yet serious. "And in this case, it's evoking quite the response from you."

"Let's hope my response doesn't lead me to a nervous breakdown," I quipped, glancing at the crowd. They leaned in, captivated, faces lit by a combination of awe and confusion. Just then, I felt a tap on my shoulder.

I turned to see a tall, lean figure with tousled hair and an easy smile—a face that was both familiar and comforting. "Hannah, there you are!" It was Leo, an old friend from college whose charm was as effortless as a summer breeze. "I was wondering if you'd make it."

"Leo! What a surprise!" My heart lifted at the sight of him, his laid-back demeanor a welcome contrast to the tension that had settled in my chest. "You're here, too?"

"Of course. Lark throws a killer party, but let's be honest, it's mostly a chance for us all to gawk at the rich and ridiculous." He gestured with a playful flourish. "I had to see this spectacle for myself."

"You have no idea," I replied, unable to suppress a grin. "I feel like I've walked into a high-stakes game of poker, and I'm the only one without a clue about the rules."

"Ah, but you've got Marcus. He's like a card shark in a sea of fish." Leo winked, his gaze drifting to Marcus, who stood a few feet away, conversing animatedly with another guest. "I've always admired his knack for blending in and standing out at the same time."

"I think it's called being charming," I shot back, though a flicker of warmth danced in my chest at the compliment. "But charming is a double-edged sword when you're surrounded by people like Lila and Lark."

"Just keep your wits about you," Leo said, his expression turning serious for a moment. "This place has a way of exposing insecurities. You never know who might be watching, waiting for a moment of weakness."

A wave of unease washed over me, the gravity of his words settling in. I glanced around, suddenly aware of how closely people seemed to be monitoring our every interaction, their eyes flicking between Marcus, Leo, and me. I could almost feel the gears turning in their minds, speculating, plotting.

"Let's get a drink, shall we?" Leo suggested, breaking through my spiraling thoughts. "I could use something strong to cut through all this pretense."

I laughed, grateful for the distraction. "Lead the way. I need something to keep me grounded before I float away into this sea of high society."

As we made our way toward the bar, the world around us blurred slightly, the laughter and chatter fading into a distant hum. I felt a renewed sense of determination; whatever secrets lurked behind the elegant facades, I wouldn't let fear hold me captive. I was here for a reason, and with Marcus by my side and friends like Leo around me, I could navigate this treacherous landscape.

"I'll take a gin and tonic, please," Leo said to the bartender, while I opted for a simple whiskey on the rocks. The moment the glass slid into my hand, I savored the coolness against my palm, a refreshing contrast to the heat of the room.

"Here's to surviving the night," Leo raised his glass, a twinkle in his eye.

"To surviving and thriving," I echoed, clinking my glass against his with a renewed sense of resolve. Just as I took a sip, Marcus joined us, a curious glint in his eyes.

"Are we toasting without me?" he asked, feigning offense.

"Only if you promise to keep us safe from the lions lurking about," I replied, the playful challenge igniting the air between us.

"Safety is my specialty," he grinned, leaning in closer, the warmth of his presence wrapping around me. "Now, let's see if we can uncover what Lark is hiding before the night takes a turn."

The night unfolded like a tapestry, threads of laughter, tension, and hidden agendas weaving together in a mesmerizing dance. As the shadows lengthened, I felt the thrill of the unknown coursing through me, pulling me deeper into a world where art, ambition, and danger collided with every breath.

The crowd swelled around us, laughter punctuating the air like the soft pop of a cork, and I found myself nestled deeper into this tapestry of wealth and secrets. As I surveyed the room, I noted the way the guests adjusted their postures and voices, performing for an audience that included everyone and no one at all. It was both fascinating and unnerving, as if we were all trapped in an elaborate play where the script was yet to be written.

"Look over there," Marcus leaned in, his voice low and conspiratorial, directing my attention toward a pair of elegantly dressed women engaged in a heated discussion. Their perfectly coiffed hair swayed with animated gestures, the air thick with something unspoken. "That's Vanessa and Margo. They're rumored to be in cahoots with Lark on some dubious dealings. If we're lucky, we might overhear something interesting."

"Or we might get caught eavesdropping and end up on the wrong end of a champagne bottle," I countered, casting a wary glance their way. The idea of being discovered felt like an electric jolt; the thrill of adventure mixed with the very real danger of exposure. "I'm not exactly dressed for a fight, after all."

Marcus chuckled, his eyes dancing with mischief. "Don't worry; I'll be your knight in shining armor. Though, I suspect it would be a rather shabby suit of armor, considering the price of these drinks."

"Ah yes, a knight who charges for his services. I see how it is." I couldn't help but smile, feeling the tension ease slightly in his presence. There was an intoxicating blend of danger and camaraderie in our venture, a bubbling excitement that coursed through the evening like a hidden river.

With a conspiratorial nod, we sidled closer to the pair, discreetly positioning ourselves near an oversized sculpture that towered over us, its abstract form casting elongated shadows on the floor. The women's voices became clearer, the tension in their conversation palpable.

"Sebastian is getting impatient," Margo hissed, her voice a velvet whisper, sharp enough to cut through the laughter around us. "He wants the shipment delivered by the end of the week, and you know how he gets when things don't go his way."

"Impatient? More like a petulant child," Vanessa scoffed, her disdain dripping from her words. "But if he thinks we're going to risk everything just because he can't sit still, he's mistaken. We're already treading on thin ice with this deal."

Marcus's brow furrowed slightly, and I felt a rush of exhilaration at the prospect of getting a glimpse into Lark's dealings. This was exactly the intel we needed, a thread to pull that might unravel the whole tapestry.

"Do you think they're talking about the same shipment?" I whispered, my curiosity piqued. "Could it be connected to the rumors of art theft?"

"Exactly what I was thinking," Marcus replied, a spark of excitement in his voice. "If we can connect the dots, we might just uncover something big."

But as we leaned in closer, a sudden shift in the atmosphere caught my attention. The crowd's laughter faded, the air thickening with an unspoken tension. My heart raced as I noticed Sebastian Lark himself weaving through the throng, his gaze sharp and predatory. It was as if he sensed the very heartbeat of the party, and he was determined to take control.

"Speaking of trouble," I murmured, my voice barely a whisper. "Looks like the lion has entered the den."

"Stay close," Marcus instructed, his tone shifting to one of caution. "If Lark is here, we need to be smart about how we proceed."

I felt a rush of adrenaline as I clutched my drink, forcing myself to remain calm while my instincts screamed at me to flee. As Lark approached, I could see the sharpness in his features, the way his lips curled into a smirk that didn't quite reach his eyes. He exuded a confidence that was both captivating and terrifying, like a magician who reveled in the secrets of his craft.

"Ladies and gentlemen!" he called out, his voice booming over the crowd, silencing the chatter. "Welcome to an evening of art and ambition! I hope you're all prepared for a night of revelation."

The guests responded with polite applause, their eyes wide and eager, as if he were about to unveil a grand illusion. Yet I sensed an undercurrent of tension—a predator making his intentions clear.

"Revelation? Or manipulation?" I muttered under my breath, shooting a glance at Marcus.

"Let's see what he has planned," Marcus replied, his eyes narrowing as he studied Lark's movements.

Lark continued, gesturing grandly toward a large canvas shrouded in velvet, the centerpiece of the evening. "Tonight, we unveil a masterpiece—one that has been kept secret for far too long. A piece that will change the very fabric of our collection."

Gasps rippled through the crowd as he pulled the velvet away with a flourish, revealing a painting that took my breath away. It was a stunning piece, full of color and chaos, yet beneath the beauty lay a darker story, a tumult of emotions captured in strokes of paint.

"This," Lark declared, "is an original from a troubled artist, long forgotten. But the story doesn't end here. It is rumored to hold secrets, treasures buried deep beneath its surface."

The guests leaned in closer, enthralled, their expressions shifting from curiosity to greed. I could feel the collective desire in the air, a hunger that matched the intensity of the gathering.

"Is he serious?" I whispered to Marcus, feeling a mix of awe and disbelief. "What secrets could it possibly hold?"

"He's baiting them," Marcus replied, his voice steady. "The allure of hidden treasures. It's a classic play in the world of art, and Lark knows how to work the crowd."

Just then, as if sensing the energy shifting, Lark turned his piercing gaze toward us, his smile transforming into something predatory. "Ah, Marcus! You've brought a friend. I do love a fresh perspective. Care to share your thoughts on my latest acquisition?"

The air shifted, the weight of his attention pressing down on me like a lead blanket. My heart raced as I felt every eye in the room turn toward us, curiosity flickering like candle flames. I could sense the tension rising, an electric charge weaving through the crowd.

"Just an admirer of the arts," I said, forcing a smile despite the fluttering in my chest. "Though I have to admit, I find the allure of secrets quite captivating."

"Secrets, indeed," Lark replied, his voice smooth as silk, laced with hidden intentions. "But secrets can be dangerous, don't you think? They have a way of surfacing when least expected."

Marcus's hand brushed against mine, a grounding touch amidst the chaos. I could feel the weight of the moment settling in, a pause filled with uncertainty, a flicker of danger flaring just beneath the surface.

"What are you suggesting, Mr. Lark?" Marcus asked, his tone even but his body coiled with tension, like a spring ready to release.

Lark stepped closer, his presence overwhelming as he lowered his voice, an intimate whisper just for us. "I suggest you tread carefully. Curiosity can lead to perilous paths."

Before I could respond, the lights flickered momentarily, casting the room in shadows before they returned, brighter than before. Gasps filled the air, but it wasn't just the lights—something else had shifted.

In that moment of confusion, a loud crash echoed through the gallery, followed by a chorus of startled screams. My heart stopped as I turned toward the source of the sound, dread pooling in my stomach. A figure darted past the entrance, cloaked in darkness, moving with the urgency of a storm.

"Stay here!" Marcus commanded, his voice a low growl as he turned to follow the shadow. But as he moved, I caught a glimpse of Lark's expression—a predatory gleam flickered in his eyes, a hint of satisfaction that sent chills racing down my spine.

I stood frozen, torn between the desire to follow Marcus and the instinct to stay rooted to the spot, my pulse racing in tandem with the chaos erupting around me. Shadows danced across the walls, whispers of intrigue filling the air, and somewhere in the depths of the gallery, secrets began to unravel.

And then, as the night teetered on the edge of an abyss, a voice pierced the turmoil, sharp and unmistakable. "You've gone too far this time, Lark!"

I turned, my breath hitching in my throat as I recognized the voice—an unexpected arrival, a twist in the tale that threatened to unravel everything.

Chapter 13: Beneath the Surface

The soft glow of chandeliers painted the grand hall in golden hues, casting flickering shadows across the polished marble floor. I stood in the middle of a sea of opulence, surrounded by glimmering gowns and sharply tailored suits that whispered tales of privilege and power. The hum of laughter and clinking glasses filled the air, a symphony of social machinations that both enchanted and unnerved me. My heart raced, not solely from the excitement of the gala, but from the undercurrent of tension that twisted through the evening. Marcus stood at my side, a steadfast presence amidst the throng, his dark eyes scanning the crowd with a vigilance that only deepened my intrigue.

As we glided through the crowd, our hands brushing occasionally—a fleeting touch that sent sparks racing up my arm—I felt the weight of unspoken words between us. The mission hung over our heads like a dark cloud; we were not here just to admire the masterpieces adorning the walls, nor to sip expensive champagne. The threat of an underground art syndicate loomed, and we were determined to uncover its secrets, even if it meant dancing with danger in the guise of this extravagant affair.

I caught snippets of conversation, a tangled web of gossip and intrigue. "Have you seen the new acquisition?" a woman whispered, her voice laced with a mix of awe and envy. "I heard it was sourced from a notorious collector in Paris." My ears perked up; the name of that collector had come up in our previous investigations. I leaned closer to Marcus, hoping my curiosity was mirrored in his expression.

"What do you think?" I murmured, my lips barely moving, a conspiratorial glint in my eye. "Can we follow that thread?"

He gave a slight nod, his jaw tightening ever so slightly. "We will, but we need to tread carefully. These people don't play by the same rules."

Just then, the crowd parted as a tall figure approached, cutting a striking silhouette against the backdrop of shimmering lights. The man had an air of confidence, the kind that spoke of influence and authority. As he reached us, I felt the electricity in the air change; an almost magnetic pull drew my gaze to him.

"Ah, Marcus! You've finally graced us with your presence," the man boomed, his voice rich and velvety, dripping with charm. "And who is this delightful companion you've brought with you? I don't believe we've been introduced."

"Clara," I said, extending my hand, a mixture of confidence and caution swirling within me. "I'm here with Marcus, just enjoying the evening."

His grip was firm, his smile disarming, but something in his eyes flickered like a shadow passing over a sunlit field. "A pleasure, Clara. You have excellent taste in company."

Marcus stiffened beside me, and I could feel his protective instincts kick in, as though he sensed something I couldn't. I fought the urge to glance up at him, to seek reassurance in those deep, watchful eyes. The man introduced himself as Victor, a prominent collector known for his dubious dealings, the kind that left a lingering taste of ash in the mouth.

"We're just admiring the art," I said, forcing a bright smile. "It's a fascinating world, isn't it?"

"Oh, it is," Victor replied, his voice smooth as silk, yet edged with something darker. "But art is only a facade, my dear. Beneath its beauty lies a labyrinth of deception. You never know what lurks behind the brushstrokes."

I exchanged a glance with Marcus, a silent understanding passing between us. The game was afoot, and we were deep in the thick of it. Victor leaned in closer, lowering his voice. "If you're interested in the real stories, I can offer you a glimpse into that world."

Before I could respond, a commotion erupted at the far end of the hall. A woman in a crimson dress shrieked, her voice piercing through the revelry. The crowd turned, curious eyes drawn to the scene unfolding. My heart raced as I caught a glimpse of chaos—a scuffle, perhaps, or an unwanted confrontation.

Marcus's hand found mine, his grip tight. "Stay close," he murmured, his tone a blend of command and concern.

I followed him, weaving through the crowd as we approached the source of the disturbance. A man, unkempt and wild-eyed, stood in stark contrast to the polished attendees, clutching a painting that looked more like a crime scene than a work of art. His desperation was palpable, and I felt a surge of sympathy mingled with fear.

"Get away from me!" he yelled, shaking the painting in the air like a weapon. "They're coming for me! You don't understand!"

The crowd recoiled, whispers of shock rippling through the guests. My instincts kicked in, urging me to step forward. "What do you mean? Who's coming for you?" I called out, my voice cutting through the tension.

He turned to me, eyes wide with panic. "The collectors—they don't like loose ends! They'll stop at nothing to keep their secrets buried!"

Before I could reply, a figure emerged from the shadows, a sleek silhouette gliding forward. The tension thickened as the crowd parted, revealing a woman with a calculated demeanor and icy blue eyes that seemed to slice through the chaos like a knife.

"David," she said coolly, her voice dripping with disdain. "You really shouldn't be here. This is not your scene."

Marcus instinctively moved in front of me, his body a protective barrier, and I could feel the heat radiating from him. "What's going on?" he demanded, his tone firm.

The woman smiled, but it didn't reach her eyes. "Just a minor dispute, nothing to concern yourself with."

The standoff pulsed in the air, thick and electric. My heart raced as I realized we were caught in a tangled web of art, deception, and peril. The stakes had suddenly escalated, and the night, once filled with the promise of elegance, now dripped with a sense of foreboding.

With every heartbeat, I felt the looming threat closing in, and the realization settled deep within me—we were no longer just spectators in this dance of danger; we were players, unwittingly entangled in a game where the rules were still shrouded in mystery.

The tension crackled in the air like static electricity as I stood there, sandwiched between Marcus's solid presence and the cool, poised woman who had just appeared. She exuded an aura of control, as if she held the keys to secrets I could only begin to fathom. Her eyes flicked over me with a mixture of curiosity and disdain, and I felt the urge to shrink back under her gaze.

"David," she said again, her tone icy, "you need to go home. You're not equipped for this world."

The wild-eyed man, still clutching the painting like a lifeline, shifted nervously. "You don't understand! This piece is worth millions! They'll kill me for it!" His voice rose, desperation threading through his words. "They'll kill anyone who gets in their way!"

The crowd had turned into an audience, their faces a blend of intrigue and fear. The whispers swirled around us like the smoke from a dying fire, igniting the atmosphere with uncertainty. I could feel Marcus's muscles tense beside me, ready to act at a moment's notice. His protectiveness was a warm embrace in the chaos, a reminder that I wasn't alone in this dangerous dance.

"Who are they?" I pressed, feeling a surge of adrenaline as I tried to keep my voice steady. "Who's coming for you?"

The woman laughed softly, a sound devoid of humor. "Oh, sweet naïve Clara. You really think you want to know? Knowledge is a dangerous thing in this world." She took a step closer to David, her smile sharp as a knife. "You should consider finding a nice, quiet place where you can hide until this all blows over."

David's eyes widened, fear dawning on him like the first light of dawn. "You can't do this! I won't let you!"

Marcus stepped forward, a protective barrier between me and the brewing storm. "I think it's time for you to leave, miss." His voice was steady, but there was an edge to it that suggested he wouldn't tolerate her intimidation tactics.

"Oh, Marcus, always the knight in shining armor," she purred, unfazed by his bravado. "But sometimes, the armor gets rusty, and the knight ends up losing his head."

"Enough," he said, voice low and menacing. The atmosphere thickened, charged with unspoken threats and hidden agendas. I felt a surge of admiration for him, standing tall against the onslaught of danger, yet I couldn't help but wonder how deep the rabbit hole went.

With a flick of her wrist, the woman gestured to a pair of burly men standing at the edge of the gathering. They were dressed in dark suits, their expressions impassive, as if they were merely shadows given form. "You really think you can protect him?" she mocked, her voice silky smooth. "You have no idea who you're dealing with."

In that instant, my heart raced. The tension surged to a boiling point, and the crowd, once merely a backdrop, felt like a living, breathing organism, watching, waiting for the next act in this unfolding drama. I caught a glimpse of a small silver object glinting in the corner of my eye—a phone or perhaps a hidden camera capturing the unfolding spectacle for an unseen audience.

"David, listen to me," I said, my voice steady despite the chaos. "If there's something you know, you need to tell us. We can help you." I reached out, instinctively wanting to draw him into our protective circle.

He hesitated, glancing between us, the fight in his eyes fading under the weight of reality. "I—I can't. They'll find me. They always do."

"Then let us help you!" I pressed, my voice a lifeline in the storm. "We're not just here for the show. We want to uncover the truth."

Marcus shifted slightly, his presence radiating strength, but I could sense a shift in him as well. He understood the stakes better than I did, and I hoped he saw what I saw—a fragile opportunity to unearth the dark truths hidden beneath the surface.

Victor, the charming collector from earlier, appeared at the fringes of the crowd, an amused smile gracing his lips. "Ah, a touch of drama. How delightful!" he exclaimed, clearly relishing the spectacle. "But tell me, what's the value of a man's life in the grand scheme of art? Some would say priceless; others would say it's simply collateral damage."

The words sent a chill down my spine, as if the very air around us had shifted to something darker. I felt Marcus's hand tighten around mine, a silent promise that we wouldn't let this slip away.

"Enough of this charade," the woman said, her voice slicing through the tension. "David, you have one chance. Walk away now, or face the consequences."

Just then, the lights dimmed slightly, the ambience shifting as if the very atmosphere was holding its breath. The party felt like a masquerade, with every guest playing a role in a deadly game. As the shadows deepened, my instincts kicked in.

"David!" I shouted, a spark of determination igniting within me. "If you have any chance of escaping this, you need to trust us. You can't do it alone!"

He looked torn, fear battling with a flicker of hope in his gaze. I could almost hear the wheels turning in his mind. Just as he opened his mouth to speak, a sudden crash echoed from the other side of the hall. A glass had shattered, and the crowd gasped collectively, the moment drawing attention away from our standoff.

In that brief distraction, the tension shifted palpably. The woman's expression hardened as she realized the precariousness of our situation. "We're not done here," she hissed, shooting daggers at Marcus and me before slipping back into the crowd, her two bodyguards retreating with her.

David's shoulders sagged as if the weight of the world had suddenly pressed down upon him. "I—I don't know what to do. If I stay, they'll find me. If I run... I don't know who to trust anymore."

"Stay with us," Marcus said firmly, his voice low and urgent. "We can figure this out together. You're not alone."

As the remnants of the chaos began to settle around us, I realized we had stepped into a world far more dangerous than I had anticipated. The stakes were higher than art and prestige; lives were at risk, and the darkness beneath the surface threatened to swallow us whole.

My heart raced with a mix of fear and exhilaration. This was a twisted game, and I had a feeling we were only just beginning to scratch the surface. With Marcus at my side and David caught in our orbit, I knew we were in deeper than ever. We were no longer mere players; we had become the very heart of this unfolding drama, entwined in a tale that promised both danger and discovery.

The crowd was a swirling mix of glimmering jewels and soft laughter, yet beneath that facade, I could feel the undercurrent of anxiety that was palpable. David stood between us, visibly shaken, as if the very walls of the elegant venue were closing in around him. I glanced at Marcus, whose jaw was set in determination, the very essence of resolve. "We need to get out of here," he said, his voice low but urgent, the chaos around us fading into a mere backdrop.

Before I could respond, David's eyes darted to the entrance, where Victor loomed, an ominous shadow in the glittering hall. "If he sees me..." David's voice trailed off, panic threading through his words.

"Then we can't let him," I interjected, my mind racing. "We need a distraction. Something to keep his attention elsewhere."

Marcus nodded, and a mischievous glint flickered in his eyes. "I've got an idea." He moved closer to me, lowering his voice as if the walls themselves had ears. "When I say go, I want you to create a scene, something that'll draw everyone's focus."

I raised an eyebrow, a rush of adrenaline surging through me. "What do you have in mind?"

"Just trust me," he said, a confident grin breaking through the tension. "You have a flair for the dramatic."

With that, Marcus slid back into the crowd, his tall frame cutting through the sea of onlookers. I turned back to David, who was fidgeting anxiously. "You need to stay close to me. Don't look around, just follow my lead."

He nodded, though uncertainty still flickered in his eyes. The world felt as if it were tilting on its axis, the laughter of the guests morphing into an eerie symphony of impending doom. I focused on the task at hand, my heart hammering in my chest as I waited for Marcus to signal.

Moments later, I spotted him across the room, locked in conversation with a group of guests, gesturing animatedly. It was as if he was conjuring a spell, captivating his audience while subtly diverting their attention. I took a deep breath, then stepped into the spotlight.

"Excuse me!" I called, my voice slicing through the noise. Heads turned, surprised gazes landing on me. "I couldn't help but notice the exquisite arrangement of hors d'oeuvres. However, I must say, these canapés leave much to be desired!"

A ripple of laughter and curious glances spread through the crowd, my boldness sparking intrigue. "I mean, who serves caviar on a cracker? It's simply an affront to culinary arts!" I continued, drawing upon my theatrical flair, my tone exaggerated and playful.

To my delight, the laughter grew, and I could see some guests shifting their attention away from the tense scene. I spotted Marcus out of the corner of my eye, flashing a triumphant smile. It was working.

David moved closer, a hesitant grin breaking through his worry. "You're pretty good at this," he muttered, glancing around as if half-expecting Victor to appear at any moment.

"Thanks," I replied, keeping my voice light despite the tightening knot of fear in my stomach. "But I wouldn't call this a career path just yet."

Suddenly, the crowd shifted as Victor stepped forward, his presence demanding immediate attention. "What's all this commotion?" he called, his voice booming and authoritative. "Are we hosting a gala or a comedy club?"

I froze, heart racing as he fixed his gaze on me, an unsettling smile stretching across his face. "Clara, is it? Your humor is as sharp as your dress. I must admit, I'm intrigued."

With a flick of his wrist, he gestured toward David, who paled under Victor's scrutiny. "And you've brought a friend. How charming."

"Just here to appreciate the art," I replied, forcing a bright smile despite the tremor in my hands. "Isn't that what we're all doing?"

Victor's gaze narrowed, his smile fading into something more sinister. "Art is a curious thing, isn't it? It can evoke such passion—sometimes leading to desperate measures."

The atmosphere shifted, the laughter dying down as the crowd held its breath, caught in the web of Victor's words. I sensed David tensing beside me, a storm of anxiety brewing just beneath his surface.

"Desperate measures?" I echoed, feigning innocence as I tried to keep the conversation from spiraling into darker territory. "I can't imagine what you mean."

"Oh, but I think you can," he replied, his voice smooth and calculated. "After all, Clara, you seem to be quite well-informed for someone who's simply here for the hors d'oeuvres."

Before I could respond, Marcus surged back to my side, his expression fierce. "Let's not forget the art we're here to celebrate, Victor. Surely, a collector of your stature wouldn't want to sully this evening with threats and accusations."

"Ah, Marcus," Victor purred, turning his attention to him. "Always the peacemaker. But tell me, how much do you truly know about what lies beneath the surface of our precious little art world?"

The tension spiraled, sharp and electric, as I felt the eyes of the crowd shift back and forth, the spectacle of our standoff drawing them in. My mind raced, frantically searching for a way to turn the tide.

Just then, David's phone buzzed in his pocket, breaking the tense silence. He fumbled to pull it out, his face twisting into a mask of dread. "It's—it's them!" he gasped, staring at the screen as if it were a venomous snake ready to strike. "They found me!"

"What?" I barely managed to stammer, my heart pounding in my ears. "Who found you?"

Before he could answer, the doors of the gala burst open, and two figures clad in dark suits strode in, eyes scanning the room with lethal precision. The crowd parted, gasps of shock echoing through the hall as a palpable fear settled over everyone.

Marcus stepped closer to me, his posture radiating protectiveness. "We need to get out of here," he said urgently, glancing at David, whose face was a canvas of panic. "Now."

But before we could make our move, one of the men locked eyes with David, a predatory smile creeping onto his lips. "There you are," he said, his voice dripping with menace. "We've been looking for you."

A wave of dread washed over me, and I realized we were on the precipice of something monumental, a dangerous game of cat and mouse where the stakes were suddenly life and death. My heart raced as I exchanged a frantic glance with Marcus, the chaos swirling around us like a tempest.

And just as I opened my mouth to shout for everyone to run, the lights flickered ominously, plunging us into darkness. The screams began almost instantly, echoing off the walls, drowning out the chaos. I could barely see through the murky haze, but I felt the panic radiating from the crowd, fear clinging to the air like smoke.

"Clara, hold on to me!" Marcus shouted, and I grabbed his hand, the warmth of his grip anchoring me in the tumult.

But then, amid the fray, a sharp crack pierced through the chaos—gunfire. It rang out like a death knell, sending a jolt of icy fear straight through my veins.

And just like that, everything fell apart.

Chapter 14: The Turning Tide

The city pulsed with a rhythm all its own, the kind that thrummed beneath my skin, urging me to step out of the shadows and into the neon glow of streetlights. The air was thick with the scent of rain-soaked asphalt, mingling with the heady fragrance of jasmine from the nearby park. I leaned against the cool stone of the building, feeling the dampness seep into my clothes, my heart racing not just from the chill but from the chaos swirling in my mind. Marcus was inside, shrouded in a haze of his own making, obsessively rifling through documents, poring over leads that felt more like threads fraying at the edges than any solid truth.

I could hear the faint echoes of his movements, the soft scrape of papers, the muffled sound of his frustration as he worked through the night, the only illumination in the room a flickering bulb casting elongated shadows that danced across the walls. The passion that had drawn us together—his fiery determination, my fierce loyalty—was now threatening to burn us apart. I took a breath, steeling myself for the confrontation that had been brewing for days, an electric tension hanging in the air like the scent of impending rain.

"Marcus," I called, my voice firm yet tentative, as though stepping into a ring where I didn't quite know the rules. Silence followed, a heavy blanket that wrapped around me, amplifying my resolve. "We need to talk."

He appeared in the doorway, his dark hair tousled, eyes reflecting a storm that mirrored the one outside. The lines on his face had deepened, etched by late nights and relentless worry. "Can it wait?" he asked, his tone a mix of desperation and exasperation. "I'm close to something. I can feel it."

"Can it wait?" I repeated, more forcefully this time, stepping closer so the weight of my presence could not be ignored. "It's been days since you've looked at anything but those papers. You're drowning, Marcus. We're drowning."

He ran a hand through his hair, frustration boiling beneath the surface. "I'm not drowning. I'm fighting for us, for the truth. Don't you see? Everything we've worked for could fall apart if I don't get this right."

I crossed my arms, heart racing not just from anger but a flicker of fear at what our lives had become. "But at what cost? I can't watch you slip away, consumed by this obsession. You're not alone in this fight. We're in it together."

For a moment, the room crackled with tension, the silence thick as fog, and I could see the conflict waging war in his eyes. He stepped closer, the scent of his cologne mingling with the dampness in the air, a blend that had always made my heart flutter. "I can't let you down, not now. Not when we're so close."

"Close to what?" I shot back, my voice sharper than I intended. "More questions? More sleepless nights? You're losing yourself in the process, Marcus. You're the man I fell in love with, not a detective on a relentless quest."

"Maybe I have to be both," he replied, his voice a low growl. "Maybe that's what it takes to survive this."

And there it was—the unspoken fear that had been lurking between us, like a beast ready to pounce. I reached out, taking his hands in mine, feeling the warmth of his skin against my chilled fingers. "But what if we don't survive? What if we lose each other in this fight?"

The vulnerability in my voice seemed to crack through the wall he'd built around himself, his shoulders sagging under the weight of it all. "I can't lose you, either," he murmured, squeezing my hands. "But I can't let this go. There's something bigger at play here, and if we don't uncover it..." His voice trailed off, the unspoken implications hanging heavily between us.

"Then what? We give up on each other?" I asked, searching his eyes for clarity, for understanding. "We let the chaos dictate our love? I refuse to be a casualty of your quest."

He stepped back, the air between us shifting, thickening with the unsaid words that danced in the space where intimacy once thrived. "You don't understand," he said, the fire in his voice reigniting. "If I don't do this, it will be worse for us. For everyone."

I stepped forward again, not letting him retreat further into his spiraling thoughts. "Then let's do it together. Share the burden, Marcus. Don't make this a solitary fight."

His gaze softened, and I felt a shift, a crack in the armor he wore like a second skin. "You really mean that?"

"Of course I do," I replied, my heart racing, my pulse quickening. "But it means you have to promise not to shut me out. I won't stand by and watch you disappear."

He took a deep breath, running a hand over his face, as though trying to brush away the doubts that clouded his thoughts. "I promise," he said at last, the words a solemn vow that hung in the air like a fragile thread.

"Good," I said, relief flooding through me, mingled with the tension that still lingered. "Now, let's tackle this mystery together, as partners. Just promise me one thing—no more secrets."

He nodded slowly, and in that moment, I felt the connection between us rekindle, the flickering flame reigniting into something fierce and bright. We were bound together not just by love but by the shared determination to face whatever awaited us. As I pulled him into an embrace, I felt the weight of our struggles shift, and for the first time in days, I dared to hope that we might just emerge from the storm stronger than before.

The rain had subsided, leaving the streets glistening under the bright glow of street lamps, a pristine canvas reflecting the chaos of the night. I stepped outside, my shoes splashing in the puddles as I ventured into the cool evening air. The city felt alive, its heartbeat matching my own—fast and erratic, yet pulsing with promise. I wrapped my arms around myself, seeking warmth, both physical and emotional. Marcus's words still hung in the air, a delicate promise that felt like a lifeline thrown into turbulent waters.

We had agreed to face this together, but the uncharted territory we were entering left me with a sense of trepidation that twisted in my stomach. What had once been a bond fueled by laughter and shared dreams now felt like a tenuous thread, frayed and ready to snap under the weight of the looming secrets. I could sense the shift in our dynamic, an unspoken understanding that the path ahead was littered with shadows that could engulf us if we weren't careful.

As I wandered, my thoughts tangled around the possibilities, I found myself at our favorite café, a cozy nook tucked away from the city's clamor. The aroma of freshly brewed coffee wafted through the air, mingling with the sweet scent of pastries that called to me like a siren. I slipped inside, the warmth enveloping me like a hug, and I sought solace in the familiar ambience. The café was nearly empty, save for a few late-night patrons hunched over their laptops, lost in their own worlds.

"Hey there, thought you'd disappeared," the barista, Anna, greeted me with a knowing smile as she wiped her hands on her apron. "The usual?"

"Please," I replied, forcing a smile that didn't quite reach my eyes. "And maybe a chocolate croissant? I think I need it."

She nodded, her brow furrowing in concern as she prepared my order. "Everything okay with you two? You've been looking a little... intense lately."

"Intense is one word for it," I said, letting out a soft laugh that felt like a release valve on a pressure cooker. "More like navigating a minefield with a blindfold on."

Anna placed my steaming cup in front of me, and I wrapped my hands around it, feeling the warmth seep into my chilled fingers. "Just remember, sometimes stepping away from the chaos can give you clarity. Take a breath, you know?"

"Easier said than done," I murmured, but I appreciated her concern. As I sipped my coffee, the rich bitterness grounded me, reminding me of the importance of savoring life even amid turmoil.

After a few moments of quiet contemplation, I pulled out my phone, scrolling through messages that had piled up while we wrestled with our demons. A few texts from Marcus caught my eye, his words laced with urgency yet tinged with vulnerability. "Let's meet," one said, "I need to talk."

My heart raced at the thought of our upcoming conversation. Would it be another round of intense debate or a breakthrough? I hoped for the latter, but anxiety gnawed at me like a persistent itch. I pushed the phone back into my pocket and took another sip, feeling fortified by the caffeine. I couldn't let uncertainty dictate my emotions any longer.

The café door chimed as it swung open, and I looked up to see Marcus stepping inside, shaking off raindrops like a dog after a swim. His expression was serious, eyes scanning the room until they landed on me. He approached, and for a brief moment, the world outside faded into oblivion.

"Hey," he said, sliding into the seat across from me, his presence both a comfort and a reminder of the storm we faced together.

"Hey," I replied, trying to read his expression, but the shadows lurking in his gaze told me he was still grappling with his thoughts. "I ordered your favorite—because I know you can't resist a chocolate croissant."

A small smile tugged at the corners of his lips, the tension easing slightly. "You know me too well. Thanks for meeting me here."

"I figured a change of scenery might help," I suggested, studying him closely. "So, what's on your mind?"

He hesitated, taking a deep breath, as though steeling himself for what was to come. "I found something," he said slowly, the weight of his words pulling the air tight around us. "Something that might change everything."

My pulse quickened. "What do you mean?"

"Remember the names we stumbled across? The ones that seemed so unconnected but...?" His voice trailed off, and I could see the gears turning in his mind, the connections he was desperately trying to articulate.

"Go on," I urged, leaning forward, instinctively reaching for his hand.

"I think they're all linked to something bigger—a conspiracy, maybe. There are whispers of a group that manipulates things from behind the scenes, pulling strings to benefit themselves, no matter the cost."

I frowned, processing the implications of his words. "And you think this group is behind everything that's been happening? The threats, the chaos?"

"Exactly," he replied, his voice low and urgent. "But I need more information, and I don't want you involved. It's too dangerous."

A surge of indignation washed over me. "Dangerous? You think I'm going to sit back and let you dive into this alone? We agreed—together, remember?"

He rubbed his temples, frustration flickering in his eyes. "You don't understand what I'm up against. This isn't just about us anymore. It's bigger."

"And I won't let you push me away," I said firmly, feeling the fire of determination ignite within me. "Whatever it is, we face it together."

The silence stretched between us, a fragile truce as we both contemplated the gravity of our circumstances. He exhaled sharply, his shoulders relaxing just a fraction. "Fine. Together then. But you need to promise me something—if it gets too dangerous, we stop. No questions asked."

"Deal," I said, the tension transforming into an unspoken bond, a renewed commitment forged in the fire of uncertainty. The challenges ahead loomed larger than life, but for the first time in what felt like forever, I wasn't afraid. With Marcus by my side, I knew we could face whatever darkness lay ahead.

The café buzzed with a low hum of conversation, the aroma of coffee and baked goods swirling around us like a comforting embrace. But beneath that surface, I felt the weight of our agreement hanging heavily between Marcus and me. I could sense the storm brewing, a cyclone of danger and uncertainty that had begun to draw us in with its magnetic pull. As I watched him, I could almost see the thoughts tumbling through his mind, colliding and clashing like storm clouds threatening to burst.

"Okay," he said, finally breaking the silence. "If we're going to do this together, we need a plan. We have to be smart about it." His voice held a seriousness that made me sit a little straighter, as though bracing for impact.

"I'm listening," I replied, my pulse quickening. "What's your idea?"

He leaned forward, eyes narrowing as he scanned the room. "First, we need to dig deeper into those names—the ones we found on that list. I've managed to get a few leads, but we can't trust anyone. Not yet."

"Agreed," I said, feeling the adrenaline kick in. The thrill of danger was intoxicating, and the idea of unraveling this mystery together sparked a fire within me. "So, what's next? We hit the books?"

He chuckled, the tension breaking just a little. "If by books you mean databases and hidden forums, then yes."

"Sounds riveting," I said, rolling my eyes playfully. "I can't wait to pull an all-nighter with you and the wonders of the internet."

"Don't sound too enthusiastic," he teased, but his smile faded as quickly as it had appeared. "Seriously, though. This isn't a game. If there really is something bigger at play, we need to be careful."

"Careful is my middle name," I replied, feigning innocence, but my heart raced at the prospect of the unknown.

He raised an eyebrow, clearly unconvinced. "More like reckless, but I appreciate the optimism."

With a sigh, I nodded, the reality of our situation settling back in. "Okay, I'll tone it down. So, what's our first move?"

"First, we need to visit the library—specifically, the archives." His expression shifted to one of determination. "I have a hunch that some of the history behind those names is buried in old newspaper clippings. If we can connect the dots, we might find something concrete."

"Sounds like a plan," I said, excitement bubbling within me. "When do we start?"

"Now."

The urgency in his tone propelled us forward, and we quickly made our way through the bustling streets, navigating the throngs of people with purpose. Each step echoed with the potential for discovery, and the air crackled with anticipation.

As we arrived at the library, the grandeur of the building loomed over us, a relic of a bygone era. The tall columns seemed to whisper secrets of the past, and I felt a shiver of excitement dance down my spine.

Once inside, the scent of aged paper filled my lungs, grounding me in the moment as we moved deeper into the labyrinth of stacks. The atmosphere was serene, the soft rustle of pages turning and the quiet footsteps of patrons creating a soothing backdrop. I felt a sense of belonging in this place—a stark contrast to the chaos of our lives outside.

"Let's start here," Marcus said, leading me to a section that appeared to be dedicated to local history. We began sifting through old newspapers, the yellowed pages crinkling under our fingertips.

The further we dug, the more engrossed I became, piecing together fragments of stories long forgotten. I could feel the pulse of the city, its history intertwining with our own journey.

"What about this?" Marcus called, his voice sharp with excitement. "Look at this article—seems like there was a scandal involving one of the names on our list."

I leaned closer, my heart racing as he pointed to the headline: "City Councilman Linked to Secret Society." The words leaped off the page, igniting a sense of urgency that surged through me. "This could be it! This could be the connection we've been searching for."

Marcus nodded, his eyes scanning the article. "We need to find out more about this society. If they were involved in something back then, they might still be operating now."

The thrill of discovery coursed through my veins, but just as quickly as the excitement bubbled up, a creeping sense of dread began to settle in. "But if this is true, we're dealing with something dangerous. What if they're still watching?"

"Then we'll just have to be smarter than they are," he replied, his voice laced with confidence. "We can't back down now."

We continued to sift through articles, and each revelation felt like a layer peeled back from a hidden truth, revealing the dark underbelly of the city we thought we knew. Hours melted away as we buried ourselves in the past, the outside world fading into a distant murmur.

Then, just as I felt we were on the brink of a breakthrough, the library's doors swung open with a force that sent a jolt of tension rippling through the air. I glanced up to see a figure standing just inside the entrance, silhouetted against the bright light from outside. My heart dropped when I recognized him—a man we had seen in the background of one of the photographs, a face that sent chills down my spine.

"Marcus," I whispered, panic threading through my words. "He's here."

"Stay calm," he replied, his voice low and steady. "We'll just keep our heads down."

But as the man's gaze swept over the library, lingering just a beat too long on our table, my blood ran cold. He began to move through the aisles, his footsteps echoing like a drumbeat of impending doom.

"What do we do?" I asked, barely able to keep my voice steady.

"Don't panic," Marcus said, but the tension radiating from him was palpable. "We'll act natural."

I fought the urge to look over my shoulder, every instinct screaming that we needed to get out. But before we could make a move, the man turned abruptly and headed straight for us. His expression was unreadable, but the aura surrounding him was charged with a sense of authority that made my heart race.

"Marcus," he said, his voice smooth as silk, yet laced with a threat that made the hairs on the back of my neck stand on end. "We need to talk."

And just like that, the air around us shifted, the vibrant world we had been building now teetering on the edge of a precipice, and I knew we were standing at the threshold of something far darker than we had ever anticipated.

Chapter 15: Into the Abyss

The air hummed with a tension that hung like a shroud, thick and electric. As I flipped the sign in my studio from "Open" to "Closed," the warm glow of the hanging lights flickered slightly, casting long shadows against the walls adorned with vibrant canvases. Each stroke of paint reflected my journey—of heartbreak, healing, and hope. But tonight, as the sky darkened to a velvet black, an unsettling chill crept into the room, wrapping around me like an unwelcome cloak.

I had just begun to gather my brushes when a flicker of movement outside the window caught my attention. I turned, the hairs on the back of my neck prickling in anticipation. There, standing just beyond the reach of the streetlamp's glow, was a figure—a dark silhouette that seemed to pulse with a life of its own. My heart thudded in my chest, a frantic drumbeat that drowned out the soft rustle of the autumn leaves outside.

Instinctively, I stepped back, my fingers trembling as I grasped my phone, dialing Marcus's number with a speed that felt both urgent and futile. The eerie figure remained motionless, its presence a stark contrast to the warmth of my little studio, which had always been a sanctuary. I could hear the ringing in my ear, each tone a reminder that I was utterly alone in this moment.

"Please, pick up," I whispered, my voice barely breaking above a breath.

Finally, Marcus's voice crackled through the line, a beacon of reassurance amidst the rising tide of fear. "What's wrong? You sound panicked."

"There's someone outside," I said, my voice shaking. "I think... I think I recognize him from your stories."

"Stay inside. I'm on my way." His tone was firm, laced with an urgency that sent a shiver down my spine. I could almost hear the engine of his motorcycle roar to life, the sound a promise that he would be here soon.

I pressed my forehead against the cool glass, peering through the darkness. The figure was still there, a haunting reminder of the shadows from Marcus's past that threatened to claw their way back into our lives. I held my breath, feeling time stretch and warp as if the universe itself was holding its breath along with me. Just then, the figure turned slightly, enough for me to catch a glimpse of his profile. The sharp lines of his jaw, the way his hair fell over his forehead—it all felt disturbingly familiar, as if I had stumbled into a memory I never wished to relive.

Moments later, the sound of Marcus's motorcycle broke the stillness, a throaty growl that signaled his arrival. Relief washed over me like a wave, but it was quickly undercut by the anxiety gnawing at my insides. I opened the door before he could knock, his presence spilling warmth into the cool night air.

"What's going on?" he asked, his brow furrowed as he took in the scene before him. His eyes narrowed at the shadow lingering outside, and in that moment, the fierce protector in him ignited.

"There," I pointed, my voice steadying as I took a step back, letting him take the lead. "That's the guy. I think he's connected to you."

As if sensing our gaze, the figure shifted, his expression unreadable. "Marcus," he called, his voice deep and dripping with a nonchalance that made my skin crawl. "Long time, no see."

My stomach twisted as Marcus clenched his fists at his sides. "What do you want?"

The man stepped forward, the light catching the sharp angles of his face. He was handsome in a rugged sort of way, the kind that would turn heads but also send a shiver down your spine. "I just wanted to talk," he replied, the smirk playing at the corners of his lips sending a wave of unease coursing through me.

"Talk?" Marcus echoed, his tone icy. "After everything?"

The figure leaned against the wall, a casual demeanor that belied the weight of his presence. "You can't run from your past, Marcus. I'm here to remind you of that."

I felt the air grow thick with unspoken tension, a chasm widening between us. This was not just a random encounter; it was a deliberate intrusion. My instincts screamed for me to back away, to retreat into the sanctuary of my studio, but I stood my ground, aware that this was no longer just Marcus's fight.

"Whatever you think you know, it's not the same anymore," Marcus shot back, stepping closer, his silhouette a protective barrier against the encroaching threat.

The man chuckled, a low sound that echoed in the silence of the night. "Things have a way of changing, don't they? But the past... it never really disappears."

I glanced at Marcus, searching his eyes for a flicker of the man I knew. The tension between them felt palpable, a heavy blanket pressing down on us, suffocating and invasive.

"Who sent you?" Marcus demanded, his voice a low growl, cutting through the atmosphere.

"Sent me?" The man laughed, a sound devoid of warmth. "I'm just a messenger, my friend. But you need to know that the game isn't over yet. There are pieces still to be played."

I felt the ground beneath me shift as a sudden realization gripped my heart. This wasn't just about Marcus anymore; it was about everything we had built together—the dreams, the plans, the love. This figure was a specter from the past, and I was terrified of what he might unleash.

The stranger leaned against the wall, an insufferable calm radiating from him as if he relished the chaos he was orchestrating. I could sense the tension in Marcus beside me, a taut string ready to snap. "You really think I'd just forget?" Marcus snapped, his eyes narrowing. "You have no idea what I've built since you vanished."

A wry grin creased the stranger's lips. "Oh, I know all about your little life here. You've done well for yourself. But a nice little art studio can't protect you from the past." His gaze shifted to me, piercing and invasive. "And who's this? Your new muse? She looks like she's seen too much already."

"Back off," Marcus growled, stepping protectively in front of me, his frame a wall I wished I could hide behind. "This isn't your playground anymore."

"Isn't it? You act like you've escaped, but the truth is, we're all tied to our choices. Some choices are harder to outrun." The stranger shrugged, a nonchalant dismissal that stoked the fire in my chest.

"Maybe you should worry about your own choices," I interjected, finding my voice despite the icy grip of fear tightening around my throat. "You've clearly made plenty of them."

His eyes flared with surprise, and for a fleeting moment, I thought I'd managed to rattle him. But the smirk returned, full of bravado. "Feisty. I like that. But don't think you can protect him. Marcus and I have history—one that won't just fade away because he's found himself a new canvas to paint on."

The atmosphere thickened, the weight of his words hanging heavy in the air like storm clouds ready to burst. I shifted uneasily, the shadows of my studio suddenly feeling far too intimate, too confining.

"History is just a series of mistakes, isn't it?" I said, trying to keep my tone light even as my heart raced. "And some mistakes should be left in the past."

Marcus turned slightly, giving me a look that said he admired my attempt at bravado but was equally worried about where this conversation was headed. "You're right," he said, his voice steady but low, "and I'm not interested in revisiting it."

"Ah, but it seems you don't have a choice," the stranger mused, pulling out his phone and tapping it with a deliberate slowness. "You see, I'm just the warm-up act. There's a bigger show coming, and you two are front-row guests."

My stomach dropped as the implications of his words sank in. "What do you mean by that?" I asked, my voice steadying as the adrenaline surged.

"Oh, you'll find out soon enough. Let's just say that some of your little secrets are about to come to light. Isn't it amusing how the universe has a way of balancing things out?" He slipped his phone back into his pocket, the motion casual yet heavy with menace.

"Is that a threat?" Marcus's voice was low, a rumble of thunder ready to unleash a storm.

"More of an invitation to play. But I understand you have your little art world to hide in. Just remember, Marcus—when you play with fire, sometimes you get burned. And it looks like your pretty little artist might just get singed in the process."

With that, he turned, his form fading into the darkness, leaving behind an eerie silence that echoed in my ears. I felt a shiver race down my spine, a cold dread settling in my bones as the door clicked shut behind him.

"Are you okay?" Marcus asked, his voice softer now, filled with concern. He turned to me, his eyes searching my face as if trying to decipher the secrets hidden behind my startled expression.

"I'm fine," I lied, even as my insides churned with uncertainty. "I just—"

"Let's get out of here." He took my hand, leading me away from the remnants of that encounter, the weight of the stranger's words still pressing heavily on my heart.

As we stepped out into the crisp night air, the stars above twinkled like diamonds scattered across a velvet blanket. The world felt both enchanting and ominous, each glimmer a reminder of the shadows lurking just beyond the edges of our lives.

"Where to?" I asked, my voice barely above a whisper as we walked, the streetlamps casting flickering halos around us.

"Somewhere safe," he said, his tone resolute. "We can't stay here."

"Do you think he'll come back?" I felt the need to voice my fears, to put words to the chaos swirling in my mind.

Marcus glanced down at me, his expression serious. "I don't know, but we can't take that chance. We need to regroup, figure out our next steps."

"Next steps," I echoed, the phrase hanging between us like a lifeline. "What do you even mean? This isn't just about you anymore, Marcus. It's about me too."

He paused, turning to face me, his eyes fierce and protective. "I know that. But you need to understand—I've been in situations like this before. I won't let anyone hurt you."

"Yet here we are," I said, frustration bubbling over. "You can't just dismiss what he said. If he has something on you—something that could jeopardize us—"

"Then I'll handle it," he said firmly, his jaw tightening. "You don't need to worry about my past. You should be focusing on keeping yourself safe."

I crossed my arms, a defensive posture I hoped would shield me from the rising tide of anxiety. "Safe? I'm already neck-deep in this mess. We both are. It's not just your fight anymore."

"I never said it was," he shot back, the tension between us crackling like the electricity in the air before a storm. "But you can't act like you know what I'm capable of. You've seen a fraction of my life."

"And you've seen only a fraction of mine," I countered, unwilling to back down. "I'm not a damsel waiting to be rescued. I can fight my own battles."

Marcus stepped closer, his presence a powerful force that sent my heart racing. "This isn't about proving anything. This is about keeping you safe while I figure out how to deal with the past trying to claw its way back in."

The words hung between us, heavy and unresolved, as we stood beneath the glow of the streetlamp, the shadows stretching out like fingers reaching for something they could not grasp. The world felt like it was shifting beneath our feet, the balance of power teetering dangerously.

And in that moment, I realized that the fight we were facing was not just with the figure from Marcus's past; it was a battle against the unknown, a struggle for the life we had begun to build together. I could feel the stakes rising, a palpable tension that coiled in the air like a live wire, ready to snap.

"Then let's figure it out together," I said, my voice steady, determination coursing through me. "I won't let you go into this alone."

He looked at me, a mix of surprise and admiration in his gaze. "You really mean that, don't you?"

"More than anything," I replied, a small smile breaking through the tension. "Besides, I've never backed down from a challenge, have I?"

A hint of a smile tugged at the corner of his lips. "No, you definitely haven't."

The moment felt charged, a spark igniting between us as we faced the uncertainty ahead. Together, we would navigate the treacherous waters of Marcus's past and carve a path through the darkness, determined to hold on to what we had built.

As we stood in the glow of the streetlamp, the remnants of that unsettling encounter still clung to us like a fog, I could feel the uncertainty between us thickening. "So, what's next?" I asked, trying to inject some levity into the situation, my mind racing through a hundred scenarios. "Are we supposed to set up camp and wait for a shadowy villain to strike again? Maybe get some popcorn and a good movie?"

Marcus chuckled softly, the tension easing just a fraction as he turned to me. "As much as I love a good horror flick, I think this is one movie we need to write ourselves."

I admired his attempt to lighten the mood, but a lingering unease settled deep within me. "I just hope we can avoid the worst plot twists. I've had enough drama for one night."

He nodded, a grim determination flickering in his eyes. "Then let's come up with a plan. The last thing I want is for him to get under your skin. If he's going to play games, then let's make sure we're two steps ahead."

The assertiveness in his tone stirred something fierce within me, a mixture of resolve and fear, the urge to fight side by side surging to the forefront. "Okay, so what do we know?" I asked, my brain churning as we began to strategize. "He's clearly got some dirt on you. What does he want? A reunion tour of your past?"

"More like a vendetta," Marcus replied, pacing a few steps as he ran a hand through his hair, frustration etched across his features. "There are things I'd rather not drag back into the light. But I'm not going to let him scare me—or you. This isn't just about me anymore; it's about us."

"Then let's not let him dictate the terms," I said, crossing my arms, trying to channel some of that boldness I felt building within. "We can turn this around. We can find out what he's planning and counter it before it even starts."

A flicker of admiration sparked in his eyes, and I realized that in this moment, we were two warriors gearing up for battle, ready to face whatever the night had in store. "You're right. I just need to know what his next move is."

As if summoned by the very mention of his name, my phone buzzed in my pocket. I fished it out, heart racing as I saw a new message lighting up the screen. The familiar dread unfurled in my chest. "It's from him," I breathed, my fingers trembling as I tapped to open it.

The message was simple yet ominous: I hope you enjoyed the show. The real fun is just beginning.

"Damn it!" I exclaimed, anger flaring up. "He's toying with us. He thinks he can just waltz in and unsettle everything."

"Let me see," Marcus said, his voice low and steady, yet there was a fire in his gaze. I held out my phone, and he read the words, his expression darkening with each syllable. "He's not going to get away with this. We need to put an end to it now."

"What are you thinking?"

"I know someone who might have answers. Someone who can dig into this guy's background."

"Now we're talking," I replied, a sense of purpose replacing my earlier anxiety. "Who do we need to call?"

"His name's Felix. He's... well, let's just say he's a bit of a rogue in his own right, but he knows how to get things done."

"Rogue sounds promising," I said, imagining the kind of person who would thrive in the shadows. "Do you trust him?"

"I trust him to get the job done, but trusting him with our lives? That's a different matter." He paused, the weight of his words lingering in the air. "He can be unpredictable."

"Unpredictable sounds like our theme for the night," I replied, trying to keep the mood light despite the gravity of our situation. "Let's get him on the line. We need every advantage we can find."

Marcus pulled out his phone, his thumb hovering over the screen as he dialed. The tension in the air was palpable, a silent agreement that we were diving into something we could not fully control.

As the phone rang, I glanced around, hyper-aware of our surroundings. The world felt different now, every shadow an echo of our earlier encounter. My heart raced as the call connected, and I could hear Felix's unmistakable voice on the other end.

"Marcus," Felix drawled, a hint of amusement coloring his tone. "To what do I owe the pleasure? Trouble in paradise?"

"Not exactly," Marcus replied, a sharp edge in his voice. "We need information—fast. There's a guy who's resurfaced from my past, and I need to know what he's after."

"Sounds serious. What's his name?"

I held my breath, wondering how deep we were about to wade into Marcus's history.

"Damon. He's been sniffing around," Marcus said, his voice low, the name slipping from his lips like a dark secret.

"Damon?" Felix's tone shifted instantly, the teasing lilt replaced with a more serious edge. "I thought that ghost was buried. What does he want?"

"Whatever it is, it's not good," Marcus said, frustration creeping into his voice. "He's already tried to rattle me, and I don't want him going after her."

"Her?" Felix asked, the curiosity evident in his voice. "Interesting. You've got a new muse. I'd love to meet her."

"Not the time, Felix," Marcus snapped, irritation rising. "Just find out what Damon is up to, and we'll deal with the rest later."

"Right, right. I'll dig into it. But you know how these things work—if he's back in the game, it's likely not just for a chat. Keep your guard up."

"Always," Marcus replied, hanging up with a determined set to his jaw.

I studied him, the intensity in his eyes a mixture of concern and anger. "What now?"

"Now, we wait."

"Wait?" I echoed incredulously. "You know I'm not good at that."

"I know," he said, a hint of amusement flickering across his lips. "But we can't jump to conclusions until we have more information. Let's get some rest. We'll need our strength."

Resting was a luxury I wasn't sure I could afford. "I'd rather not sleep, to be honest," I said, trying to mask my unease.

Marcus stepped closer, his voice lowering. "Neither would I. But you need to trust me on this. I'll make sure you're safe."

The sincerity in his gaze softened the edges of my anxiety, and I nodded reluctantly. "Okay, I trust you. But only until the end of the night. After that, it's fair game."

"Deal," he said, a faint smile breaking through the tension.

Just as we turned to head back toward my studio, the hairs on the back of my neck prickled once more. A noise, faint but unmistakable, echoed through the night—heavy footsteps advancing toward us, cutting through the quiet like a knife.

"Did you hear that?" I whispered, adrenaline surging through me again.

Marcus stiffened, his body coiling with tension. "Stay behind me."

I watched as his posture shifted, an instinctive readiness taking over, and I felt the weight of the moment settle over us like a heavy blanket. The footsteps grew louder, an ominous rhythm that sent my heart racing.

"Who is it?" I asked, my voice trembling despite my attempt at bravado.

But Marcus didn't answer; he was already scanning the darkness, his eyes sharp and focused.

Then, just as the silhouette of a figure emerged from the shadows, my breath caught in my throat. It was Damon, a smile curling his lips, that unsettling glint in his eye promising trouble.

"Miss me?" he said, the words laced with a mockery that made my skin crawl.

As the world around us faded, I realized we were standing at the edge of an abyss, and there was no turning back now.

Chapter 16: The Breaking Point

Fear crackled in the air, sharp and electric, as Marcus and I stood in the dim light of the warehouse. Shadows stretched along the walls like dark fingers grasping for something they could not hold. The acrid scent of rust and aged wood mixed with the sharp tang of sweat clung to us as we moved deeper into the belly of this forsaken place, our hearts beating a frantic rhythm that echoed against the cold, concrete floor.

"Are you sure we should be here?" My voice trembled, betraying the steely facade I desperately tried to maintain. I caught a glimpse of Marcus's profile, etched in the sparse light spilling from the overhead fixtures, his jaw set and resolute, a man prepared to dance with danger. The faintest glimmer of doubt flickered behind his eyes, but he turned to me, and that spark ignited into something fierce.

"We can't run anymore. This ends tonight." His words, laced with urgency, shot through me, igniting a fire I thought had long been extinguished. I nodded, knowing that the stakes were higher than ever. Marcus had been haunted by his past long enough, and I was done standing on the sidelines, watching him carry this burden alone.

We pressed on, the chill of the air wrapping around us like a suffocating blanket. Each step felt monumental, the sound of our footfalls swallowed by the oppressive silence. I clenched my fists, the pulse of adrenaline coursing through me pushing aside the fear that tried to creep in. It was almost laughable how quickly I had transformed from an onlooker in Marcus's life to a player in a deadly game, where the rules had yet to be written.

As we rounded a corner, the silhouette of a figure emerged in the distance. My heart stuttered before settling into a rapid race. The dim light flickered, illuminating a man hunched over a table, the flicker revealing the glint of something metallic—a knife, perhaps, or worse.

I could feel the tension crackling between us like static electricity, drawing us closer together.

"Stay behind me," Marcus hissed, instinctively moving to shield me with his body. I wanted to protest, to remind him that I could handle myself, but the sight of the stranger's broad shoulders and the cruel twist of his mouth silenced my bravado. I moved a fraction closer, feeling the heat radiate from Marcus, his resolve a comforting presence amidst the chaos.

"You don't belong here, Marcus," the man snarled, his voice a low growl that sent a shiver down my spine. "You should have stayed away. This is bigger than you, and certainly bigger than her."

The words hung in the air, heavy with implications that curled around us like smoke. I felt Marcus stiffen beside me, the weight of those words settling over him like a shroud. I couldn't help but grip his arm tighter, wanting to anchor him to this moment. The realization hit me hard: this wasn't just about Marcus and the shadows that chased him; it was about me, too. I had chosen to stand by his side, to face whatever darkness lurked in his past, and I wouldn't back down now.

"What do you want?" Marcus's voice was steady, though I could hear the tension threading through it like a coiled spring ready to snap.

The stranger chuckled, a low, menacing sound that echoed off the walls. "What do I want? I want to show you what happens when you decide to play hero. You think you can just waltz in here and take back control? You have no idea who you're dealing with."

Without thinking, I stepped forward, the sudden movement drawing both their gazes. "He's dealing with me, too," I said, my voice ringing out, louder than I intended, cutting through the tension. The adrenaline surged, and with it, a newfound confidence. I met the stranger's glare head-on, willing my heart to keep pace with my resolve. "Whatever you think you're going to do, we're not afraid of you."

A pause followed my declaration, and in that fleeting moment, I felt the weight of the world shift slightly. Marcus's hand slipped around my waist, a grounding touch that reaffirmed our shared strength. The stranger's expression morphed into one of disbelief, then irritation, as if I had dared to disrupt the carefully crafted narrative he believed he controlled.

"You think you're brave?" he spat, stepping closer. The knife gleamed ominously in his hand, reflecting the flickering light. "You have no idea what true bravery is."

A laugh escaped my lips, surprising even myself. "Bravery isn't the absence of fear; it's facing it head-on, and here we are. So let's get this over with, shall we?"

Marcus's grip tightened around me, but I could see the corner of his mouth twitching upward, a flicker of pride mingled with disbelief. The stranger's bravado faltered for a brief second, and I seized the moment. "What's your name? Let's at least make this a bit more personal."

The challenge hung in the air, bold and defiant. It was a gamble, but as I glanced at Marcus, I knew I couldn't let fear take hold. We were in this together, and I refused to let anyone take that away from us. The tension thickened, an invisible thread binding us in this precarious dance, each move drawing us closer to an inevitable confrontation that could unravel everything we had fought for.

The stranger's sneer returned, but something shifted in his demeanor. "You want my name? Fine. Call me whatever you want, but just know that your little romance ends here."

As he lunged forward, a surge of panic surged through me, but my instincts kicked in. I pushed Marcus aside, stepping into the path of the oncoming threat, my heart pounding fiercely in my chest. I had come too far to back down now.

My instincts screamed as the stranger lunged, a whirlwind of adrenaline and instinct propelling me forward. In that heartbeat, clarity struck. I wasn't just protecting Marcus; I was fighting for our chance at a future that hadn't even begun. The metallic glint of the knife was a stark reminder of how quickly everything could spiral out of control, but I wasn't about to let fear dictate my actions.

"Is that really the best you've got?" I retorted, my voice sharper than the blade aimed at us. The audacity of my words hung in the air, bold and foolish, but they seemed to catch the man off guard. He hesitated, eyes narrowing in confusion. I seized the moment, stepping to the side just as he reached for me. My heart thundered, but I could feel a fierce determination surging through me.

Marcus moved with a fluidity I had never seen before, shifting his weight as he prepared to counter the man's aggression. "Get behind me," he commanded, but I shook my head, refusing to be sidelined again. This was our fight, and I wouldn't let him bear the burden alone.

The stranger, realizing we were not the frightened prey he anticipated, roared with frustration, "You think you can stand against me?"

I exchanged a glance with Marcus, the unspoken bond between us strengthening in that moment. "Oh, sweetheart, we're not standing against you. We're standing together."

A flicker of uncertainty crossed the stranger's face, but it was quickly masked by rage. He charged again, and I prepared myself, adrenaline coursing through my veins like wildfire. In a heartbeat, the world around us shrank to the space between us and the threat looming ahead.

Marcus moved to intercept, his powerful frame creating a wall between me and the danger, but I couldn't let him take all the risks. With a swift motion, I darted forward, grabbing a rusty pipe lying abandoned on the ground, and swung it toward the attacker. The metal connected with a dull thud, catching him off balance.

He stumbled back, momentarily disoriented, his eyes wide with shock. "You—" he began, but I cut him off, my voice a fierce echo of defiance. "You underestimated us."

"Don't get cocky," Marcus growled, his focus unwavering as he prepared to make the next move. I nodded, grounding myself in the reality of our situation. We were outnumbered by fear and uncertainty, but we were not outmatched. Together, we formed a shield against the darkness that had come to claim us.

The stranger, regaining his footing, glared at me, hatred simmering beneath his cool exterior. "You think this is a game? You have no idea what you're up against. The people behind this... they won't just walk away."

"Neither will we," Marcus shot back, his voice a steady anchor. "You've threatened my life for the last time."

The tension in the air was palpable, a coiled spring ready to snap. I felt the adrenaline coursing through my body, sharpening my senses. Everything was heightened—the faint rustle of fabric, the distant hum of city life outside the warehouse, the electric charge of anticipation crackling around us.

As we squared off against the stranger, I felt the weight of everything we had faced together pressing down on us. The shadows that haunted Marcus were now entwined with my own fears. We were entwined in a web of threats that had grown far too complex, yet here we stood, unified against the looming darkness.

With a sudden twist, the stranger lunged again, this time aiming for Marcus. I couldn't stand by. "Look out!" I shouted, my voice slicing through the chaos like a knife. I lunged forward, swinging the pipe once more, adrenaline fueling my resolve. This was it—this was our moment.

My swing caught him in the side, sending him sprawling across the floor. "Get up, Marcus!" I urged, my heart pounding as I turned to help him.

He was already on his feet, determination radiating from him as he moved to flank the man. Together, we advanced, a united front ready to confront whatever lay ahead.

The stranger scrambled back, his bravado faltering as he realized the tide had shifted. "You think this is over?" he spat, panic creeping into his voice. "You have no idea what you're dealing with."

"Then enlighten us," I shot back, refusing to let fear invade this moment. "Who are you working for? What do they want with Marcus?"

The man hesitated, his expression a mix of fury and uncertainty, as if my words had cracked the facade of confidence he wore like armor. "You really want to know?" he sneered, but there was a tremor beneath his bravado.

"Yes," Marcus pressed, stepping closer, his eyes locked onto the stranger's with an intensity that dared him to lie. "Tell us."

He seemed to weigh his options, and I could almost see the gears turning in his mind, the struggle between loyalty to his employer and the primal instinct for self-preservation. Finally, he let out a bitter laugh, a sound devoid of humor. "Fine. If you want the truth, you're already in over your heads. You think you can outsmart them? They're everywhere, watching, waiting. This isn't just about me; it's about something much larger."

"What are you saying?" I demanded, urgency lacing my voice. The threat that loomed was no longer just a personal vendetta; it was a shadow that stretched far beyond our current battle.

He looked between us, and for a fleeting moment, I saw something resembling fear flash across his face. "They're coming for you. Both of you. And when they do, you won't stand a chance."

"Try us," Marcus said, stepping forward, the fire in his eyes a reflection of my own. We were no longer simply defending ourselves; we were ready to strike back, to reclaim our lives.

The man's bravado faltered again, his confidence crumbling under the weight of our resolve. "You think you can take them on? You're playing a dangerous game."

"Maybe," I replied, my heart racing. "But I'd rather play a dangerous game than stand idly by and let fear dictate my life."

As his expression darkened, I sensed the tide of our confrontation shifting yet again. He wasn't just a man; he was a symbol of everything we were fighting against, and I wouldn't let him walk away without facing the truth of his threats.

With one last flicker of defiance, he turned and bolted toward the exit. "You'll regret this!" he shouted over his shoulder, the echo of his words lingering like a specter in the air.

"Not if we catch you first!" I called after him, the adrenaline still surging as Marcus and I exchanged a glance filled with determination and purpose.

"Are you okay?" he asked, his voice low as we stood amidst the remnants of chaos, breathing heavily as reality settled in.

"I will be," I replied, my heart still racing. "But we need to move. If he's right, we don't have much time."

As we pushed through the shadows of the warehouse, a newfound sense of purpose ignited between us. The night was far from over, and whatever awaited us outside was no longer just a threat; it was a battle we were ready to fight together.

The echoes of our confrontation faded as we slipped out of the warehouse, the night air heavy with an uneasy silence that felt charged with potential. I could still taste the metallic tang of adrenaline on my tongue, a stark reminder of the dangers we faced. The streetlights flickered overhead, casting long shadows that danced like specters along the cracked pavement. Every rustle of leaves and distant car horn seemed magnified, an unwelcome reminder that we were not yet safe.

"Do you think he'll come back?" I asked, glancing at Marcus, who walked beside me, his presence a comforting weight against the uncertainty that loomed over us. He ran a hand through his tousled hair, a gesture I had come to recognize as a sign of contemplation.

"He might," he said, his tone serious but laced with a hint of amusement. "If he does, he's going to regret it. I've got a few tricks up my sleeve."

I laughed, the sound a welcome relief amidst the tension. "You think you're the only one who can swing a pipe? I took him by surprise. Who knows what else I'm capable of?"

"True, true," he replied, smirking. "You were quite the warrior back there. I almost didn't recognize you."

"Oh please," I countered, rolling my eyes. "Don't let it go to my head."

As we walked, the streetlights dimmed slightly, casting us into deeper shadows. The quiet hum of the city felt both soothing and foreboding, the calm before a storm that we both sensed brewing on the horizon. I couldn't shake the feeling that we were being watched, the adrenaline from our confrontation morphing into a more persistent, gnawing fear.

"We need to find a place to regroup," Marcus said, his voice low and deliberate. "Somewhere we can figure out our next move without looking over our shoulders."

"Agreed," I replied, scanning the street for any familiar signs of safety. "But where do we even go? I don't exactly have a secret hideout."

He stopped abruptly, turning to face me, and the earnestness in his gaze sent a jolt through my system. "What about the old café on Fifth? It's closed now, but the back room is usually locked up tight. We could hunker down there for a bit."

"The one with the terrible coffee?" I teased, a playful smile creeping onto my lips despite the situation. "I'd rather drink dirt."

"It's a place, and it's off the radar," he replied, his tone lightening as he walked ahead, casting a glance over his shoulder. "Plus, it'll give us a chance to figure out how deep this rabbit hole goes."

We made our way to the café, navigating through narrow alleys and dimly lit streets, our bodies moving in sync like a well-rehearsed dance. Each step felt charged with possibility and danger, the air thick with unspoken words.

As we approached the café, an unsettling sensation pricked at my instincts. The usual hum of the city felt muted, as if the world had pressed pause. I hesitated, a chill creeping down my spine. "Marcus, do you feel that?"

He turned, brow furrowing slightly. "Feel what?"

"Like we're not alone," I murmured, my eyes darting around the darkened corners. The street was nearly empty, the only sound the soft rustle of leaves above us.

"Let's keep moving," he urged, quickening his pace toward the café's entrance. As we slipped inside, I couldn't shake the feeling that something was waiting just beyond the door, poised to strike.

The air inside was stale, the remnants of coffee and pastries lingering like ghosts in the corners. Dust motes floated lazily in the dim light, creating a surreal atmosphere that felt oddly disconnected from the chaos outside. Marcus pushed through the door to the back room, his movements practiced, and I followed closely behind, the unease settling in my stomach like a lead weight.

The back room was just as I remembered: dimly lit and cluttered with forgotten furniture. A rickety table stood in the center, surrounded by mismatched chairs that looked like they'd seen better days. I took a deep breath, forcing myself to focus on the task at hand. "Okay, we need a plan."

"Right," Marcus replied, scanning the room. "First, we need to figure out who that guy was and who he's working for. Then, we can decide how to handle this."

I nodded, pulling out my phone. "I can start looking up any recent threats or incidents. Maybe there's something in the news."

"Good idea. But be careful; we don't want anyone tracing our steps."

As I swiped through news articles, a knot formed in my stomach. The headlines were a dizzying mix of violence and corruption, each more disturbing than the last. "Marcus, this doesn't make sense. There are reports here about gang activity, but none of it seems connected to you."

"Maybe they're just trying to intimidate me," he suggested, but his voice lacked conviction. "I've been trying to stay under the radar, but clearly, that didn't work out."

A sudden noise interrupted our conversation, a soft scuffling sound outside the door that made my heart leap into my throat. Marcus held his breath, his gaze locked on the entrance, muscles tensed as he prepared for whatever threat lay just beyond.

"Did you hear that?" I whispered, creeping closer to him, my senses heightened.

He nodded, eyes narrowing as he stepped toward the door. "Stay behind me."

With a deep breath, he swung the door open, revealing a darkened hallway that stretched into the unknown. The café felt like a haven turned haunted house, and the air thickened with the possibility of danger.

"Hello?" Marcus called, his voice steady but edged with caution.

No response came, only the silence of the empty café wrapped around us like a shroud. The tension was palpable, a tightrope stretched thin between us and the unseen threat.

Just as I was about to say something, a loud crash echoed from the other side of the café, causing me to jump. My heart raced as Marcus spun around, eyes wide. "What was that?"

"I don't know, but we need to move," I said, urgency threading through my voice.

Before we could react, a figure emerged from the shadows, a dark silhouette that sent a jolt of fear through me. I barely had time to register the flash of a knife before the figure lunged toward us.

"Get down!" Marcus shouted, pushing me aside as he braced himself for impact. The world slowed in that instant, my heart pounding as the figure advanced, and I realized we were about to face yet another reckoning—one that could change everything.

As the knife glinted in the low light, I felt a surge of adrenaline and determination. Whatever lay ahead, I would face it with Marcus by my side, and together, we would fight against the encroaching darkness. But the uncertainty of what was to come gnawed at me, leaving a bitter taste in my mouth as the shadows closed in.

Chapter 17: The Confrontation

The scent of rust and decay greeted me like a long-lost friend as we stepped into the warehouse. Every creak of the floorboards beneath my feet echoed like a ghostly whisper, and the dim light filtering through grimy windows cast a pallid glow over the scattered debris—broken pallets, shattered glass, and the remnants of forgotten dreams. The walls, once painted a vibrant industrial gray, now dripped with the weight of despair and neglect, a fitting backdrop for the confrontation that awaited us. My heart thrummed in my chest, a relentless reminder of the stakes at hand.

Marcus stood beside me, his silhouette sharp against the gloom, exuding a mix of confidence and dread that made my skin tingle. I could sense his apprehension, the way he tightened his grip on the strap of his bag. The man we were here to face was a specter from his past, a reminder of battles fought and lost, a name whispered in the dark corners of his mind—Lucas. A chill danced down my spine at the mere thought of him, a man whose reputation for cruelty had etched itself into the fabric of Marcus's life.

"Are you ready?" I asked, my voice a mere thread against the oppressive silence. I was aware that I needed to be the anchor, the steadfast rock in the storm.

Marcus inhaled sharply, his eyes narrowing as if he could peer through the shadows to where Lucas waited. "I don't think anyone is ever truly ready for this," he replied, his tone heavy with the weight of unspoken memories.

A shiver crawled up my spine as I nodded, understanding the gravity of what lay ahead. "Then let's do this together."

The words were an incantation, a rallying cry against the tide of fear that threatened to wash over us. As we moved deeper into the warehouse, the light dimmed further, leaving us to navigate through the darkness as if wading through thick molasses. Each step was measured, cautious, my instincts screaming for me to turn back, to flee from the impending confrontation. But I couldn't abandon Marcus; I had promised him my unwavering support, my courage.

The room opened up into a vast expanse, the ceiling looming like a threat. At the far end, a figure emerged from the shadows, a silhouette hardened by time and experience. Lucas. The mere sight of him sent a pulse of adrenaline racing through me, igniting every nerve ending as I braced myself for what was to come. He was tall, imposing, with an air of menace that crackled in the stagnant air. His smirk was a serpent's, coiling with contempt, and my stomach twisted at the sight.

"Well, well, well," Lucas drawled, his voice a smooth caress laced with malice. "Look who decided to show up. Marcus, my old friend."

The air thickened, charged with tension. I felt Marcus stiffen beside me, his jaw clenching as he prepared to face the man who had haunted his every step. "This ends tonight, Lucas," he said, his voice low and fierce.

"Does it?" Lucas's laughter echoed off the walls, a sound devoid of warmth. "I've seen you try to outrun your past, but it always finds you, doesn't it?"

My chest tightened at his words, and I stepped forward, determined to inject my own voice into this chaotic dance. "You're not the monster he fears anymore," I declared, my voice steady despite the flutter of nerves in my stomach. "You're just a man hiding behind the remnants of your past."

The shift in Lucas's demeanor was palpable, the flicker of surprise in his eyes giving way to anger. "And who might you be?" he sneered, dismissing me with a wave of his hand. "Some little girl playing hero?"

"I'm someone who knows how to face down bullies," I shot back, surprised at the fierceness of my own words. "And you're nothing but a coward hiding in the shadows."

For a moment, the air crackled with disbelief, and I could see Marcus's astonishment reflected in his wide eyes. I pressed on, fueled by an unexpected well of bravery. "You think you can intimidate us? That you can control Marcus with fear? You're mistaken."

Marcus finally turned to me, a flicker of admiration breaking through his facade of tension. "You shouldn't have done that," he murmured, the words both a warning and a plea.

But the challenge had been laid, and Lucas wasn't going to let it slide. "Is that so?" He stepped closer, his imposing figure casting a long shadow over me. "And what makes you think you can protect him? You don't even know the depths of his darkness."

"Neither do you," I shot back, my heart racing. "You think you know Marcus? You think you can define him by your past? You're wrong. He's more than your shadow."

In that moment, the warehouse fell silent, the tension hanging heavy in the air like the dust motes swirling in the meager light. I could see the change in Marcus, the way his shoulders squared and his chin lifted. He was no longer the scared boy haunted by his past; he was a man, ready to reclaim his story.

"Let's not forget who truly holds the power here," Marcus said, his voice a low rumble, echoing with newfound strength. "You've lost your hold over me, Lucas. This isn't about you anymore."

With those words, I felt the shift in the atmosphere, a crack forming in Lucas's façade of control. For the first time, he seemed uncertain, vulnerable beneath the weight of Marcus's defiance and my unwavering stance.

"You think you can just walk away from me?" Lucas's voice was tinged with desperation now, and the flicker of fear in his eyes sparked something deep within me.

"Yes," Marcus said, his voice steady, unyielding. "We can and we will."

And in that charged moment, I knew we were on the brink of something monumental. The confrontation was no longer just about Marcus facing his past; it was about us—two souls standing together against a storm, defying the darkness that had threatened to consume him. The outcome remained uncertain, but as long as we stood side by side, I felt a flicker of hope igniting in the shadows, a promise of light breaking through the dark.

The silence that followed Marcus's declaration hung like a heavy curtain, thick with unspoken challenges and simmering tensions. Lucas's eyes narrowed, and for a brief moment, I could almost see the gears turning in his mind, calculating how best to regain control. The air crackled with an energy that felt almost tangible, as if the walls themselves held their breath, waiting for the next move in this dangerous chess game.

"Well, well, aren't we feeling brave today?" Lucas finally retorted, a mocking smile spreading across his lips. "Is this how you've decided to fight back? With your little girlfriend beside you?"

I felt the heat rise in my cheeks, not from embarrassment, but from a simmering indignation. "I'm not just here to hold his hand, Lucas. I'm here to remind you that you don't have a monopoly on fear." My voice rang out, slicing through the tension like a knife, though I could feel Marcus tense beside me, a silent warning in his posture.

Lucas's smirk faltered for a second, his bravado flickering like a faulty bulb. "Oh, sweet girl, you have no idea what you're dealing with," he sneered, taking a step forward.

"Try me," I shot back, feeling a rush of adrenaline surge through me. It was a reckless move, perhaps, but something deep within me refused to back down, refused to let fear dictate my actions any longer.

Behind me, Marcus inhaled sharply, his eyes darting between us, a storm of emotions churning in his gaze. I could feel the weight of his history pressing against us, the scars of his past threatening to overshadow our moment. It was as if the very air was charged with memories that neither of us wanted to confront.

"Do you really think you can protect him?" Lucas's voice dripped with sarcasm, yet beneath it lay an unsettling truth. "You're just a distraction. He's always going to be tied to me, and you won't change that."

Marcus shifted, his body radiating a tension I had only felt when facing my own demons. "No one's tied to you anymore, Lucas. That's the whole point of this meeting." The certainty in his voice was both a surprise and a comfort, and I could see the spark of defiance igniting in his eyes.

"What a delightful little pep talk," Lucas drawled, his gaze darting to me. "But sweetheart, you're still in over your head. You don't know what it's like to be haunted by your past."

Before I could respond, Marcus stepped forward, breaking the invisible barrier between us and Lucas. "You don't know her. You think you can intimidate us with your empty threats? You've lost your hold over me. I won't let you manipulate me any longer."

Lucas's expression shifted, a flicker of genuine surprise crossing his features. "Oh, you've really grown, haven't you?" He leaned back, crossing his arms as he assessed Marcus like a predator sizing up its prey. "But let's not kid ourselves. You're still that scared kid I remember."

"Keep talking," I urged Marcus softly, my voice barely above a whisper. "You're stronger than you think."

With a deep breath, Marcus continued, his voice firm. "I was scared, yes. But I've faced my fears, and I'm not going to let you drag me back into that darkness."

Lucas's facade cracked just enough for me to sense the desperation beneath. "You think you can just walk away from this? From me?"

A sly smile danced on my lips as I replied, "You've already lost, Lucas. You don't get to dictate the terms of our lives anymore."

In a flash, the mood shifted. Lucas's facade of confidence slipped, revealing a vulnerability that took me by surprise. For a fleeting moment, he seemed like a man cornered, grappling with the reality that the grip he once had was slipping away. "You're wrong," he said, his voice low and raw. "You don't understand what I've done for you, Marcus. You don't see the big picture."

"And what picture is that?" Marcus asked, his tone steady. "The one where you use fear to control everyone around you? That's not power, Lucas. That's weakness."

Lucas's eyes flared with anger, the mask of confidence slipping further as he took a step closer, invading our space. "You think you've escaped? I know your secrets, Marcus. I know your weaknesses."

"Then you don't know me at all," Marcus countered, his voice resonating with newfound strength. "I've faced those weaknesses and come out the other side. You're just a relic, a fading memory of a life I'm done with."

The confrontation intensified, every word a calculated strike, every breath a potential explosion. I could feel the air growing heavy with anticipation, each second stretching into eternity. It was a precarious dance, one that could tip either way at any moment.

With a sudden surge of emotion, I found myself stepping between Marcus and Lucas, my heart racing as I met Lucas's eyes with fierce determination. "You've had your time, Lucas. You don't get to dictate our futures any longer. We're moving forward, and there's nothing you can do to stop us."

For a moment, the tension snapped like a taut wire, and Lucas recoiled slightly, his arrogance faltering. "You really think you can just push me aside? I'll make you regret this."

"Regret is a weak currency," I replied, feeling emboldened by the strength of my own convictions. "You don't scare us anymore, and you certainly don't own the rights to our story."

Lucas's expression darkened, his eyes narrowing to slits as the anger boiled beneath the surface. "You're making a big mistake."

"Maybe," Marcus interjected, his voice cutting through the tension like a knife. "But I'd rather make mistakes on my own terms than live in fear of you."

And just like that, the dynamic shifted again. The power had subtly turned in our favor, and I could feel the tide of confidence swelling around us. The past was still there, lurking in the corners, but we were no longer its prisoners. We were the architects of our own narrative, standing at the threshold of a future unwritten, ready to break free from the chains of fear that had bound us for too long.

The warehouse, once a tomb of despair, now felt like a crucible, a place where the fire of our resolve burned bright. We would face whatever came next together, and for the first time, I felt truly hopeful that the shadows might finally begin to recede.

Lucas stood before us, a mix of menace and disbelief etched into his features. The silence stretched, thick and electric, the kind that makes your skin prickle. Marcus stood resolute, his chin lifted slightly as if preparing for a storm, but I could see the slight tremor in his fingers—a reminder that this confrontation was more than just words; it was a reckoning.

"You think you've got everything figured out, don't you?" Lucas challenged, his voice oozing with sarcasm. "You've got your little girlfriend here, cheering you on, but it won't change a thing. I still own a piece of you."

"Ownership isn't the same as control," I interjected, stepping forward with a confidence I didn't quite feel. "You may think you can dictate Marcus's life, but you're a relic—a footnote in his story, not the author."

Lucas's eyes narrowed, amusement morphing into irritation. "And what do you know about his story? You're just a distraction, a sweet little face that won't last long in the real world."

His words cut deep, and I could feel Marcus's body tense beside me, the pain of old wounds surfacing. "You're wrong," I replied, my voice steady as I turned to Marcus. "You're not just a scared kid anymore. You're a man, and together, we'll write our own narrative."

"Cute," Lucas scoffed, though there was a hint of uncertainty flickering behind his bravado. "But narratives can change in an instant, and I know how to turn the page."

With a sudden shift in energy, I caught sight of movement in the shadows—a flash of something that made my heart race. My instincts kicked in, and I felt an urgent need to protect Marcus from whatever darkness Lucas still wielded. "What do you mean by that?" I demanded, my voice cutting through the tension.

Lucas grinned, and it was the kind of smile that made my stomach turn. "Let's just say your precious little love story has some unexpected twists ahead."

Just then, the heavy clang of a metal door echoed through the warehouse, drowning out any retort I could muster. My heart raced as I turned toward the sound, my eyes widening at the sight of a figure emerging from the shadows. A familiar figure, one that sent a wave of dread crashing over me.

"Lucas, you always were the drama queen," the newcomer drawled, a smirk dancing across her lips. It was Angela, the very person I had hoped would remain a specter of Marcus's past—a ghost that had no place in our future.

"Angela," Marcus said, his voice barely above a whisper, a mixture of shock and disbelief flooding his features.

She stepped further into the light, revealing the glint of something sharp tucked into her belt. "Surprised to see me?" she taunted, her eyes darting between us like a predator sizing up her prey. "You thought you could just walk away from everything, didn't you? How naive."

The tension shifted again, this time laden with a new threat. I could feel the hair on my arms stand on end as I squared my shoulders, unwilling to let fear dictate my response. "What do you want, Angela?" I asked, my voice sharper than before.

"Just a little reunion," she purred, tilting her head as if appraising us. "I've come to collect what's owed. You think you can just sever ties with the past? No one walks away from me unscathed."

Marcus's jaw clenched, and I could feel the storm brewing inside him. "You're not collecting anything," he said, his voice now laced with a cold fury. "You have no power here."

"Oh, but I do." She stepped closer, her confidence radiating like a dark cloud. "You see, Lucas might have been the one to scare you, but I was the one who held the leash. You've only seen the tip of the iceberg."

Marcus shook his head, disbelief mingling with rage. "You're not going to manipulate me anymore. I'm done playing your games."

Angela laughed, a chilling sound that echoed off the walls, mingling with the dust motes caught in the shafts of light. "Games? Oh, darling, this isn't a game. This is survival. And I plan to come out on top."

In a flash, I grasped Marcus's hand, squeezing it tightly. "We can face this together," I said, my voice steady despite the chaos swirling around us. "You're not alone."

"Together?" Angela sneered, her gaze darting between us like a viper ready to strike. "How sweet. But you really think that's enough? I know things about you, Marcus, things that could shatter your little fairytale."

"What do you mean?" I demanded, fear threading through my veins.

"Let's just say your precious bond is built on secrets, and secrets have a way of coming to light." She stepped closer, her presence suffocating as she leaned in, her voice dropping to a conspiratorial whisper. "I know about your father, Marcus. I know what he did."

The words hit like a punch to the gut, the impact reverberating through me. I felt Marcus's grip tighten, his eyes wide with a mix of anger and disbelief. "You wouldn't dare," he said, a dangerous calm settling over him.

"Oh, I would. And I will," she replied, the satisfaction in her voice unmistakable. "You thought you could bury the past, but it's clawing its way back to the surface. Your family isn't what you think. There are debts to be paid, and I'm the one who collects."

The tension became palpable, a suffocating weight pressing down on us. Marcus's face darkened, and I could see the conflict churning within him, the shadows of his past battling against the light of his present. I was desperate to keep him anchored, to pull him back from the precipice.

"Don't listen to her," I urged, my heart racing as I glanced between them. "She's trying to manipulate you."

Angela laughed again, a cruel sound that sliced through the air. "Oh, sweet girl, you don't understand the stakes. This isn't about manipulation. This is survival. And I plan to survive, with or without you."

In that moment, the world felt like it was unraveling around us. Lucas, once the embodiment of Marcus's fears, now stood silent, watching the exchange with a mix of bemusement and caution. I could sense the shift, the way the power dynamics were in flux.

"You're wrong," Marcus said, his voice a low growl. "I won't let you control me anymore."

Before Angela could respond, a loud crash echoed through the warehouse, the sound reverberating off the walls. The moment hung, suspended in time, as all eyes turned toward the source of the commotion—a door slamming open, revealing the silhouettes of several figures stepping into the light.

"Looks like we have company," Lucas said, his voice dripping with sarcasm as he stepped back, a wicked grin forming on his face.

Panic surged through me as I recognized the faces emerging from the shadows. "What are they doing here?" I whispered, feeling the walls close in around me, my pulse racing in my ears.

"Time to choose sides," Angela said, her voice low and menacing. "Let's see how brave you really are."

In that moment, the weight of uncertainty crashed over us, and I knew that the stakes had just risen higher than I could have imagined. As the figures moved closer, I braced myself for the confrontation that lay ahead, a rush of adrenaline mingling with fear. The path forward was no longer clear, and as the shadows began to close in, I realized we were standing at the edge of a precipice, teetering on the brink of something far more dangerous than I had ever anticipated.

Chapter 18: A Fragile Peace

The dim light of my studio cast long shadows, making the once-vibrant hues of my paintings seem muted, as if they were aware of the weight we carried. Marcus and I sank onto the battered sofa, its fabric frayed yet comforting beneath us. The air was thick with the smell of turpentine and linseed oil, mingling with the subtle scent of burnt sage from earlier attempts to cleanse the space of lingering tension. I wrapped my arms around my knees, the fabric of my faded jeans cool against my skin, and let out a sigh that felt too large for my body. "So, that was a lovely evening," I quipped, attempting to lighten the heavy atmosphere, though my voice wavered slightly.

Marcus chuckled, a sound that momentarily pushed away the darkness threatening to engulf us. "I've had worse dates," he replied, his eyes sparkling with a hint of mischief, even amidst the uncertainty. "Remember the time I spilled wine on your canvas? I'm pretty sure that was worse."

I couldn't help but smile, the memory flooding back of red wine pooling across the white canvas like a gory sunset. "I do recall contemplating whether to cry or laugh. You know, art is all about perspective."

He shifted closer, the warmth of his body radiating against the chill of the room, and for a moment, I felt as if we were cocooned in our own little universe, insulated from the chaos that had just unfolded. But even in this sanctuary, the remnants of our confrontation loomed like ghosts. The crack in the wall—a recent casualty of our frantic escape—seemed to whisper secrets I wasn't ready to confront.

"Do you think it's really over?" My question hung in the air, fragile as a spider's web. I picked at a loose thread on my jeans, the soft material yielding to my anxious fingers. The silence stretched, heavy and oppressive, before Marcus answered.

"I don't know," he admitted, the vulnerability in his voice surprising me. "It feels like we've crossed a line, but I can't shake the feeling that something else is coming." His gaze drifted toward the window, where the moonlight bathed the city in a silvery glow, illuminating the dust motes dancing in the air like lost dreams.

The city beyond my studio felt both familiar and foreign, a paradox I couldn't quite grasp. Each building stood tall, a monument to countless stories, yet I felt isolated, our world narrowing down to the two of us and the decisions we had yet to make. The stillness outside was deceiving; I could almost hear the city breathe, its pulse synchronizing with the quiet chaos inside me.

"I wish I could just paint it all away," I murmured, my fingers tracing the edges of a canvas that remained blank, an abyss awaiting creation. "Sometimes I think if I could capture this moment, freeze it forever, I'd be safe."

"Or stuck," Marcus countered, his tone playful yet serious, drawing me back from the precipice of despair. "Art is all about movement, isn't it? It's the evolution that makes it beautiful."

I turned to him, a spark of inspiration igniting in the depths of my uncertainty. "You're right. Maybe I need to embrace the chaos rather than fight it." The thought was exhilarating, yet frightening. Embracing chaos meant confronting the storm within me, acknowledging the shadows lurking beneath the surface.

Marcus reached out, his fingers brushing against mine, a simple touch that sent electric shivers up my arm. "Whatever happens, we'll figure it out together," he said, his voice steady, but I could see the flicker of doubt in his eyes. It was there, hanging like an uninvited guest, and I knew we both felt it.

"Together," I echoed, allowing the word to fill the space between us. It felt like a promise wrapped in uncertainty, yet I clung to it. "I guess that's all we can do."

The night unfolded slowly, filled with the rhythm of our unspoken fears and hopes. I painted, letting the brush glide over the canvas, strokes becoming more frantic as the emotions surged within me. Each color I mixed bled into the next, creating a chaotic symphony of reds and blues, echoing the tempest in my heart. Marcus watched, his presence grounding me even as my mind danced on the edge of the abyss.

"You're an artist," he said, admiration lacing his words. "You can turn chaos into beauty. If anyone can navigate this storm, it's you."

His encouragement was a lifeline, yet I still felt the weight of impending shadows. The thought of our confrontation replayed in my mind—a vivid reel of faces and words that danced like flames. I couldn't escape the feeling that the echoes of our past were not done with us yet.

As I mixed colors, the vibrant hues began to morph into a scene that felt hauntingly familiar—a stormy sky, dark clouds swirling ominously above a distant horizon. "Look at this," I said, stepping back to assess my work, the painting pulsating with energy. "It's both beautiful and terrifying, just like us."

"Maybe it's a sign," Marcus suggested, his brow furrowing in thought. "A reminder that even amidst the storm, there's beauty waiting to be found."

His perspective offered a flicker of hope, igniting a spark within me. "Or maybe it's just my overactive imagination," I replied, chuckling softly, even as a part of me clung to the notion that the storm was only beginning.

The night wore on, shadows creeping further into the corners of the studio, each brushstroke a testament to our struggle. As we fell into an easy rhythm, our shared laughter weaving through the silence, I realized that while the past may loom large, we had the power to shape our future. The canvas was still wet, and so was our story, waiting for us to take the next step together.

The following morning was a cruel contrast to the restless night that had passed. Sunlight poured into the studio through the wide windows, illuminating dust particles that hung in the air like tiny, sparkling secrets. The vibrant colors on my palette seemed almost mocking in their cheerfulness, a stark juxtaposition to the heaviness still lodged in my chest. I moved through the space with a disquieting energy, halfheartedly preparing my coffee while stealing glances at Marcus, who was curled up on the couch, his features softened in sleep.

The sight of him, so peaceful yet vulnerable, sent a rush of warmth through me. I remembered the intensity of the night before—the way we had leaned into each other, the silence stretching comfortably between us until I could almost hear his thoughts. Yet even now, with daylight chasing away the shadows, I sensed the weight of unspoken words lingering in the air.

I poured the steaming coffee into my favorite mug—one I'd decorated with swirling blues and yellows, a reminder of warmer days—and turned back to see Marcus stirring. His eyes blinked open, and he regarded me with a drowsy smile, a flash of sunlight breaking through the clouds. "Is that coffee or are you just trying to seduce me with your artisanal mug?"

"Why not both?" I grinned, my heart racing at the banter. "You know, a little caffeine and a splash of charm can go a long way."

He pushed himself up, the cushions sighing beneath him as if in reluctant protest. "I must say, it's quite effective," he replied, his voice still gravelly with sleep, sending a shiver of delight through me. I watched as he ran a hand through his tousled hair, the sunlight catching the edges of his jaw, making him appear more rugged and handsome than ever.

"Careful," I teased, leaning against the kitchen counter. "You'll make me think you're actually a morning person."

"Only when there's coffee involved," he shot back, his smile widening. "I prefer to keep the charm reserved for later in the day when I can truly appreciate it."

As we exchanged playful jabs, I felt a shift in the air, a subtle reminder that beneath our lighthearted repartee lay a fragile foundation. "What's the plan for today?" I asked, attempting to infuse my tone with casual curiosity while hiding the tremor of anticipation beneath.

Marcus took a sip of his coffee, eyes narrowing as he thought. "Well, ideally, I'd like to forget that warehouse incident ever happened and enjoy a lovely day free of threats to our existence."

"Right, because ignoring problems always works out splendidly." I raised an eyebrow, fighting back a smile, but deep down, I felt the weight of his words.

"Okay, fine, but can we at least pretend for a moment that we're normal people? Let's go for a walk, maybe explore the art district."

"Normal sounds overrated," I mused, leaning into the challenge, my heart fluttering at the thought of stepping out into the world with him. "But a stroll through the art district could be nice. Just as long as we avoid any warehouses."

"Deal." His eyes danced with mischief, and I felt a spark of excitement at the prospect of stepping into the sunlight together.

After a quick change of clothes, we set out into the crisp morning, the city alive with possibilities. The vibrant streets greeted us with a symphony of colors, vendors selling everything from handmade jewelry to bold street art that splashed across the walls like confessions. The intoxicating aroma of fresh pastries wafted through the air, luring us toward a nearby café where we indulged in sweet croissants, their flaky layers crumbling against our fingertips.

"I swear," Marcus said, biting into his pastry, "if we're chased down by any pastry thieves today, I'm blaming you."

I laughed, shaking my head. "A bold accusation, considering I'm the one feeding you."

As we wandered, we fell into a comfortable rhythm, our conversation flowing easily between art, dreams, and the uncertain future that loomed over us like a heavy fog. I pointed out a mural that caught my eye, an explosion of color depicting a phoenix rising from the ashes. "This one reminds me of you," I said, my voice laced with sincerity. "You've faced your demons, and you keep rising."

Marcus stopped to examine it, his expression thoughtful. "And yet, the ashes always linger. It's a messy transformation."

"True, but it's also beautiful," I countered, hoping to illuminate the flicker of hope hidden beneath his thoughtful demeanor. "Messy doesn't mean it isn't art."

He nodded, but the shadows didn't fully dissipate from his gaze. "I just hope that whatever is waiting in the wings doesn't drag us back into those ashes."

Just then, a sudden commotion erupted a few blocks away, voices raised in alarm. We exchanged worried glances, the earlier lightness in the air shifting abruptly. The crowd ahead parted like a curtain revealing chaos—a group of artists had gathered, their voices a mix of anger and passion, demanding recognition for their work, their struggles echoing louder than the city's heartbeat.

"This is not our fight," Marcus said, glancing at me, concern flickering in his eyes.

I hesitated, torn between the instinct to retreat and the urge to engage. "But isn't it part of our world? Artists fighting for their place?"

Before he could respond, a familiar face emerged from the crowd—Maya, a fiery painter I had collaborated with in the past. Her hair was a wild explosion of curls, and she wielded a paintbrush like a sword, rallying the artists with fervor. "We cannot let them silence us! Our voices matter!" she shouted, her passion igniting the crowd.

"Looks like we're getting pulled into this after all," Marcus muttered, amusement and trepidation mingling in his tone.

As I watched Maya lead the charge, I felt a familiar flame ignite within me. This was more than just a movement; it was an embodiment of everything we had fought for. "Let's see where this goes," I said, glancing at Marcus. "After all, art is about pushing boundaries, right?"

"Right," he said slowly, a grin creeping onto his face. "Just remember to keep your paintbrush at the ready."

With that, we plunged into the crowd, ready to join the rally. The atmosphere buzzed with electricity, and for the first time that day, the shadows that clung to my heart felt lighter, the call to action transforming our fragile peace into a shared purpose.

The crowd surged around us, a living entity fueled by a collective passion that pulsed through the air like a drumbeat. Maya's voice rose above the din, her calls for recognition and respect echoing off the buildings that towered like silent witnesses to our struggle. Marcus and I stood at the edge, drawn into the maelstrom of emotion and energy, our earlier lightheartedness replaced by a sense of urgency.

"I didn't think today would turn into a revolution," Marcus murmured, his eyes scanning the fervent faces surrounding us.

"Neither did I, but here we are," I replied, my heart racing as I watched Maya rally the crowd with the fervor of a general leading troops into battle. "This is what we fight for—art, freedom, and the right to be heard."

As the voices rose in unison, I felt a fire ignite within me, propelling me forward. I pushed through the throng, the energy electrifying, the scent of paint and sweat mixing with the crisp autumn air. "Maya!" I called out, reaching for her amidst the sea of bodies. She spotted me, her eyes sparkling with determination as she beckoned me closer.

"Join us!" she shouted over the din, brandishing her paintbrush like a sword. "We need every voice, every brushstroke in this fight!"

Before I knew it, I was swept into the front lines, a sudden wave of adrenaline coursing through my veins. "We are artists!" Maya proclaimed, and the crowd echoed back, their voices rising in a chaotic chorus that filled the street with an infectious energy. "And we demand to be seen!"

"Demanding is one thing," Marcus said, sidling up beside me, his tone light yet laced with seriousness, "but I'd rather not end up in jail today."

I shot him a playful glare. "Just roll with it, Marcus! Sometimes you have to get your hands dirty to make an impact."

His lips curled into a smirk. "Just so long as those hands don't end up in handcuffs."

With every rallying cry, every brush of the paintbrush against canvas that Maya made, I felt the tension coiling around me, an electric charge that made my skin tingle. Each artist around us was a vibrant thread in a vast tapestry, each voice a brushstroke on a canvas that begged to be painted anew. We were more than individual pieces; together, we created something grand, something undeniable.

As the crowd surged forward, Maya began to paint on a large canvas propped against a nearby wall, her strokes wild and free, embodying the very essence of rebellion. "This is our moment!" she shouted, splattering colors across the surface with abandon. "Let's create a mural of defiance!"

Marcus stepped back, his expression both bemused and captivated. "This is what you do, huh? Just throw paint and hope for the best?"

"Pretty much," I laughed, the excitement bubbling within me. "But it's all about intention! We'll put our feelings out there for everyone to see."

As I stepped closer to the canvas, I felt a tug at my heartstrings—a deep-seated desire to transform our chaotic emotions into something beautiful. I grabbed a brush, and together, we painted our fears, hopes, and everything in between. Each stroke was cathartic, a release of pent-up energy that felt both exhilarating and terrifying.

But as we lost ourselves in the art, a sudden crack of thunder rolled across the sky, shaking the ground beneath us. The vibrant day morphed in an instant; dark clouds rolled in like a tide, the atmosphere shifting from jubilation to foreboding. People began to murmur, unease creeping through the crowd like a cold wind.

"Uh-oh," Marcus said, his playful tone now tinged with worry. "I think Mother Nature is joining the protest."

Before I could respond, the first drops of rain began to fall, plopping against the canvas and our skin like warning shots. Maya, undeterred, continued to paint, her determination only amplifying. "Don't stop! This storm can't wash away our voices!"

The crowd, however, was less convinced. Some began to scatter, seeking shelter, while others hesitated, caught between the thrill of the moment and the threat of the impending storm. I glanced at Marcus, uncertainty flickering in my gut. "Should we stay or go?"

He grabbed my hand, his grip firm. "If we leave now, it'll feel like we're running from something. We've already fought so hard to be here."

"Okay, we stay."

With the rain picking up, we found ourselves working feverishly, painting against the elements, transforming our fears into colors that splashed onto the canvas, soaking up the energy of the crowd and the storm. But just as I began to lose myself in the moment, a sudden flash of lightning illuminated the sky, followed by a crack of thunder that reverberated through the air, sending a ripple of panic through the crowd.

People screamed, and chaos erupted as they darted for safety. I turned to Marcus, my heart pounding in rhythm with the storm. "We need to get to cover!"

But as I moved to pull him away, the ground shook beneath us. A sound like a roaring freight train filled the air, drowning out the rain and chaos. My eyes widened as I turned to see a large section of the nearby scaffolding buckling, wooden beams splintering under the sudden weight of the storm and the crowd's panic.

"Maya!" I screamed, my voice barely rising above the din, but she was lost in the crowd, a bright spot of determination amidst the growing turmoil.

The world around us shifted, the crowd scattering like leaves in a tempest, and for a moment, time stretched. I felt as though I was trapped in a slow-motion nightmare, fear and adrenaline colliding.

Marcus pulled me back, just as the scaffolding crashed down, the sound sharp and unforgiving, echoing through the air like the final note of a tragic symphony. My breath caught in my throat as debris flew, and I grasped his arm, our eyes locking in a moment of unspoken understanding.

"Go!" he shouted, urgency lacing his voice.

But before I could respond, the ground beneath me trembled again, and a horrifying realization struck—this storm was more than just nature's fury; it felt like a dark omen, the past clawing its way back into our lives with a vengeance.

As the rain pounded down, I searched for Maya through the chaos, panic bubbling in my chest. "We can't leave without her!"

"Then let's find her!" Marcus replied, determination etched across his features. Together, we pushed forward, bracing against the wind and rain, ready to confront whatever lay ahead. But just as we moved deeper into the chaos, a shadow emerged from the fray—one that I recognized all too well.

"Surprise!" the voice echoed, sending chills down my spine as I turned to face the very embodiment of our past—a figure I thought was long gone, now standing amidst the storm, the storm within my heart igniting once more.

Chapter 19: Secrets and Lies

The sun hung low in the sky, casting a warm golden hue over the quiet street where our little apartment nestled between a bakery and an old bookshop, each emanating its own distinct scents—freshly baked bread and the musky aroma of well-loved pages. It was in this vibrant yet unassuming sanctuary that I had carved out a semblance of normalcy, a world filled with laughter, shared meals, and cozy evenings spent wrapped in each other's arms. Yet, as the day drifted lazily into twilight, the familiar comfort began to crack, revealing fissures that had previously gone unnoticed.

I returned home, arms laden with groceries and a heart full of anticipation, ready to whip up Marcus's favorite pasta dish. The door creaked open, the gentle sound barely cutting through the hum of the city outside. My eyes swept across the living room, taking in the scattered remnants of our lives together: a pair of shoes left haphazardly by the door, a half-drunk mug of coffee forgotten on the coffee table, and the faint echo of laughter that lingered like a ghost from earlier that morning.

"Hey, love! I'm back!" I called out, my voice light, buoyed by the evening's promise.

There was no reply. Just the muted sound of music drifting in from the kitchen. It was an unfamiliar tune, one I had not heard before, and something about it set off an inexplicable unease within me. As I walked down the narrow hallway, the scent of garlic and tomatoes wafted toward me, mixing oddly with an underlying hint of something sharper, something more... secretive. My pulse quickened, a subtle warning I couldn't ignore.

Marcus stood by the stove, a spatula in hand, his brow furrowed in concentration. He was handsome in that rugged way that had first caught my attention—a scruffy beard, tousled hair, and an old band t-shirt that hugged his shoulders just right. But tonight, his charm felt like a mask, one that I wasn't sure I could trust.

"Smells amazing," I said, forcing a smile that felt strained. "What's cooking?"

He turned, surprise flickering in his hazel eyes, but it quickly morphed into an expression I couldn't decipher. "Just experimenting with some new spices. Hope you don't mind."

I shrugged, feigning indifference while my gut twisted in knots. "Not at all. I brought back the ingredients for that pasta you like." As I reached for the grocery bag, my fingers brushed against something that felt out of place, something that didn't belong to me. My breath caught as I pulled out his phone, the screen illuminating with a flurry of notifications—messages blinking away like fireflies in the dusk.

"Marcus," I said, unable to mask the tremor in my voice, "is this your phone?" I held it up, the weight of my discovery pressing heavily against my chest. "I thought you were going to put it away."

"Uh, yeah," he replied, his voice tinged with uncertainty. "I was just—"

"Can I see it?" I cut him off, my heart racing. I didn't even know why I felt compelled to ask, but the moment felt charged, like the air before a storm.

"Why do you want to see it?" he asked, the edge of defensiveness creeping into his tone. "It's just a bunch of work messages."

"Just let me see it, Marcus." The words fell from my lips like shards of glass, sharp and urgent. "Please."

He hesitated, his fingers tightening around the phone. In that pause, I felt the world tilt, the foundation of everything we had built together beginning to tremble. The flickering lights overhead dimmed as shadows stretched across the room, deepening the weight of the moment.

"Fine," he said finally, surrendering the device with a sigh. "But I promise it's nothing. Just... don't read too much into it."

I could hear the tension in his voice as I unlocked the screen. The messages scrolled before me, and with each word I read, my heart sank deeper into a chasm of confusion and dread. There were names I didn't recognize, conversations that felt cloaked in secrecy. The air turned thick with the scent of betrayal, each exchange revealing layers of intimacy I had never expected.

"Marcus," I whispered, my voice barely carrying the weight of the revelation. "Who is Chloe?"

His face blanched, the color draining from his cheeks as if the very essence of the truth was being siphoned away. "I can explain," he stammered, stumbling over his words as the reality of his situation became palpable.

"Explain?" I echoed, incredulity mingling with hurt. "You've been talking to her like she's... someone important. Why wouldn't you tell me?"

"I didn't want to worry you," he said, desperation lacing his words. "It's not what you think. She's just a colleague—someone I've been working with on that project. It's all professional."

The jagged edges of his excuses only deepened my skepticism. "Professional?" I shot back, a sharp laugh escaping my lips that felt almost foreign. "This doesn't sound like just work. Why hide it, then?"

"I swear, there's nothing between us. I was going to tell you. I just... didn't know how," he pleaded, his eyes pleading with me to believe him.

But with every word he spoke, the fortress of trust we had built began to crumble. What had felt like a fortress now seemed more like a façade, its cracks revealing a stark truth: I was no longer sure what to believe. In that moment, the kitchen, once a haven of warmth and laughter, felt cold and cavernous, echoing with unanswered questions that hung heavily in the air like the scent of burnt garlic.

As the silence stretched between us, the music faded into the background, replaced by the rhythmic pounding of my heart. How had we come to this? I had never imagined that the man I loved, the one I had trusted with my heart, could be harboring secrets that threatened to unravel everything we had shared.

The silence that followed my accusation hung in the air like a thick fog, obscuring clarity and revealing nothing but shadows. I watched Marcus closely, searching for a flicker of honesty in his expression, but all I found was a tangled web of emotions that mirrored my own. His eyes darted, a mixture of anxiety and frustration swirling in their depths, and I could feel my own heart thrumming in sync with the mounting tension.

"Look, it's complicated," he finally managed, his voice wavering. "Chloe and I have been working on this project for months. We've spent late nights together, brainstorming, you know how it goes."

"Late nights?" I echoed, my voice rising just slightly as the words dripped with skepticism. "And this didn't strike you as something you should mention? Did you think I'd just... what, not care? That it was fine for you to share your evenings with someone else?"

He opened his mouth to respond, but no words came out. The weight of the truth—whatever it was—sat heavily on his tongue, and I could see him grappling with it, wrestling with his thoughts like a boxer trying to land a punch but missing every time.

"Okay," I pressed, crossing my arms defiantly. "Let's break this down. You've been spending time with someone else and decided to keep that a secret. For months. It sounds pretty straightforward to me."

"Please, just listen to me," he pleaded, stepping closer, desperation evident in his eyes. "Chloe is... she's just a friend. We've been working together, yes, but it's strictly professional. I didn't tell you because I didn't want to make you feel insecure. I wanted to protect you."

"Protect me?" I let out a laugh that had more edge than amusement. "You think hiding this from me is protecting me? You're not some knight in shining armor; you're just making it worse. You can't protect me from something you're creating yourself!"

He ran a hand through his hair, the gesture familiar but laced with an unfamiliar intensity. "You're right, I messed up. I should have told you, but I didn't want to worry you. I thought I could handle it, and it wouldn't be a big deal."

"Handle what, exactly? A secret life?" I shot back, the words like daggers between us. "You're acting like this is a trivial inconvenience, but I don't feel like you're taking it seriously. I mean, do you even understand how this looks?"

"Of course I do," he said, his voice rising defensively. "But you have to trust me. We're still us. You know that."

"Us?" I repeated incredulously. "What does 'us' even mean now? Is it built on secrets? Are you telling me I have to just overlook this? This isn't just a misunderstanding, Marcus. It's a betrayal."

The atmosphere crackled with unresolved emotions as I stepped back, needing space from the intensity of our confrontation. I felt like a marionette whose strings had been cut, a puppet unravelling with every word. The life we had crafted together suddenly felt fragile, as if it could shatter at any moment.

"Why did you even have your phone out when I got home?" I asked, frustration bubbling up. "Were you waiting for her to text you, or were you just being sneaky?"

"I wasn't waiting," he said, desperation tinging his voice. "I had a meeting earlier, and she sent over some notes. I swear it was nothing. You've got to believe me!"

The sincerity of his words was swallowed by my rising suspicion. "Then why was your heart racing just now? You're sweating bullets."

"I—" he began, and the look in his eyes was one I hadn't seen before. Not fear, not anger, but something deeper. A truth buried beneath layers of confusion and remorse.

"Look," I said, letting my voice soften just a fraction. "If you want this to work, I need honesty. Not just about Chloe but about everything. About us."

"Okay," he said, exhaling sharply, as if a weight had finally lifted from his chest. "I'll tell you everything, but you have to promise to hear me out without jumping to conclusions. Can you do that?"

"Fine," I replied, the word escaping me like a breath I had been holding. I was willing to listen, though the thought of what I might hear sent chills racing down my spine.

He paused, his gaze steadying as he shifted to face me fully. "When Chloe and I started working together, I was initially drawn to her ideas. She's brilliant, and I admired that. But there was never anything more than professional respect. It just... grew complicated. And then, before I knew it, I found myself sharing things with her that I never intended to. Ideas, jokes... a connection. But I promise you, it never crossed the line."

"And yet, you hid it from me," I interjected, the sharpness of my words slicing through the honesty of his confession.

"Yes," he admitted, his shoulders sagging. "And I regret that every single day. I didn't want to hurt you, and I didn't want to make you feel like you weren't enough. You're everything to me."

"Everything?" The word tasted bitter, as if laced with irony. "If I'm everything, then why is this happening? Why does it feel like you've been living a double life?"

"Because I didn't know how to talk to you about it," he confessed, the weight of his admission settling heavily between us. "I was scared of how you might react. And scared of losing you."

My heart ached at his words, the vulnerability in his eyes a stark contrast to the betrayal I felt. "Losing me? You're the one who put this at risk."

"Maybe so, but it was never intentional. I didn't think it would lead us here," he said, his voice thick with emotion. "I love you, and I don't want to lose what we have. Please, let's work through this together."

"Together," I repeated, letting the word roll off my tongue, trying to find a sense of comfort in it. But how could we move forward when trust had been severed, when every word felt laced with potential deceit?

"I need time," I finally said, the weight of my decision pressing heavily on my chest. "I can't just forget this, Marcus. It's going to take more than words to rebuild what's been broken."

"I understand," he replied softly, the sincerity in his eyes making my heart ache for the man I had loved so fiercely. "Whatever you need, I'll be here."

As I stepped away from him, the reality of our situation settled like a storm cloud above us, dark and brooding. It felt like standing at the edge of a precipice, a long way down, unsure of whether to leap or retreat. But in that moment, I knew one thing for sure: I had to find my own ground before I could decide whether to extend my hand or let it slip away.

I could feel the air between us thickening, as if it were a tangible entity, heavy with unspoken thoughts and unyielding tension. Each word Marcus uttered hung in the atmosphere, both a lifeline and a potential noose, and I struggled to navigate the intricate maze of my emotions. My mind was a cacophony of questions, hurt, and an unsettling sense of betrayal that wormed its way into every crevice of my thoughts.

"Do you realize how easily this could have been avoided?" I finally said, the sharpness of my tone surprising even me. "A simple conversation, an ounce of honesty, and we wouldn't be standing here on the brink of... whatever this is."

"I know," he replied, running a hand through his tousled hair, a gesture I used to find endearing but now felt like a desperate plea for understanding. "But it wasn't just about me. I didn't want to burden you with my work drama. I thought I could manage it on my own, and that if it ever became something more—"

"Something more?" I interrupted, the thought hitting me like a punch to the gut. "You mean something more than just a 'professional respect'? That's rich."

His expression shifted, a flicker of guilt passing through his eyes. "It wasn't like that. I didn't mean for it to get complicated. I just... wanted to keep you out of it."

"Keep me out of it," I echoed incredulously. "What makes you think I wouldn't want to be in your life? All of it, including the complicated bits? We're partners, aren't we?"

"Partners," he mused, his gaze dropping to the floor, as if searching for the right words among the scattered crumbs of our shared life. "Yeah, we are. But I didn't want to risk losing you over something that might be nothing."

"Or it could be everything," I countered, frustration bubbling beneath the surface. "What's next? Are you going to start telling me about other women in your life? Because at this point, I'm not convinced I'm the only one you've kept in the dark."

His expression turned from guilt to surprise, and for a fleeting moment, I regretted the words. "There's no one else," he said firmly, his voice regaining strength. "I promise you that. It's only ever been you. Please, believe me."

"I want to," I admitted, the weight of vulnerability crashing over me like a rogue wave. "But how can I when you've kept so much from me?"

The kitchen was suddenly too small, the walls closing in as the truth of our situation hit me with a vengeance. The laughter we once shared felt distant, drowned out by the tidal wave of secrets now crashing down upon us. I glanced at the half-prepared dinner on the stove, a stark reminder of the mundane life we had built amidst this emotional chaos. A life that now felt irrevocably altered.

"Let's start over," Marcus suggested, his voice softer now, a hint of hope glimmering in the depths of his eyes. "Let's find a way to be honest with each other, no matter how messy it gets. I can share everything with you. Just give me a chance."

I wanted to take that chance, to reclaim the sense of security that had once enveloped me, but the fear of what he might reveal next gnawed at my insides. "What if I don't like what I hear?" I said, my voice trembling slightly. "What if the truth is even worse than I imagine?"

He stepped closer, his expression earnest. "Then we face it together. Just like we always have."

His words, though laced with sincerity, felt like a thin thread of hope, fragile and easily severed. I took a deep breath, attempting to find steadiness in the whirlwind of emotions swirling around us. "Okay," I finally said, my heart pounding with uncertainty. "But this needs to be real. No more half-truths, no more secrets."

"I promise," he replied, reaching for my hand. I hesitated for a moment, but eventually, I let him take it, feeling the warmth of his touch seep into my skin like a promise of better days.

But before we could delve deeper into the conversation, a loud knock echoed through the apartment, the sound jolting us apart like lightning splitting the sky. My heart raced as I exchanged a glance with Marcus, uncertainty etched across his face. "Who could that be?" I asked, the earlier tension reigniting with the sudden intrusion.

"I have no idea," he replied, his brow furrowing in concern.

I walked cautiously to the door, every step heavy with apprehension. The knock came again, more insistent this time, as if the person on the other side was impatiently waiting for a revelation to unfold. My mind raced with possibilities, each one more absurd than the last. Was it Chloe? Had she come to confront us about something that I couldn't even fathom?

I peered through the peephole, my heart pounding in my chest. A figure stood just outside, shrouded in shadows, but there was something unmistakable about the stance—the tension radiating from them felt all too familiar.

"Who is it?" Marcus asked, moving closer, his voice barely above a whisper.

"It's... it's someone I know," I stammered, my stomach tightening with a blend of fear and disbelief.

"Someone you know? What do you mean?"

Before I could answer, I opened the door, the hinges creaking ominously as I revealed the figure on the other side.

"Emma," the woman said, her voice cool and steady, but there was an undercurrent of something more—a tension that suggested more than mere casual conversation. "We need to talk. Now."

The air thickened as realization dawned upon me, the world tilting on its axis. Emma was not just an old friend; she was a ghost from a past I thought was buried—a truth I had tried to forget. And now, here she stood, a harbinger of secrets that could unravel everything I had fought so hard to hold together.

"Talk about what?" I managed, the words feeling heavy in my throat.

Her gaze flicked to Marcus, and in that fleeting moment, I saw something dark and unsettling pass between them. "About Marcus," she replied, her voice firm, as if she held all the cards in a game I had no idea I was playing. "And everything he hasn't told you."

The walls around me seemed to close in, the room spinning as I struggled to catch my breath. Just when I thought I had begun to grasp the threads of my relationship, a new layer of complexity unfurled before me, threatening to drag me down into the depths of uncertainty once more.

Chapter 20: The Breaking Point

The clatter of my coffee cup echoed in the nearly empty café, a fitting backdrop to the whirlwind of emotions swirling within me. I sat at a table that bore the scars of countless conversations, the wood scratched and marked like the heart I was desperately trying to piece back together. The rich aroma of freshly brewed coffee mingled with the faint scent of cinnamon from the pastry display, creating a comforting ambiance that stood in stark contrast to the storm brewing in my mind. Outside, autumn leaves danced chaotically in the brisk wind, mirroring the turmoil I felt inside. I traced the rim of my cup, each circular motion grounding me momentarily, but it was futile; my thoughts were a cyclone, pulling me back to Marcus.

The last argument replayed in my mind like a well-worn record. His voice had been calm, collected—a stark contrast to my rising fury. "You don't understand," he had said, and with those words, he had pulled away just enough to keep a wall between us, a barrier I could no longer see how to breach. The sharpness of my own words had cut through the air, leaving us both gasping in the aftermath. I was torn, teetering on the edge of anger and longing, my heart a battlefield where love and betrayal fought for dominance.

As I sipped my coffee, I couldn't help but replay the moment when he had looked at me with that familiar spark—one that once ignited a fire within me. It was a look that had always whispered promises, tales of togetherness against all odds, yet now it felt laced with something darker, like a bitter reminder of trust fractured by secrets. I had tried to convince myself that I could walk away, that I was strong enough to close that chapter, but the truth was more complex. The warmth of our shared moments lingered like a ghost, hovering just out of reach.

My phone buzzed, jolting me from my reverie. I glanced at the screen, my heart quickening as I saw Jenna's name flash. An old friend from college, her vivacious spirit had always been a balm for my wounds, a reminder of simpler times when our biggest worries were exam schedules and what to wear to the next party. I answered, feeling the weight of her familiarity wash over me like sunlight breaking through a gloomy sky.

"Hey, stranger!" Her voice was bright and playful, an echo of the laughter we shared during late-night study sessions and adventurous weekends. "I was in the neighborhood and thought I'd see if you were up for some coffee. You sound like you could use it."

Her perceptiveness was unnerving, but also a comfort. I nodded, though she couldn't see me. "Sure, I'm at Café Sol. You remember it?"

"Of course! Meet you in ten!" The line went dead, and I felt a spark of anticipation mingling with my lingering heartache.

When she arrived, Jenna breezed in like a gust of wind, her curly hair bouncing with each step, her smile bright enough to light up the dimmest corners of my mind. She embraced me tightly, the familiar scent of her floral perfume enveloping me, reminding me of summers spent laughing under the sun. We settled into a cozy corner, and the world outside faded as we fell into easy conversation. I could feel the tension in my shoulders easing with every shared anecdote, every laugh.

"Okay, spill," she said, leaning in conspiratorially, her eyes sparkling with mischief. "You can't hide behind that cup forever. What's really going on with you and Marcus?"

Her straightforwardness cut through my defenses. I hesitated, searching for the right words as the scent of freshly baked pastries wafted past us, teasing my senses. "It's complicated," I admitted finally, the confession tasting bitter on my tongue. "I don't know how we got here. We were so good together, and now..."

"Now you're at each other's throats?" she finished for me, her tone a mix of sympathy and encouragement. "Relationships aren't supposed to be easy, but they're worth fighting for. What's the root of the problem?"

Jenna's probing was a balm, forcing me to confront the truths I had been skirting around. "I feel like he's hiding things from me. It's like there's this shadow between us, and I can't reach him anymore."

"Have you talked to him about it? I mean, really talked?"

"Of course!" I exclaimed, frustration creeping back into my voice. "But every time I bring it up, he deflects. It's like he doesn't trust me enough to be honest."

"Or maybe he's scared of what the truth might bring," she suggested, her tone softening. "You need to remind him why you're worth fighting for. People are messy; love is messy. But it can also be beautiful, you know?"

Her words hung in the air, heavy with meaning. I felt a flicker of clarity pierce through the fog of my uncertainty. Maybe I had been so wrapped up in my own hurt that I hadn't considered how Marcus was feeling. The memory of his eyes, filled with both sorrow and longing, resurfaced in my mind, and I realized that perhaps we were both prisoners of our fears.

"Maybe I'm just scared," I confessed, a wave of vulnerability crashing over me. "What if we can't go back to what we had?"

"Or what if you can create something even better?" she countered, her voice firm yet encouraging. "You won't know unless you try. Don't let fear win."

With every sip of my coffee and every word we exchanged, the knot in my stomach began to unravel. Maybe it was time to confront my own fears, to take that leap of faith. I needed to find Marcus, to reach out through the darkness that had encroached upon us. I wanted to fight for our love, for the future we had once envisioned together, and Jenna's unwavering support reminded me that I wasn't alone in this struggle.

The warmth of the café embraced us as laughter echoed around, a vibrant contrast to the seriousness of my thoughts. I left with a renewed sense of purpose, ready to face whatever lay ahead, determined to bridge the chasm that had formed between Marcus and me.

The sunlight poured through the café window, casting a warm glow that felt almost like an embrace, pulling me from the remnants of doubt that had clung to me like a damp fog. My heart raced with a renewed sense of purpose as I stepped outside, the cool autumn air refreshing and invigorating. Each breath felt sharper, as if the crispness was scouring away the shadows of uncertainty. I made my way down the bustling street, the sounds of the city humming around me—a symphony of laughter, distant car horns, and the faint clinking of coffee cups from nearby shops.

As I approached Marcus's apartment building, my pulse quickened. The path to his door felt both familiar and daunting. Memories of our shared laughter, whispered secrets, and gentle touches danced in my mind, but so did the hurt, the bitter words that had been flung during our last encounter. I stopped short at the entrance, hesitating as a wave of doubt washed over me. Was this the right thing to do? The door loomed ahead, a threshold that divided what was from what could be. I took a deep breath, willing myself to cross that divide.

The elevator ride felt interminable, each ding of the floor numbers mocking my indecision. I could picture Marcus in there, likely lost in thought or perhaps pacing like a caged animal. When the doors slid open, I stepped out, the plush carpet underfoot softening my footsteps. I approached his door and knocked, each tap reverberating through my chest.

Silence hung thick in the air, and for a moment, I was convinced I'd made a colossal mistake. Just as I was about to turn away, the door creaked open, revealing Marcus, tousled hair and those deep, soulful eyes that still sent shivers of affection down my spine. He looked surprised, his expression shifting quickly between joy and confusion.

"Hey," I said, the word slipping from my lips, thick with unspoken emotions. "Can we talk?"

His brow furrowed, but he stepped aside, allowing me to enter. The apartment felt as familiar as an old sweater—comforting yet frayed at the edges. I noticed the coffee table cluttered with takeout containers and a few books stacked haphazardly, a stark reminder of the chaotic weeks we'd endured. The air was tinged with a scent of something rich and savory, a half-eaten meal left to grow cold.

"Um, I wasn't expecting you," he said, rubbing the back of his neck, a gesture I recognized well. "Is everything okay?"

"Can't we just be honest for once?" I asked, the frustration of our previous conversations bubbling to the surface. "I'm tired of pretending things are fine when they're not."

His expression hardened, walls rising like a fortress around him. "You know it's not that simple."

"Isn't it, though?" I countered, planting my hands on my hips. "You're hiding things from me, and I'm tired of feeling like I'm standing outside looking in."

His gaze dropped, and I could see the conflict in his eyes, the turmoil mirrored in the lines on his forehead. "It's not about you," he muttered, almost as if trying to convince himself.

"It always feels like it's about me!" I shot back, my voice rising in frustration. "We're in this together. So why are you acting like you have to shoulder everything alone?"

"Because I can't drag you into my mess," he replied, his voice barely above a whisper, but the weight of his words hung heavily between us. "I don't want to hurt you."

"Hurt me? Marcus, I'm already hurting! You think shutting me out is protecting me? It's doing the opposite!" My heart pounded in my chest as the heat of the moment simmered, the air thick with unvoiced fears and unguarded truths.

We stood there, breaths mingling in the tense space, each waiting for the other to make the next move. My resolve wavered slightly, but I pressed on, determined to peel back the layers he had wrapped around himself. "What are you so afraid of? What is it that you think I can't handle?"

He opened his mouth, hesitating as if weighing his words. "What if I'm not good enough? What if I fail you?"

The vulnerability in his eyes caught me off guard, and I softened, stepping closer. "Marcus, love isn't about perfection. It's about accepting each other's flaws and growing together."

He searched my face, uncertainty flickering across his features. "You make it sound so easy, but it's not. I don't want to be a burden."

"You're not a burden; you're my partner. It's not a one-way street, and it shouldn't be. We need to fight for this," I urged, reaching for his hand, feeling the warmth and strength of him against my palm.

For a heartbeat, he hesitated, but then he gripped my hand tightly, his thumb brushing over my knuckles in a soothing motion that ignited a flicker of hope within me. "I just don't know where to start," he admitted, vulnerability pouring from his voice.

"Start by telling me the truth," I replied, keeping my tone gentle yet firm. "Whatever it is, I'm here to listen. We can figure this out together."

He took a deep breath, his chest rising and falling in a steady rhythm as he grappled with the weight of his thoughts. "I've been struggling with my job. I thought I could handle it, but it's spiraled out of control, and I didn't want to drag you down with me. I thought if I just fixed it myself, it would all go away."

My heart clenched at his words. "Marcus, you're human. We all have our struggles. It doesn't make you weak or unworthy. It makes you real. Please don't hide that from me."

The dam broke then. He sank onto the couch, pulling me down beside him, and the tears that had been pent up rushed forth. "I just feel like I'm failing at everything—work, us. I don't want to lose you."

My chest tightened at his admission. "You're not losing me," I said softly, brushing a stray tear from his cheek with my thumb. "We can face this together. Just let me in."

He nodded, his grip on my hand tightening, as if afraid I would slip away if he didn't hold on tight enough. "Okay, let's try. I don't want to be afraid anymore."

With those words, a fragile bridge began to form between us, one built on the shaky foundation of honesty and vulnerability. I felt the sharp edges of our previous arguments soften, and the air hummed with the promise of a new beginning. The sun dipped lower in the sky, casting a golden hue across the room, illuminating the path ahead as we began to navigate the intricate dance of trust once more.

The air around us felt charged, as if the room itself held its breath, waiting for the next wave of emotion to crash upon us. Marcus's gaze remained locked onto mine, his eyes a mixture of vulnerability and resolve. I could feel the walls we had both erected beginning to crack, and the thought of what lay beneath filled me with a bittersweet longing. As he released a shuddering breath, I leaned closer, willing him to see that we were still on the same team, navigating a labyrinth of uncertainty together.

"You don't have to shoulder everything alone, you know," I said softly, still holding his hand, my thumb gently stroking his knuckles. "Whatever's going on at work—let's tackle it. I'm in this with you."

He blinked, surprise flickering in his eyes. "You really mean that?"

"Of course I do! I may not have all the answers, but I can definitely help with the questions," I said, trying to infuse a little humor into the moment. "And we can brainstorm over pizza. You can't go wrong with pizza."

A small smile crept onto his lips, and for the first time in weeks, I saw a glimmer of the man I had fallen for, the one whose laughter once filled the spaces between us like music. "I could go for some pizza. But we have to talk about this."

"Absolutely. I promise not to hold back," I replied, a surge of determination coursing through me. "So, what's really going on? Is it just work, or is there more?"

His expression darkened slightly, and I felt my stomach twist. "It's a little more complicated than that. My boss has been breathing down my neck, and I'm starting to think he's trying to push me out. I've never been in a situation like this before, and I'm scared."

The raw honesty in his voice struck a chord deep within me, and I squeezed his hand tighter. "Scared of what? Losing your job? Losing us?"

"Both, I guess," he admitted, his vulnerability peeling back another layer of his defenses. "If I can't provide for us, what kind of partner am I?"

"Marcus, you are so much more than your job. I've never cared about the money; I care about you." My heart swelled with the urge to assure him, to bolster his fading confidence. "We can figure out a plan. You're talented and smart. You'll find a way to make this work."

He studied me for a moment, a mixture of admiration and uncertainty flickering across his face. "You really think I can fix this?"

"Absolutely," I said, my voice unwavering. "Together, we can navigate this mess. Just remember that you're not alone anymore. We'll tackle it head-on."

Just then, a sudden vibration startled us both. My phone buzzed violently against the table, shattering the fragile moment we were sharing. I glanced at the screen and saw Jenna's name flashing again.

My heart dropped. Why was she calling now? "Excuse me for a second," I said, lifting my phone to answer. "I'll be right back."

Marcus nodded, but I could see the flicker of concern in his eyes. I stepped into the kitchen, trying to distance myself from the emotional weight of our conversation. "Hey, Jenna," I said, trying to keep my voice light, but the tension was palpable.

"Hey, I'm sorry to bother you again, but I just got a text from Sophia," she said, her tone urgent. "You might want to hear this. It's about Marcus."

My stomach dropped, a cold wave of dread washing over me. "What about him?"

"She heard some stuff from a mutual friend. There's been a lot of talk at the office. Rumors flying about him potentially being laid off," she said, her voice filled with concern. "It sounds serious."

"No, no. That can't be right." I felt the ground beneath me shift. "He just told me he was feeling overwhelmed, but he didn't mention anything about that!"

"Maybe he's trying to protect you from it. You know how he gets—he doesn't want you to worry."

"But I have a right to know!" I exclaimed, a wave of anger rising within me, mixed with fear. "Why didn't he tell me? I just talked to him!"

"I think he's caught in a tough spot. You need to talk to him about this. You can't let it fester. This could be a big deal," Jenna urged.

"I will. I promise," I said, my mind racing. "Thanks for telling me."

After hanging up, I took a deep breath, my heart racing as I returned to Marcus. He was still on the couch, a furrowed brow indicating that he sensed something had shifted in me.

"Everything okay?" he asked, his eyes scanning my face for any signs of trouble.

"No," I admitted, the words tumbling out. "Jenna just told me there are rumors at work about layoffs, and you didn't say anything."

His expression shifted, vulnerability replaced by a flash of defensiveness. "I didn't think it was important. I didn't want to worry you."

"Not important? Marcus, this is huge! You should have told me. We could have faced it together," I said, my voice rising in frustration.

"I didn't want to add to your stress. You're dealing with your own issues!" he fired back, frustration creeping into his tone.

"Is that really what this is about? Protecting me, or is it just easier to keep me in the dark?"

"Maybe I thought it would just blow over!" he snapped, and the tension between us thickened like fog, obscuring the clarity we had just begun to find.

"Or maybe you're scared," I shot back, my heart racing as anger and fear intertwined. "Scared that if you share too much, you might lose me."

The moment hung suspended in the air, our breaths mingling with the palpable tension. I could see the realization dawning in his eyes, and for an instant, I thought we might reach a breakthrough.

But just then, there was a loud crash from the kitchen, the sound of something heavy hitting the floor. I jumped, my heart lurching in my chest. "What was that?" I exclaimed, glancing towards the noise.

Marcus stood up, his expression morphing from frustration to alarm. "I don't know. Stay here."

He moved toward the kitchen, and I followed closely behind, my heart pounding in my ears. As we rounded the corner, the sight that greeted us was shocking: the refrigerator door stood ajar, and the contents had spilled out, a cascade of groceries strewn across the floor.

But it wasn't just that. I spotted a shadow moving near the back door, a figure slipping through the entrance, dark and menacing. My stomach twisted, a primal fear racing through me.

"Who are you?" I shouted, the challenge ringing in my voice, but the figure paused, glancing back with a gaze that sent chills down my spine.

The stranger hesitated, and in that moment, the tension reached a breaking point. Just as I was about to take a step forward, a loud bang echoed, and the lights flickered ominously, plunging us into darkness.

"Marcus!" I yelled, the world spinning around me, my heart racing with an urgency I couldn't understand.

And then there was silence.

Chapter 21: A Dangerous Revelation

The moment I crossed the threshold into Marcus's studio, a shiver darted down my spine, not from the chill of the autumn air that seeped through the cracks in the windows, but from the weight of revelations hanging in the air like thick fog. I could smell the paint, a fragrant reminder of his artistry, yet today it felt suffocating, layered with an unspoken tension. The walls, adorned with vibrant canvases swirling with color and emotion, stood as stark contrast to the muted turmoil brewing inside me. Here, art should have inspired, but instead, it felt like a gilded cage, each frame a prisoner of secrets that clawed at the edges of my consciousness.

"Are you ready for this?" Marcus's voice cut through my spiraling thoughts, grounding me. He stood by a canvas splattered with hues of indigo and gold, a tempest of passion frozen in time. The way he leaned against the easel, arms crossed and brow furrowed, made my heart flutter and twist with equal parts admiration and dread. It was a look I had grown accustomed to, that deep furrow of concentration that bespoke both brilliance and vulnerability.

"Does anyone ever feel ready?" I replied, forcing a lightness into my tone that barely masked the tremor beneath. The truth he was about to share felt like a freight train barreling down the tracks, a collision I both craved and feared.

He stepped closer, the scent of turpentine mingling with his musky cologne, a blend that always set my senses on high alert. "You deserve to know everything, and I won't let this fester any longer."

I nodded, my throat dry as sandpaper. My mind raced through the possibilities: perhaps the man from the warehouse had been just a loose thread in a grand tapestry of corruption, or maybe he was the harbinger of something more sinister—an architect of our undoing.

Marcus's gaze flickered to the window, the late afternoon sun casting long shadows across the wooden floorboards, creating a tapestry of light and dark that seemed to dance in time with my racing heart. "The man we encountered at the warehouse... he's not just some rogue player. He's connected to a larger network. A network that we've only just begun to scratch the surface of."

I swallowed hard, the implications of his words settling heavily in my stomach. "How deep does this go?"

"Deep enough to encompass everything—dealers, collectors, even some of the biggest names in the art world," he said, each word dripping with gravity. "We're talking about money laundering, stolen art, and worse. It's not just about us anymore; it's about exposing a monster."

The thought of a sprawling web of corruption left a bitter taste in my mouth. I had always loved art for its beauty, its ability to evoke emotions and tell stories. But now, those stories twisted into something dark and malevolent, the very heart of creativity tainted by greed.

"So, what's our play here?" I asked, trying to harness the whirlwind of thoughts swirling in my mind.

A spark ignited in his eyes, a glimmer of the fearless man I had fallen for. "We gather evidence, trace the connections. We'll expose them for what they are."

I felt a rush of exhilaration. The thrill of the chase coursed through my veins, pushing away the trepidation that clung to me like a second skin. "And how do we do that without getting ourselves killed?"

He chuckled, a sound that rang with both irony and warmth. "We're going to have to be smart about this. Subtle. I know people—contacts who can help us infiltrate the circles we need to reach. We'll start small, gather intel."

"Sounds like we're diving headfirst into a rabbit hole," I said, my voice steady despite the rising adrenaline. "What if they catch us?"

"Then we make sure they don't," he replied, his tone fierce, and it struck a chord deep within me. In that moment, the lines between fear and excitement blurred into a single, intoxicating sensation.

"Alright," I said, steeling myself. "Let's do this. But if we're going to take on a monster, we need to ensure we have our weapons ready."

With that, we launched into a flurry of plans and strategies, brainstorming ways to gather intel without drawing attention to ourselves. The excitement ignited a fire within me, propelling us through the dimly lit space as ideas flew between us like sparks. I felt the walls of his studio closing in, not as a trap but as a sanctuary, where we could huddle against the chaos outside.

As dusk settled around us, casting a warm glow through the studio, I noticed the way his hands moved with fervor, animated as he explained the intricacies of art auctions, the sly tactics employed by those who thought themselves untouchable. I couldn't help but admire the way his passion spilled over, illuminating not just the room but my heart as well.

"Marcus," I said, pausing amidst the whirlwind of our plans, "why are you so invested in this? It's dangerous."

He met my gaze, and in his eyes, I saw something profound. "Because this isn't just about art for me; it's about integrity, about protecting what we love from being twisted into something unrecognizable. If we don't fight for it, who will?"

A surge of admiration swelled within me, intertwining with the threads of attraction I had long since tried to untangle. In that moment, amidst the chaos of our endeavor, I realized I wasn't just in this for the art or the thrill. I was in it for him, for the man willing to stand against the tide, to fight for what was right even when shadows loomed large.

Together, we were standing at the precipice of something monumental, the stakes higher than I had ever imagined, yet with every plan we forged, every word exchanged, the dangerous thrill of what lay ahead electrified the air between us, binding our fates as tightly as the colors on his canvas.

The night unfurled around us, draping the city in a silken embrace as we mapped out our strategy beneath the flickering light of Marcus's studio. Shadows played against the walls, twisting and curling like the whispers of secrets we were about to unearth. I had never imagined I'd find myself in the midst of a clandestine operation, but here I was, heart pounding and blood racing, every nerve ending alight with the thrill of the chase.

Marcus leaned against the workbench, his hands moving in grand gestures as he outlined the next steps. "We need to blend in, find a way into one of the high-stakes auctions," he said, his voice steady but laced with excitement. "That's where the real players will be."

"Ah, yes, because nothing says 'we belong here' quite like pretending to be rich art collectors," I quipped, rolling my eyes with a smile. "I'm not sure I can pull off a thousand-dollar scarf and a taste for pretentious wine."

A playful grin danced across his lips, and he stepped closer, his presence filling the space with warmth. "Don't worry, I'll teach you the art of feigned sophistication. It's a skill I've mastered over years of mingling with the elite."

"Is that so? I can't wait to learn from the master of pretense." I shot back, teasing him. The tension from earlier eased just a bit, replaced by a shared laughter that rang through the studio, shattering the weight of our previous conversation.

As the banter hung in the air, a thought crept into my mind—a tiny voice whispering of the danger that loomed ahead. Still, I couldn't ignore the exhilarating spark of possibility. Together, we were an unstoppable force, two artists in our own right, ready to paint a new picture from the chaos.

"Okay, so how do we get into this auction?" I asked, my curiosity piqued.

Marcus straightened, his expression shifting into one of seriousness. "There's a gala coming up at the Eastside Gallery. It's a charity event, and many of the art world's big names will be in attendance. If we can secure invitations, we'll have a perfect opportunity to gather intel."

"Right, because nothing screams 'trustworthy informants' like mingling with the wealthy elite at a charity gala," I remarked, crossing my arms. "What's the plan? We show up in our best outfits and act like we belong?"

"Exactly," he replied, his enthusiasm infectious. "We'll network, drop names, listen in on conversations. It's all about finding the right connections."

The thought of rubbing shoulders with the art elite made my stomach flutter with equal parts excitement and apprehension. I had spent countless evenings admiring their work from afar, yet now I would be standing among them, a mere pretender to their crafted lives. "And what if someone sees through our façade?" I asked, the anxiety creeping back in.

Marcus took a step closer, his hand brushing against mine in a gesture both casual and electric. "Then we improvise. We're quick on our feet, remember? Besides, we'll have each other's backs. I won't let anything happen to you." His promise settled over me like a warm blanket, reassuring yet dangerously intoxicating.

The weight of his words lingered in the air, intertwining our fates with an intensity I hadn't anticipated. "Okay, I'm in," I said, a newfound resolve igniting within me. "But only if you promise to dress like a total snob. I can't be the only one faking it."

"Deal," he laughed, the sound brightening the dim room. "Let's find you the perfect gown. You'll outshine everyone there."

And just like that, our next phase became an adventure of its own. We spent the next few days scouting local boutiques, scouring vintage shops, and even rummaging through his expansive collection of eclectic clothing. Each fitting turned into a game, the playful back-and-forth punctuated with laughter and the occasional accidental brush of hands. As I twirled in a floor-length emerald dress that hugged my curves just right, I caught Marcus staring, his eyes darkened with a mix of admiration and something deeper.

"You look stunning," he murmured, his voice low and intimate.

"Thanks, but I think the dress is doing most of the work," I replied, a teasing smirk dancing on my lips. "The real question is: will this work for our elaborate deception?"

"Trust me, you'll be the highlight of the evening," he assured me, his tone shifting to something serious. "But remember, it's not just about how we look. We need to stay focused. This isn't just a party—it's our chance to dig deeper."

The night of the gala arrived, and as I slipped into the dress, the soft fabric against my skin felt like a second layer of armor. The air was thick with anticipation, and my heart raced as I caught a glimpse of myself in the mirror. The gown shimmered with every movement, reflecting the light and draping around me like a cloud of confidence.

Marcus arrived dressed to the nines, his tailored suit fitting him as if it had been custom-made for the evening. "Wow," he breathed, his eyes wide as they roamed over me. "If looks could kill, you'd be a weapon of mass destruction."

"Flattery will get you everywhere," I shot back, playfully adjusting my earrings. "Just make sure you keep up with me tonight."

As we stepped into the gala, the atmosphere buzzed with life. Laughter and conversation floated through the air, mingling with the rich scent of fine cuisine and expensive perfumes. I felt like a fish out of water, yet the thrill of the unknown electrified me. Every glance we exchanged, every playful quip, deepened our bond, threading us together amidst the swirling crowd.

"Let's grab some drinks and start mingling," Marcus suggested, and I nodded, eager to dive into the sea of strangers.

We navigated through the throng, exchanging pleasantries with artists, critics, and collectors. I listened intently, absorbing their conversations, hoping to catch a whisper of the secrets that lay beneath the polished surface. It was exhilarating and terrifying, and with each passing moment, the tension between Marcus and me intensified, a silent agreement that we were in this together, side by side against the world.

As the evening wore on, we found ourselves cornered by a particularly loquacious art dealer, his demeanor a mix of arrogance and charm. He waved his glass of champagne like a scepter, gesturing wildly as he recounted his latest acquisition—an alleged masterpiece that everyone claimed to be real but which my gut told me was a fake.

"Ah, the art world is filled with pretenders," he declared, his laugh booming through the crowd. "It's all about who you know, wouldn't you agree?"

"Or how well you can spin a story," I replied, unable to resist the urge to poke at his inflated ego.

Marcus shot me a warning glance, but I was already committed, the thrill of the challenge pushing me forward. "Isn't that right? You could sell a piece of blank canvas and call it 'The Void,' and someone would still pay top dollar."

The dealer's eyes narrowed slightly, and a flicker of surprise crossed his features, quickly masked by a practiced smile. "You have a sharp tongue, my dear. You must be new to this scene."

"Just observant," I replied, holding his gaze. Behind me, I sensed Marcus tense, the air shifting as he recognized the precarious line I was toeing.

Just then, a woman clad in a stunning silver gown stepped into our circle, her presence radiating confidence. She flashed a smile that could cut glass. "Well, darling, it seems like you've caught the attention of our friend here," she said, her voice dripping with honeyed sarcasm. "And trust me, that's no small feat."

I felt Marcus relax beside me, the tension easing just a touch. "I have my methods," I said, returning the woman's smile with one of my own.

"Good," she replied, her eyes sparkling with mischief. "You'll need them tonight. There's more than just art at stake here, and it looks like we're all playing a dangerous game."

The moment hung in the air, heavy with promise and threat, as I exchanged glances with Marcus. In that crowded room, surrounded by laughter and artifice, I felt a renewed sense of purpose. We were not merely here to observe; we were players in a world rife with deception, ready to weave our own narrative amidst the chaos.

The gallery hummed with energy, an undercurrent of anticipation that electrified the air. I found myself swept up in the throng of elegantly dressed attendees, each of them a character in a grand play where the stakes were as high as the ceilings. Crystal chandeliers twinkled overhead, casting prismatic light on the polished floor, while the soft strains of a string quartet floated through the room like a delicate veil, momentarily masking the tension simmering just below the surface.

"Now this is a perfect place for secrets," I murmured to Marcus, my voice barely audible over the clinking glasses and soft laughter. He stood close, the warmth of his body sending ripples of excitement through me, and for a moment, I was lost in the flicker of his gaze.

"Just keep your ears open," he whispered back, a mischievous grin tugging at his lips. "You never know who might slip up."

I nodded, my heart racing as we split up, moving through the crowd with a purpose that felt almost intoxicating. I mingled with a cluster of patrons who were discussing the latest trends in contemporary art, feigning interest while listening closely for any mention of the man from the warehouse or the whispers of corruption Marcus had hinted at.

As I sipped on a flute of champagne, the bubbles tickling my nose, I felt the presence of someone behind me. Turning, I found the silver-gowned woman from earlier, her expression playful yet shrewd.

"You've got quite the talent for blending in," she said, her voice laced with intrigue. "Most people would be quaking in their heels in a place like this."

"I've had my fair share of adventures," I replied, offering her a confident smile. "A little chutzpah goes a long way."

"Chutzpah, indeed. But don't let it get you too far ahead of yourself," she warned, her eyes sparkling with mischief. "The art world is full of wolves dressed in fine suits."

"I'm more of a lone wolf," I shot back, relishing the banter. "I prefer to keep my distance from the pack."

She laughed lightly, a sound that cut through the ambient noise like a clear bell. "Just be careful. Curiosity can be as dangerous as it is intriguing."

"Thanks for the tip," I said, though the weight of her words hung in the air like a storm cloud.

Just then, Marcus rejoined me, his expression serious. "We need to move. I've heard something interesting."

I felt my heart drop. "What do you mean?"

"There's talk about an undisclosed auction happening tonight in the back room," he explained, glancing around to ensure no one was eavesdropping. "They're showcasing pieces that have been blacklisted—stolen art."

My stomach twisted at the thought. "How do we get in?"

"I have a friend who might help," he replied, his voice low. "But it means slipping away unnoticed."

I glanced at the swirling crowd, anxiety and excitement mixing like paint on a palette. "Let's do it," I said, determination surging through me. "We're here for a reason, right?"

He nodded, and together we maneuvered through the throng, ducking into a hallway lined with abstract sculptures and dramatic portraits. The murmur of the gala faded behind us, replaced by the heavy silence of anticipation as we approached a nondescript door marked with a single flickering bulb overhead.

"Are you ready?" Marcus asked, his hand brushing against mine again, sending another shockwave through me.

"Ready as I'll ever be," I replied, my voice firm. He turned the knob, and the door creaked open, revealing a dimly lit room filled with flickering shadows and an air of secrecy that enveloped us like a cloak.

Inside, the atmosphere shifted dramatically. The chatter was muffled, replaced by the low hum of urgent whispers. A small crowd of suited men huddled around a table covered with various pieces of art, their eyes darting around as if they were waiting for the authorities to crash their clandestine gathering.

Marcus glanced back at me, a mix of excitement and concern in his eyes. "Stay close," he whispered, and I nodded, my heart pounding in my chest as we stepped further into the room.

As we approached, I could make out the details of the artwork: a fragmented sculpture that looked almost lifelike, a painting that seemed to drip with emotion, and another piece that sent chills down my spine, a haunting portrait with eyes that seemed to follow you no matter where you stood.

"Beautiful, isn't it?" a voice drawled from behind us. We turned to see a tall man in a crisp black suit, his demeanor confident yet predatory. He eyed us with a scrutinizing gaze, the corners of his lips curling into a smirk.

"Just admiring," Marcus replied, his tone cool. "I didn't know there was a secondary auction happening."

"Oh, this is just a little something for those in the know," the man said, his eyes narrowing. "And who might you two be?"

"Just art lovers," I replied, forcing a casualness into my voice that I didn't feel. "We heard about this through the grapevine."

"Ah, the grapevine," he echoed, chuckling softly, but there was something about his laughter that set my teeth on edge. "A dangerous place to pick up information."

The atmosphere thickened, and my instincts screamed that we were treading on dangerous ground.

Just then, another figure emerged from the shadows, and my breath caught in my throat. It was the man from the warehouse, his face twisted into a sinister smile. "Well, well, well, look who decided to crash the party," he said, his voice smooth yet menacing. "You've been quite the thorn in my side, haven't you?"

I exchanged a glance with Marcus, panic rising within me like bile.

"Let's not make this any more difficult than it needs to be," Marcus said, his bravado slipping as tension crackled in the air.

"Oh, but difficulty is precisely what I thrive on," the man replied, stepping closer, his gaze fixed on me with a predatory gleam. "I hope you two have come prepared for the consequences of your little investigation."

A wave of fear washed over me, but beneath it, I felt a flicker of defiance ignite within my chest. We had come too far to back down now.

"Maybe we're not the only ones who should be worried," I countered, my voice steadier than I felt. "You've been running from the truth, and it's only a matter of time before it catches up with you."

The man's expression shifted, a flash of annoyance crossing his features, but it was quickly replaced with a cold smile. "How quaint. You think you hold the cards here?"

Before I could respond, the room erupted into chaos as voices escalated and hands moved toward hidden weapons. Marcus instinctively stepped in front of me, shielding me from view. The tension surged, and I felt the weight of our peril pressing down like a leaden shroud.

"Get down!" Marcus shouted, and in that moment, everything exploded into a blur of motion and sound. I ducked instinctively, my heart pounding in my ears as I scrambled for cover.

The last thing I saw was Marcus reaching for me, a desperate look in his eyes, and then the room plunged into chaos, gunfire ringing out like thunder. The world fractured around me, and as I ducked behind a table, my breath quickened, fear twisting into determination.

This was the moment everything changed, and as I caught Marcus's frantic gaze through the chaos, I realized we had crossed a line that would seal our fates forever.

Chapter 22: Into the Fire

The air was thick with the mingling scents of expensive perfume and fresh-cut flowers, an intoxicating bouquet that masked the underlying tension lurking beneath the surface. Crystal chandeliers glittered like stars overhead, casting a soft glow on the silk-clad patrons twirling through the vast gallery, their laughter a sharp contrast to the secret we were determined to uncover. I could feel the pulse of the music vibrating through the polished marble floor, an insistent reminder that beneath the grandeur lay a web of deception, and we were weaving our way into its heart.

Marcus was a steady presence at my side, his fingers warm and reassuring against my palm. I stole a glance at him; his suit, tailored to perfection, accentuated the strength in his shoulders and the sharpness of his jaw. He had a way of drawing attention without even trying, his confidence magnetic in a room full of polished façades. I, on the other hand, felt like a slightly tarnished coin among gleaming gold. The deep blue of my dress hugged my figure but didn't quite manage to mask the butterflies fluttering riotously in my stomach. Still, I straightened my spine, determined to play my part as seamlessly as the wealthy elite surrounding us.

"Remember, we're just here for a little reconnaissance," Marcus murmured, his breath a warm whisper against my ear. I nodded, swallowing hard. The stakes had never been higher; if we were caught, there would be no way out. This gala was more than an art exhibition; it was a façade for a criminal empire, and we were the uninvited guests poking our noses where they didn't belong.

As we glided through the crowd, I tried to absorb every detail: the way the light caught the intricate patterns of the paintings lining the walls, the hushed conversations that flitted like butterflies, and the exquisite way the evening gowns flowed as their wearers moved. But beneath the beauty, a darker undercurrent pulsed. I scanned the faces of the attendees, searching for anyone who looked out of place or overly vigilant. They were like predators in a jungle, their smiles sharp and predatory.

A nearby group of men erupted into laughter, their voices booming over the soft strains of a piano, and I couldn't help but glance their way. They were too well-groomed, their expensive watches gleaming with the kind of wealth that came from a life lived in the shadows. One man, with slicked-back hair and a smile that could charm a snake, caught my eye. He leaned in, whispering something to his companions, their eyes darting around the room as if they were on the lookout for trouble.

"Marcus," I whispered, tugging him closer. "I think we might have our first lead."

He turned, his expression shifting into a mask of focus. "Let's blend in. We can't draw attention yet."

We moved closer, slipping into the throng of guests. My heart raced as we approached, the murmur of their conversation filtering through the din. I could hear snippets—names, vague references to shipments and transactions that sent a chill down my spine. Each mention of a figure tied to the art world felt like a breadcrumb leading us further into the labyrinthine web of deceit.

"I heard the next shipment is coming in tonight," one of the men said, his voice low but laced with urgency. "If we don't act fast, we'll lose our chance."

"Relax," the snake-charmer replied, a smirk dancing on his lips. "We've got it all under control. The gallery is just the beginning. The real prize lies in the vault beneath the museum."

I felt the blood drain from my face. A vault? Our intel hadn't mentioned anything about a hidden vault. The implications swirled in my mind, intertwining with the realities of what we were up against. This was no simple art theft; this was a full-blown operation that could ruin lives.

"Did you hear that?" I asked Marcus, my voice barely above a whisper.

"Yeah, we need to find a way down there," he said, his gaze hardening with determination.

Before I could respond, a voice boomed above the crowd, commanding attention. The gallery owner, a portly man with an air of importance, stood atop a small platform, the glittering chandeliers reflecting off his shiny bald head. "Welcome, esteemed guests! Tonight, we celebrate not just art but the very spirit of creativity that binds us. However, I must remind everyone—" he paused, scanning the audience, "—that art is best enjoyed when shared in a spirit of camaraderie and trust."

The laughter faded into a hush, and I could see the subtle shifts in the crowd, eyes narrowing as the weight of his words settled over us. Something was off. The air crackled with tension, and I felt the invisible thread of fear snaking through the room.

As the owner continued, Marcus leaned closer. "We need to split up. I'll head toward the staff area; see if I can find a way down to that vault. You stay here, keep an eye on that group. If anything changes, signal me."

"Are you sure?" I asked, the knot in my stomach tightening.

"Trust me. I'll be fine. Just don't lose sight of them."

With a final squeeze of my hand, he melted into the crowd, leaving me to navigate the sea of polished smiles and veiled intentions alone. I took a deep breath, steadying myself as I observed the group of men, their laughter now strained, a thin veneer over the rising tension that hung in the air like a storm cloud.

Just then, a woman approached me, her long, crimson gown trailing like liquid fire. She had an air of sophistication, her dark hair cascading over her shoulders, framing a face that could launch a thousand ships—or betray them. "Enjoying the gala?" she asked, her voice smooth as silk, but her eyes were sharp, slicing through the atmosphere like a knife.

"Very much," I replied, forcing a smile. "The art is stunning."

"Indeed, it is. But beauty can be deceiving." She leaned in slightly, her voice dropping to a conspiratorial whisper. "Do you know the true value of art? It's not always about what's displayed, but what lies beneath."

My heart raced, each word sending electric pulses through my veins. Was she just another attendee, or was she involved in the very scheme we sought to uncover? Her enigmatic gaze bore into mine, daring me to unearth the layers beneath her polished exterior.

"Sometimes, the greatest treasures are hidden where no one thinks to look," she continued, her smile enigmatic.

"Or perhaps they're just waiting for someone to discover them," I countered, my pulse quickening.

Her eyes sparkled with amusement, but I sensed an underlying current of danger. In this world of artifice, we were all players on a stage, and I had no idea who would be the first to take a fall.

The woman in the crimson gown studied me for a moment, her expression oscillating between curiosity and something deeper, almost predatory. The flickering candlelight danced in her eyes, and I couldn't shake the feeling that every word we exchanged was a game of chess, each move calculated. "What lies beneath, indeed," I said, summoning the bravado I didn't quite feel. "But isn't it the thrill of the hunt that makes it worthwhile?"

"Ah, a philosopher in the midst of chaos," she replied, her lips curling into a smile that sent a shiver up my spine. "Tell me, do you enjoy the chase?"

Before I could answer, a ripple of commotion broke through the crowd, and my attention shifted to the gathering of men. Their laughter had turned into tense murmurs, a signal of something amiss. The snake-charmer, now standing with his arms crossed, was scanning the room, his gaze darting toward the exit as if sensing a storm brewing. I felt my pulse quicken; whatever was happening, it was about to come to a head.

"I should see what's going on," I said, trying to maintain my composure.

"Do be careful," the woman warned, her voice a sultry whisper that dripped with intrigue. "Curiosity can lead one down dangerous paths."

"Danger is my middle name," I shot back, attempting to inject levity into the growing tension. As I turned to make my way through the crowd, I caught a glimpse of Marcus. He had slipped into the shadows, his movements fluid and deliberate, a man on a mission. My heart swelled with admiration and worry in equal measure.

Navigating through the throng of elegantly dressed patrons, I kept my gaze fixed on the group of men. The energy in the room had shifted, a palpable weight pressing against my chest. I could sense the unspoken tension; their earlier camaraderie now seemed fraught with suspicion. As I drew closer, I could overhear snippets of their conversation, words like "shipment" and "tonight" punctuating the air like gunshots.

Suddenly, one of the men, a tall figure with a sharply cut jaw and icy blue eyes, stepped forward, his tone accusatory. "You think you can just waltz in here and take what's ours? We've put too much on the line for you to mess this up!"

The others shifted uneasily, glancing toward the exits as if weighing their options. I felt the knot in my stomach tighten. They were more than just art thieves; they were part of something much larger and more sinister. I needed to find a way to alert Marcus without drawing attention to myself.

"Perhaps you should consider the consequences of your actions," the snake-charmer interjected smoothly, an unsettling calmness in his voice. "We wouldn't want an unexpected visitor ruining our plans, now would we?"

His words hung in the air, heavy with menace. My instincts screamed at me to retreat, but the impulse to uncover the truth pushed me forward. I took a step closer, my heart racing. The last thing I wanted was to get caught in their crossfire, but I was desperate for information.

In a moment of reckless courage, I called out, "Why don't you all just relax? We're here to enjoy art, after all. What's a little drama among friends?"

The men turned to me, surprise flickering across their faces. The tall one raised an eyebrow, assessing me like I was a puzzle to solve. "And who might you be, my dear?" he asked, his voice a silk-smooth drawl.

"Just a connoisseur of fine art and fine company," I replied, forcing a smile that felt more like a grimace. "I couldn't help but notice your spirited discussion. Is there a problem I can help with?"

The room felt suddenly still, the laughter and chatter of the gala fading into the background. All eyes were on me, and I could feel the weight of their scrutiny. The tension was palpable, a thick fog of suspicion and intrigue that wrapped around us like a cocoon.

Before anyone could respond, a commotion erupted near the entrance. A security guard, his face flushed with urgency, rushed into the gallery, barking orders. "Everyone, please remain calm! We have a situation!"

Panic rippled through the crowd, and I seized the moment, darting to the side as the men's attention shifted toward the commotion. I spotted Marcus slipping back through the crowd, his expression tense but determined. We locked eyes for a brief moment, and I silently willed him to be careful.

"Let's not lose our cool, gentlemen," the snake-charmer said, his charm slipping slightly. "We can handle this."

But the tall man wasn't so easily placated. "If the guard is here, it means they know something," he hissed, his voice low and dangerous. "We need to move—now."

Suddenly, they began to disperse, heading toward a side door that I hadn't noticed before. My instincts kicked into high gear, and without a second thought, I followed them, slipping into the shadows behind a column. The adrenaline surged through my veins, urging me to act.

As I crept closer, I caught snippets of their conversation again, snippets that painted a vivid picture of their desperation. "The shipment is non-negotiable. If we don't get it tonight, we're done for," the tall man growled, frustration etched into his features.

I held my breath, straining to hear every word. The urgency in their voices, the unravelling thread of their plan, ignited a fire of resolve within me. If I could gather enough evidence, perhaps we could expose their entire operation. My heart raced, knowing that every second counted.

Just as they reached the door, I stepped out from my hiding place, adrenaline propelling me forward. "You won't get away with this!" I called out, my voice more confident than I felt.

The tall man turned, surprise flashing in his eyes before anger took over. "What did you just say?"

The snake-charmer's lips curled into a sly grin. "Looks like we have a little mouse in our midst. What shall we do with her?"

Before I could respond, a loud crash echoed through the gallery, drawing everyone's attention. An entire wall of art, decorated with priceless paintings, had collapsed, sending dust and debris flying into the air. Gasps filled the room as chaos erupted, guests scrambling for the exits, and in that instant, I knew I had to act fast.

"Now!" I shouted, my instincts firing on all cylinders. "They're trying to escape!"

I dashed toward Marcus, who was weaving through the confusion, his eyes wild with urgency. "We need to get to that vault now!" he yelled, grasping my hand tightly.

Together, we sprinted toward the side door the men had just exited, hearts racing and adrenaline surging. Behind us, the sound of the crashing artwork reverberated like thunder, echoing the tumultuous storm of danger brewing around us. We pushed through the door, propelled by a shared determination to uncover the truth lurking just beneath the surface.

The door creaked open, revealing a dimly lit corridor lined with paintings that flickered with the glow of hidden security lights. The atmosphere shifted as we stepped into the narrow space, a sudden chill wrapping around us like a shroud. I could hear the distant sounds of chaos fading behind us, replaced by the eerie echo of our footsteps on the cold concrete floor. My heart raced as I glanced at Marcus, whose expression was a mix of determination and concern.

"Do you think they'll follow us?" I whispered, my voice barely breaking the tense silence.

"Let's hope they're too distracted by the mess we just left," he replied, scanning the corridor. "But we need to move quickly. If they're here, they might already be onto us."

We pressed forward, the anticipation hanging thick in the air. Every step felt precarious, as if the walls themselves were listening to our whispered intentions. The corridor branched off in multiple directions, each turn a potential dead end. My mind raced, piecing together the clues we had overheard.

"There has to be a way to that vault," I said, trying to suppress the panic rising within me. "If they're in a rush to get there, it's likely somewhere down here."

"Let's stick to the left," Marcus suggested, his voice low and steady. "I saw a staircase at the end of the hallway when we first entered. If we can find that, we might have a shot."

Just as we reached the intersection, a loud crash resonated from the far end of the corridor. We exchanged quick glances, the realization dawning on us that we weren't alone. Footsteps echoed in the distance, heavy and purposeful. My breath hitched as I felt the urgency of our situation.

"We can't stay here," I whispered, taking a step back into the shadows. "Let's find that staircase now."

As we hurried down the corridor, I could feel my heart pounding in time with the footsteps behind us. The dim lights flickered above, casting eerie shadows on the walls, making it feel as though we were being pursued by ghosts rather than men. Each step echoed our determination, and I couldn't help but feel a mix of exhilaration and terror coursing through me.

We finally reached a heavy door at the end of the hallway. Marcus pushed it open, and we stepped into a small room filled with dusty crates and old canvases, remnants of art long forgotten. The smell of paint and varnish hung thick in the air, mingling with the scent of mildew.

"Keep an eye out," he said, scanning the room for any signs of danger. "I'll see if we can find a way down."

I nodded, my pulse racing as I peered around the cluttered space. I could hear the footsteps growing closer, echoing ominously in the tight confines of the corridor. My mind raced, searching for anything that might help us.

Suddenly, I spotted a wooden ladder leaning against a stack of crates. "Over here!" I called to Marcus, pointing toward it. "That might lead us to the vault!"

"Good eye!" he replied, moving swiftly to my side. Together, we navigated through the maze of crates, our movements quick and deliberate.

As I climbed the ladder, the wood creaked under my weight, each sound amplifying the tension in the air. I could hear the voices of the men approaching, their conversation now a low murmur, punctuated by sharp laughter.

"Did you see that? That art was worth millions," one of them said, and I felt a chill run down my spine. "If we get caught, it'll be the end of us."

"Relax," the snake-charmer's voice echoed, smooth and unsettling. "We have everything under control. Just keep your eyes peeled for that girl and her boyfriend. They can't have gone far."

Panic surged through me. They were looking for us. We were running out of time.

With one last effort, I pulled myself onto a platform above, squinting into the darkness beyond. The faint outline of another staircase loomed ahead, promising an escape from the mounting danger below.

"Marcus, hurry!" I urged, glancing down as he climbed the last few rungs. He quickly joined me on the platform, his eyes darting toward the sound of approaching footsteps.

"Which way?" he asked, breathless and alert.

"Straight ahead," I replied, pointing toward the staircase. "We have to get down before they find us."

We raced toward the stairs, the sound of our footsteps drowned out by the chaos below. As we descended, I could hear muffled voices and the rustle of fabric. It was a strange blend of urgency and elegance—distant reminders that we were still in the heart of a gala while darkness encroached all around us.

The staircase twisted and turned, leading us deeper into the bowels of the gallery. Each step felt like a countdown, a clock ticking down to an inevitable confrontation. I could feel the walls closing in, the air thickening with tension.

"Do you think we're getting close?" Marcus asked, his breath coming in quick bursts.

"I have to believe so," I replied, pushing aside the panic rising within me. "This must be where they keep the real treasures."

We reached the bottom of the staircase and emerged into a vast room illuminated by a series of overhead lights. The space was cavernous, filled with crates and large, ominous-looking containers. My breath caught in my throat as I took in the sight before me—this was the vault.

"Look," Marcus said, pointing to a cluster of men gathered at the far end, their backs turned toward us. They were sorting through a pile of art pieces, their movements hurried and frantic.

"Now's our chance," I said, my heart racing with anticipation. "We need to get in close and find out what they're planning."

"Wait," Marcus warned, grabbing my arm. "We should be careful. If they see us—"

Just then, a loud crash reverberated from behind us, a sound sharp and jarring. We spun around, eyes wide, only to see the snake-charmer emerging from the shadows, his smile a cruel twist of triumph.

"Looking for something?" he taunted, his gaze locked onto us. The tension hung thick in the air, electrifying and dangerous.

I felt the world narrow down to that moment, the stakes rising like a tide. We were cornered, the walls of our world shifting, teetering on the brink of disaster.

"Get behind me!" Marcus shouted, pushing me back, the instinct to protect igniting within him. I could feel my heart pounding in my chest, the adrenaline coursing through my veins, urging me to act.

With nowhere to run, we were trapped in this dance of fate, the lines drawn sharply between danger and escape. The confrontation loomed ahead, a storm about to break, and I knew that whatever happened next would change everything.

Chapter 23: The Final Showdown

The air was thick with the scent of rain-soaked asphalt, mingling with the lingering aroma of fried dough from the nearby fair. I could hear the distant laughter of children, their carefree joy a stark contrast to the turmoil swirling in my chest. Just an hour earlier, Marcus and I had been huddled in our makeshift headquarters, piecing together the fragments of a plan that now felt more like a flimsy web than a solid strategy. Our bright ideas had dimmed, snuffed out by the stark reality of our situation. I ran my fingers through my damp hair, contemplating the consequences of our reckless pursuit of truth.

The streetlights flickered ominously, casting an eerie glow that made the shadows dance across the cobblestones. Every step I took felt weighted, as if the ground beneath me conspired to pull me back. I glanced at Marcus, whose jaw was set in that determined line I had come to know so well. He turned to me, eyes glinting with a mix of fear and resolve that mirrored my own. "We can't back down now," he urged, his voice low but charged with an electricity that sent shivers down my spine. "If we don't confront him tonight, we might never have another chance."

I nodded, though uncertainty gnawed at my insides. What did I really know about facing a man like Anton Voss? Charisma dripped from his every word, like honey tempting a bee, yet beneath that sweet exterior lurked a darkness that sent shivers through even the bravest souls. I had seen the way his gaze turned steely, his smile morphing into something predatory when he sensed weakness. It was a game to him, and we were the pawns, mere pieces on his chessboard of manipulation and deceit.

As we approached the warehouse, my heart raced, pounding a frantic rhythm against my ribcage. The dilapidated structure loomed ahead, a rusting hulk against the night sky, its windows like dark, hollow eyes staring down at us. I thought of the countless hours we had spent uncovering the labyrinthine truths of Voss's operations, connecting the dots that led us here. The evidence we had amassed felt like a fragile treasure, each piece precariously balanced on a knife's edge, and tonight, everything was at stake.

"Are you ready?" Marcus asked, his tone steady, though the flicker of doubt danced across his features. I could see the tension in his shoulders, the slight tremble of his hands as he adjusted the collar of his jacket. In that moment, I recognized a shared vulnerability between us, an unspoken bond forged in the fires of adversity.

"Ready as I'll ever be," I replied, forcing a smile that didn't quite reach my eyes.

He took a deep breath, and together we stepped through the threshold of the warehouse. The heavy scent of oil and rust engulfed us, a stark reminder of the grim realities that awaited. Shadows writhed along the walls, each creak and groan of the building amplifying the dread that settled in my stomach. My skin prickled as if we had crossed into a realm where time and morality no longer mattered.

The interior was dimly lit, the flickering fluorescent lights overhead buzzing like angry bees. As we moved deeper into the belly of the beast, I felt a chill that wasn't just from the temperature; it was the unmistakable sense of being watched. The hairs on the back of my neck stood on end, and every instinct screamed for me to turn back, to run as fast as I could away from this nightmare. But retreat was not an option. Not now.

Suddenly, laughter echoed from the far end of the warehouse, low and menacing, sending a ripple of cold fear through me. "So glad you could join us," came the smooth voice of Anton Voss, each word dripping with insidious charm. I could see him silhouetted against the faint light, a figure crafted from shadows and malice. "I was beginning to think you'd lost your nerve."

"Cut the theatrics, Voss," Marcus shot back, his bravado a thin veil over the tremors that betrayed him. "We're here to end this."

Voss stepped into the light, a smirk playing at the corners of his mouth, exuding confidence that wrapped around him like a cloak. "Ah, such passion! But you see, that's where you misunderstand this little game of ours. I hold all the cards."

I felt a rush of adrenaline, each heartbeat drumming against my temples. "And we're here to change the rules," I countered, my voice steadier than I felt.

His laughter echoed again, ringing hollow. "Change the rules? How quaint. But you're not in a position to negotiate." He gestured casually, and suddenly, figures emerged from the shadows—his enforcers, looming giants with cold eyes and menacing smiles that twisted my stomach into knots.

For a moment, I froze, a paralyzing wave of panic washing over me. But then, I felt Marcus's presence beside me, his unwavering determination igniting something fierce within me. It was time to show Voss that we weren't the frightened children he thought we were.

"Listen, Voss," I began, forcing the words through clenched teeth. "You think you can intimidate us? You're wrong. We've seen the truth, and we're not backing down."

The tension in the air crackled, thick as fog, and I could sense the shift. Voss's smirk faltered, just for a heartbeat, and I seized the moment. "We're not afraid of you. You might think you own this city, but we will expose you for the monster you are."

His eyes narrowed, the gleam of amusement replaced by a chilling intensity. "Brave words for someone standing on the edge of a precipice."

And just like that, the atmosphere thickened, the stakes rising as if the very air around us held its breath, waiting for the inevitable clash that would determine our fates.

Voss's eyes glinted like shards of glass, each one reflecting a malevolent spark that sent a shiver down my spine. My heart raced, thundering against my ribcage as the figures flanking him shifted, their bulk casting long shadows that stretched toward us like dark, grasping hands. I could almost hear the gears in Voss's mind turning, calculating, strategizing, and I was painfully aware that every second spent in this standoff put us one step closer to disaster.

"Do you truly believe your words hold any weight?" Voss asked, his voice smooth yet laced with an undercurrent of menace. "Your little crusade is nothing more than a blip on my radar. I've been playing this game far longer than you can imagine."

I swallowed hard, forcing myself to step forward, the flickering lights casting a glow on my face that betrayed none of the fear roiling inside. "Playing games with people's lives isn't a strategy; it's a crime." I felt the warmth of Marcus's presence beside me, a silent affirmation that we were in this together, ready to face the storm brewing before us.

"Ah, but that's where you're mistaken," Voss purred, his expression morphing into something almost affectionate, as if he were indulging a child's innocent fantasies. "Everything is a game. You think your resolve is admirable, but it makes you predictable. A little spark trying to ignite a bonfire."

Marcus's jaw clenched, and I could feel the tension radiating off him like heat from a flame. "We're not afraid of you," he said, voice steady but charged with the weight of our shared resolve.

Voss laughed, a sound rich with derision, and gestured to the enforcers. "I'm not sure you comprehend the severity of your situation. Fear is not just a weapon; it's a currency. And in this world, you two are broke."

Just then, a loud crash echoed from behind me, followed by the sound of a scuffle. I turned my head, heart racing, to see a shadow darting through the entrance. A flash of red hair—Elena, my spirited friend, her eyes ablaze with defiance, charging toward us like a storm. "You didn't think we'd leave you hanging, did you?" she called, a fierce grin splitting her face.

Voss's amused demeanor faltered, and I could see a flicker of irritation cross his features. "More ants at the picnic," he remarked, irritation coating his words. "How quaint."

Elena skidded to a halt beside us, breathless but undeterred. "You've underestimated us, Voss. We're not just here to play nice." She brandished a small, glinting object in her hand—a knife, its blade reflecting the harsh fluorescent lights.

"Now that's an interesting choice of weapon," Voss replied, his voice laced with mockery. "You think a little knife is going to change the outcome here? You're mistaken."

"Maybe not," I countered, heart pounding with adrenaline, "but we've got more than just knives." I nodded to Marcus, who stepped back, his eyes locking onto mine with an understanding that ignited something deep within me.

Before I could process what was happening, he lunged forward, pushing past Elena, a fierce determination radiating from him. The moment hung in the air, taut and electric, as if the universe held its breath, waiting for the first move in this high-stakes chess match.

"Enough of this," Marcus shouted, and with a quick motion, he threw a smoke bomb onto the concrete floor. It exploded with a hissing sound, enveloping us in a thick cloud that obscured everything beyond an arm's length.

"Brilliant move," Elena said, her voice slightly muffled, the tension laced with admiration. "But let's not forget who we're dealing with."

"I'm not worried about him," I replied, my voice steady despite the chaos. The smoke twisted around us, curling like tendrils of a phantom, and for a moment, I could almost taste victory.

"Then let's use the element of surprise," she suggested, her grin widening. "We can't let him think we're running scared."

The air crackled with energy, the chaos a perfect cover for the calculated moves we needed to make. With our senses heightened, we moved like shadows, gliding through the smoky haze, our breaths synchronized as we navigated the unpredictable terrain of the warehouse.

Suddenly, the sound of a scuffle erupted, a low thud followed by a grunt. I could hear Voss barking orders to his men, his voice cutting through the air like a knife. "Find them! Don't let them escape!"

I glanced at Marcus, and we exchanged a knowing look, our determination coalescing into a singular force. It was now or never. We had to strike while we still had the upper hand.

"Ready?" I whispered, adrenaline coursing through my veins.

"Always," he replied, the fire in his eyes reflecting my own.

We surged forward, the smoke beginning to clear just enough for us to see. Voss was still a figure of menace, but now we had the element of surprise on our side. He was just about to bark another order when Marcus lunged, catching Voss off-guard. The two collided, a flurry of movement as fists flew and the tension erupted into a physical confrontation.

"Don't just stand there!" I shouted at Elena, my heart racing as I watched the chaos unfold. "Help him!"

Elena darted past me, brandishing her knife with fierce resolve. I could see the resolve etched on her face, an unwavering commitment that filled me with hope.

But just as I turned to join them, a loud crash erupted behind me, sending splintered wood and debris flying through the air. I spun around, heart dropping as I saw a new figure emerge from the shadows—one I hadn't expected.

"Surprise!" It was Marco, Voss's former right-hand man, the one who had defected and given us crucial information. "Thought you could use a hand."

The tension shifted again, morphing from a battle of wills into something more chaotic and unpredictable. Voss's smirk slipped, a mixture of disbelief and anger washing over his features.

"Marco? You traitor!" he spat, venom dripping from his words.

Marco's laughter rang through the warehouse, a sound rich with satisfaction. "You had it coming, Anton. It's time someone took you down a peg."

With that, the scene erupted into an all-out brawl, the once silent warehouse now a cacophony of shouts, grunts, and the clang of bodies colliding. Each blow exchanged was fueled by our desperation, our shared desire to reclaim our lives from the iron grip of a man who had played us like puppets.

I dove into the fray, adrenaline surging, the chaos pushing me forward, and for the first time in a long while, I felt the weight of my fears lift, replaced by an exhilarating sense of purpose. The truth was finally within reach, and we would stop at nothing to seize it.

The moon hung low, casting a silvery glow over the abandoned warehouse, where dust motes danced in the dim light. My heart raced as Marcus and I crouched behind a stack of crates, our breaths shallow, each echoing like thunder in the oppressive silence. The atmosphere felt electric, charged with unspoken tension and the faint scent of rust. As shadows flickered in the distance, I stole a glance at Marcus, whose blue eyes were filled with a mix of determination and dread. His hand, warm and steady, rested against mine—a quiet promise that we would face whatever came next together.

"Remind me again why we thought it was a good idea to confront him here?" Marcus whispered, his voice barely above a murmur. I could see the way his jaw clenched, a sure sign of the apprehension that gnawed at him. This wasn't just about us anymore; it was about stopping a man who had caused so much harm in the name of his twisted ambitions.

I forced a smile, attempting to lighten the moment. "Maybe we wanted to add a little drama to our lives? Nothing says romance like a little high-stakes confrontation in a creepy warehouse."

Marcus raised an eyebrow, skepticism lacing his expression. "Sure, if by romance you mean potentially getting shot at. I'm more of a candlelit dinner type."

Before I could retort, a sudden crash echoed through the space, followed by the unmistakable sound of heavy boots approaching. The criminal mastermind we'd come to confront—Ronan Blackwood—was known for his ruthless efficiency and unnerving charm. A man who could switch from charming to deadly in the blink of an eye, he was as much a danger as he was an enigma. I clenched my fists, willing myself to be brave, even as the fear clawed at my insides.

"Stay close," I murmured, inching toward the edge of our hiding spot. Marcus nodded, his expression grave. I could feel the tension between us, thick enough to slice through. Whatever happened next would either solidify our bond or tear it apart.

Just then, the lights flickered on, bathing the warehouse in a harsh glow. There he stood, tall and imposing, with an almost theatrical flair. Ronan's presence filled the room, his smile disarming yet chilling. "Ah, my dear guests! I knew you'd come. Did you think I wouldn't notice your little scheme?"

"Nice of you to dim the lights for us," I shot back, mustering every ounce of defiance I could. "It really sets the mood."

Ronan chuckled, a sound that sent shivers down my spine. "You've always had a sharp tongue, haven't you? But we both know it won't save you tonight." He gestured dismissively, and suddenly, a group of his goons stepped from the shadows, flanking him like wolves around their alpha.

My heart sank. "This isn't just about us anymore, is it?" I muttered to Marcus, feeling the weight of impending doom settle on my shoulders.

"Not if we can help it," Marcus replied, a steely resolve creeping into his voice. He glanced at me, and in that brief exchange, I felt an unspoken understanding—this was our fight, and we weren't backing down.

Ronan strolled closer, his gaze piercing. "You're tenacious, I'll give you that. But you're outmatched. You've come to the lion's den, and you're armed with nothing but hope."

"Hope's a powerful weapon," I retorted, surprising even myself with the strength of my conviction. "And it's not just hope; it's the truth. You can't silence it forever."

At this, Ronan's expression darkened, the playful veneer slipping just enough for me to catch a glimpse of the menace underneath. "Ah, the truth. Such a noble pursuit. But you see, truths can be twisted, shaped to suit one's needs. And my truth is that you will not leave this place alive."

"Don't be so sure," Marcus said, stepping forward. "You underestimate us."

Ronan raised an eyebrow, intrigued. "Do I? Then let's play a little game." He clapped his hands, and the goons tightened their formation, a silent threat hanging in the air. "You think you can save each other? Prove it. I'll give you a chance to escape, but only one of you can go. Choose wisely."

The challenge hung between us, heavy and suffocating. I looked at Marcus, a mix of horror and disbelief washing over me. "He can't be serious."

"Oh, he is," Marcus replied, his voice steady but his eyes betraying his fear. "But we can't let him divide us. We'll find a way to outsmart him."

"Outsmart him? He's playing with our lives!" I shot back, my heart pounding in my chest.

"Or maybe he's just playing with yours," Marcus said softly, stepping closer. "We have to trust each other. No matter what."

As the tension reached a breaking point, I felt an unexpected surge of clarity. "We won't let him dictate our choices. We can face this together."

Ronan's laughter echoed around us, mocking. "Such a touching sentiment! But in the end, it's futile. You have one minute to decide. Choose."

In that moment, a new wave of determination coursed through me. I glanced at Marcus, searching for a spark of hope. "We'll both get out of here. I promise."

As the clock ticked down, the air thickened with urgency, and I felt the pressure of our situation pressing down like a vice. The warehouse, once just a backdrop to our confrontation, now felt like a trap, each second a reminder of our impending doom.

Suddenly, the lights flickered ominously, and I caught a glimpse of movement behind Ronan. A flash of silver caught my eye—something sharp and deadly glinting in the shadows. My heart raced.

"Marcus, look out!" I screamed, but the warning was too late.

With a swift motion, Ronan turned, and chaos erupted. A figure lunged from the darkness, aiming for him, and in an instant, everything changed. The sound of a struggle filled the air, accompanied by shouts and the sharp crack of a gunshot.

In that split second, everything I thought I knew unraveled.

Chapter 24: A New Canvas

The wind whistled through the cracks in the old barn, a sound that felt almost like laughter, if laughter could be cold and biting. I stood there, brush in hand, the palette cradled against my hip, its once vibrant colors dulled by the remnants of dust and despair. The barn, once a bustling hub of laughter and dreams, lay silent now, its rafters adorned with cobwebs as intricate as lace, whispering secrets of days gone by. A layer of grime coated everything, and the scent of damp wood mingled with the faint echo of hay. This was not merely a space; it was a canvas, a testament to the stories carved into its very bones.

Marcus moved beside me, his presence a comforting weight against the backdrop of our shattered world. He had a way of standing just close enough to ignite warmth but not so close as to suffocate me. His hair, tousled by the wind, caught the late afternoon light, casting him in a halo that was almost ridiculous but somehow entirely fitting for the moment. "Are you really going to paint over all of this?" he asked, gesturing to the mottled walls, remnants of my past attempts at expression. "I mean, I get that it's a bit dreary, but there's something hauntingly beautiful about it."

I chuckled softly, feeling a rush of warmth flood my cheeks. "Beautiful, yes. But haunting? Not in the way I want to capture it." The truth was, this barn was the last reminder of my childhood dreams, of the time before everything felt so fragile and broken. It represented the layers of my life—the dreams dashed, the ambitions forgotten, and the fears that had kept me chained. "I need to create something new," I added, my resolve hardening like the thick paint I was about to apply. "Something that represents who I am now, not who I was."

He tilted his head, that mischievous glint in his eye suggesting he was about to tease me. "So, you're saying you'll just erase the past like it never happened? Seems a bit... extreme, don't you think?"

With a mock glare, I swatted at his arm, feeling a giggle bubble up despite the weight of our situation. "Not erase, Marcus. Reinterpret. Reimagine." I dipped my brush into a pool of cerulean blue, swirling it against the palette with an intensity that mirrored the tumult in my heart. "I need to redefine this space—our space. We've faced enough darkness. It's time for light, color, and a little bit of chaos."

As I lifted the brush to the wall, Marcus's hand shot out to stop me, his fingers brushing against my wrist, sending a jolt of awareness up my arm. "What if the chaos is what makes it real? What if it's the chaos that connects us to who we truly are?"

His words lingered in the air, heavy with meaning. I dropped my gaze to where he held my wrist, warmth radiating from his touch. The chaos we had faced together had changed us both, and in many ways, it had woven us together like threads in a tapestry. "Maybe you're right," I admitted, letting my breath out slowly, as if releasing a tightly coiled spring. "But I can't paint chaos without finding my center first. I have to make sense of everything."

"Then let's make sense of it together," he replied, his voice low and steady, pulling me back from the edge of my thoughts. "Show me how you see it, and maybe we can find the beauty in the chaos."

His offer felt like a lifeline, and I couldn't help but smile, the corners of my lips curling upward as I found strength in his unwavering support. I took a deep breath and turned back to the canvas, dipping my brush again, this time in a riot of colors. My strokes were broad and fearless, blending hues of emerald green with splashes of fiery orange, each movement an act of rebellion against the weight of my past.

The barn walls transformed under my touch, the colors merging and clashing, creating a vibrant tapestry of emotion. I felt alive in a way I hadn't for what felt like eons. The colors danced as if they had a heartbeat of their own, swirling together to form shapes that resembled memories—a childhood dream of racing through fields, laughter ringing in the air, shadows of old friends now scattered like leaves in the wind.

Marcus stepped back, studying the progress with a look of pure admiration on his face. "It's beautiful," he said, his voice thick with sincerity. "It's raw, it's real. And it's you."

"I'm still finding me," I admitted, my voice barely a whisper as I stared at the wall. "I'm not sure what that means yet."

He stepped closer again, his shoulder brushing mine, grounding me amidst the vibrant chaos I was creating. "That's the journey, isn't it? We never really know who we are until we're faced with the fragments of our past. Maybe it's okay to be in between."

I looked at him, the shadows of doubt mingling with a flicker of hope in my heart. He was right. The path to rediscovering myself was littered with uncertainty, but it was also paved with the possibility of new beginnings. In this barn, amidst the remnants of our battle, we could forge something beautiful from the ashes of our past.

As I continued to paint, the sun dipped lower in the sky, casting a golden glow through the barn's slats, illuminating the chaotic masterpiece coming to life on the walls. And in that moment, I felt the weight of our shared experiences transform into something more—an invitation to create a future that was unafraid to embrace both chaos and beauty, hand in hand with the person who had become my greatest ally.

The vibrant chaos of my painting filled the barn, wrapping around me like a favorite sweater—familiar yet invigorating. I lost myself in the strokes, my mind dancing between memories and dreams, all while Marcus stood by, a quiet force, absorbing the transformation happening before our eyes. It felt as though the paint carried whispers from my heart, coaxing out emotions I hadn't fully acknowledged. Each brushstroke was a reminder of our journey together, a tapestry woven with threads of laughter, tears, and quiet moments that now shimmered with significance.

"Did you ever think you'd be a barn artist?" Marcus quipped, leaning against the doorframe with a playful smirk. "I mean, what's next? A gallery opening in a hayloft?"

I chuckled, shaking my head. "As long as the hay is fresh and the lighting is good, I could see it. 'Barn-icatures' might just be the next big thing. After all, who wouldn't want to hang an abstract piece surrounded by the smell of hay and manure?"

"Honestly, I'd come to that exhibit," he said, crossing his arms with a mock-seriousness that made my heart flutter. "We could charge admission and call it performance art. 'Watch the tortured artist as she battles her inner demons with the medium of oil paint!'"

I feigned exasperation, waving my brush as if to shoo him away. "Stop! You're going to ruin my artistic integrity." Yet beneath the surface, I felt a warmth blooming, something that felt both innocent and electric. With every banter, we were building not just a world of color on the walls, but something richer, something that transcended the paint.

Just then, a loud crack echoed outside, jolting me from the moment. I dropped my brush, the bright green paint splattering across the canvas like a startled heartbeat. My eyes darted toward the barn doors, where the light from the setting sun was suddenly obscured by an ominous shadow.

"What was that?" Marcus asked, his expression shifting from playful to serious in a heartbeat.

"I don't know. It sounded like it came from the woods," I replied, my heart pounding in time with the sounds around us. The wind picked up, rattling the barn with an unsettling energy that sent a shiver down my spine.

"Let's check it out," he said, a protective instinct lighting up his gaze. I nodded, swallowing the lump in my throat as I moved toward the door, my pulse quickening.

We stepped outside, the crisp air hitting me like a splash of cold water. The sun was sinking, casting long shadows that danced across the grass. The woods loomed ahead, thick with trees whose branches swayed like skeletal fingers. There was something unsettling about the silence that followed the sound—an absence of chirping crickets and rustling leaves that felt unnatural.

As we made our way closer to the tree line, Marcus reached for my hand, his grip firm yet gentle, grounding me. "You know we don't have to do this," he murmured, his voice a low rumble filled with concern. "We could just head back inside, maybe finish the painting and call it a day."

"No," I said, steeling my resolve. "We can't let fear dictate our actions. Besides, what if someone needs help?"

We stepped into the woods, the underbrush crunching beneath our feet. The shadows deepened, and I could feel the tension rising like static in the air. A few steps in, and I noticed a flicker of movement just ahead—a flash of white that darted between the trees.

"Did you see that?" I whispered, urgency lacing my tone.

"Yeah. Stay close." Marcus's voice was steady, but I could feel the tension radiating off him. We moved deeper, drawn to the source of the disturbance, our breaths mingling with the crisp autumn air.

As we rounded a particularly gnarled tree, the scene before us unfolded like a horror movie, sharp and unsettling. A small, white dog trembled against a fallen log, its eyes wide and fearful, glistening like two tiny moons in the dusk. The poor thing looked lost, its collar twisted and frayed.

"Oh, you poor thing!" I gasped, kneeling down and extending my hand. "It's okay, buddy. We're not going to hurt you."

The dog inched closer, wary yet hopeful, its little tail wagging tentatively. "Look at this little guy," I said, glancing back at Marcus, who wore a mixture of surprise and delight. "He's like a ghost among the trees."

"Maybe he's a woodland spirit," Marcus joked, crouching down beside me, the tension from moments before easing slightly. "Or a little fluffy guardian sent to protect us."

With a gentle coaxing, the dog finally approached, nuzzling my fingers. Relief washed over me as I felt its warmth against my skin. "Where do you think he came from?" I asked, my heart swelling with affection as he licked my hand, his little body vibrating with pent-up energy.

"Lost, I guess. Poor guy." Marcus rubbed his chin thoughtfully. "Maybe we should take him back to the barn and figure out where he belongs."

"Absolutely!" I smiled, my spirits lifting as I glanced back at the barn, now a comforting beacon of safety. I cradled the dog in my arms, feeling its heartbeat match the rhythm of my own as Marcus led the way back.

As we neared the barn, I felt a new sense of purpose wash over me. This wasn't just a painting. It was becoming a home, a sanctuary for more than just the remnants of my past—it was a place where love could flourish, a canvas waiting to be filled with every shade of life.

Just as we stepped inside, the dog squirmed in my arms, eager to explore its new surroundings. I set it down, and it began to sniff every corner, tail wagging furiously. The barn, once a silent witness to our struggles, was alive with the joyous energy of this unexpected addition.

"Looks like you've got a new muse," Marcus remarked, a twinkle in his eye as the dog bounded around, creating chaos in a delightful way.

"Or a little rascal who will inevitably ruin my masterpiece," I teased, laughter bubbling up between us. Yet in that moment, I realized we were both being drawn into something much larger—something that required us to embrace the uncertainty of the future while cherishing the vibrant threads of connection that had already begun to weave us together.

The barn buzzed with energy as the little dog darted between our legs, a whirlwind of fur and enthusiasm. I watched, my heart lightening with every bound he made, feeling as though he was gathering up the scattered fragments of my spirit, a playful reminder that joy often lurked in the most unexpected places. I had named him Theo in a moment of inspiration—short for Theodor, a tribute to the adventures and mishaps that lay ahead.

"Where do you think he came from?" Marcus mused, crouching down to the dog's eye level, his tone shifting to something softer, more reflective. "I mean, it's not every day you find a stray in the woods."

"Maybe he escaped a dramatic life as a secret agent," I replied with a teasing grin, my imagination igniting. "Fleeing from his former life, living off the grid, and now, look at him! He's finally found his home."

"Or he's just a simple pup looking for treats," Marcus countered, rolling his eyes playfully. "I can see it now: 'Theo the Wonder Dog, once a spy, now a barn dweller.'"

His laughter wrapped around me, blending seamlessly with the sounds of Theo's joyful barks. The barn had become a canvas of its own, filled with life and laughter, and the space that had once felt heavy with memories was now bursting with possibilities.

I dipped my brush back into the paint, my fingers moving rhythmically across the canvas, guided by instinct rather than thought. The colors flowed like water, twisting into shapes that reminded me of sunlit days spent with friends, the warmth of laughter echoing in the background. "What do you think of this?" I asked, stepping back to assess my work.

Marcus squinted, tilting his head as he considered the blending of colors. "It's bright. Bold. A bit chaotic, maybe?"

"Exactly!" I exclaimed, feeling a thrill of excitement. "I want it to feel alive, like all the messiness of life coming together. It's a reflection of us, you know?"

He stepped closer, his expression shifting to something deeper. "Yeah, I see it now. It's like you're capturing the chaos we've experienced and turning it into something beautiful."

"Or something utterly confusing," I joked, smirking as I added a splash of vibrant yellow. "Who knows, maybe it will become an avant-garde masterpiece that leaves everyone questioning my sanity."

"Just make sure to include a little sign that says 'No refunds on emotional interpretation,'" he replied with a chuckle.

As I painted, I felt a shift in the atmosphere, a quiet that enveloped us like a blanket. Theo had settled down, curling up on a pile of hay, his little body rising and falling in a peaceful rhythm. But just as I began to lose myself in the colors, a sharp sound broke the tranquility—a knock echoed from the barn door, jarring us both.

"What was that?" I whispered, glancing over my shoulder.

"Stay here," Marcus said, his voice low as he moved toward the door. I could feel the tension building between us, that familiar spark of unease. "I'll check it out."

"Yeah, because that's what everyone says before they end up in a horror movie," I muttered, half-joking, half-concerned.

"Hey, it's my job to protect you. Just... don't move, okay?" He flashed me a reassuring smile, but I could see the apprehension in his eyes.

As he opened the door, I held my breath, feeling the air thicken with anticipation. The shadows danced outside, the fading light creating a dark, foreboding silhouette that sent a shiver racing down my spine.

"Is anyone there?" Marcus called out, his voice steady despite the rising tension.

Silence hung in the air, heavy and oppressive, until a figure stepped into view, cloaked in shadow. My heart raced as I strained to see who it was, dread coiling in my stomach like a serpent.

"Marcus!" I exclaimed, moving forward instinctively, but he held up a hand, signaling me to stay back.

"Who are you?" Marcus demanded, his tone shifting to one of authority. The figure paused, illuminated by the last rays of sunlight, and I squinted, trying to make sense of the silhouette.

It was a woman, her features sharp and enigmatic, her eyes gleaming with an unsettling intensity. "I'm here for the dog," she said, her voice smooth but edged with something darker.

Theo, sensing the shift, began to growl, the sound low and warning. "What do you mean, 'here for the dog'?" I challenged, stepping out of the shadows behind Marcus, unwilling to cower even as my heart raced.

The woman smirked, a chilling expression that sent a shudder through me. "Theo belongs to me. You have something that doesn't belong to you."

"Excuse me?" I bristled, indignant. "He's a stray! He was lost! He needs us."

Her gaze pierced through the dim light, and a flicker of anger crossed her face. "He was never lost. He's been watching you. You've attracted attention, and I need him back."

"What kind of attention?" Marcus asked, stepping in front of me, protectively.

But before she could respond, a loud crash erupted from outside the barn, shaking the ground beneath us. The walls reverberated as if the very structure were trembling in fear.

"What was that?" I shouted, glancing at Marcus, our earlier lightheartedness evaporating in an instant.

"I don't know, but we need to get out of here," he said, urgency sharpening his voice.

As we turned to leave, Theo suddenly bolted toward the door, barking fiercely at the intruder. My heart raced, every instinct screaming at me to flee, yet something deeper told me we were caught in a web much larger than ourselves.

"Stop him!" the woman yelled, lunging toward the dog.

But before I could react, the barn door burst open, revealing a swirling cloud of darkness that swallowed the last of the daylight. In that moment, everything shifted—shadows blurred into chaos, and the ground beneath us began to tremble with an unsettling force.

"What the hell is happening?" I screamed, grabbing Marcus's arm.

The woman's eyes widened, a mix of fear and determination flashing across her face. "You don't know what you're dealing with!"

And just like that, the world around us exploded into chaos, a whirlwind of color, shadows, and panic as the unexpected intruders descended upon us.

Milton Keynes UK
Ingram Content Group UK Ltd.
UKHW030912121124
451094UK00001B/124